EMMA'S ARMY
How Millions of Angry, Marching Seniors Saved Their Vanishing America

A futuristic novel
by Dan Chabot
©2022 by Dan Chabot

Emma-isms

"Must we just sit here while home-grown terrorists burn down our cities, taunt and goad our police, while our schools turn out a generation of socialists and communists, while China takes over the world? Will we watch while the cancel culturists erase our culture and our history, while the media takes sides – always the same side – while we drown in political correctness and wokeness, while Big Tech tries to influence what we believe, how we vote?"

***

"To this generation we say, 'You have been entrusted with a precious gift, the beacon of democracy, liberty, freedom. Do not squander it, do not let this light go out, or you and your descendants will answer to history! We will curse you from our graves if you fritter away the precious gift that was handed on to you through our ancestors. If America goes extinct, the world will slip into another Dark Ages from which it might never emerge."

***

"We want to keep the best of the Old America we grew up in and love, while welcoming so much of what is new and good. The responsible citizens among us have been striving to perfect the great idea that is America – the idea that all men are created equal. We have come a long way. Let us finish the journey..."

***

"We have at least one good fight left in us, the most important fight of all, the fight to save our nation and our way of life before our fading voices are stilled forever. We might be the last line of defense, the last barricade protecting a vanishing America...."

***

This generation likes to march for its causes. Well, we can march, too..."

EMMA'S ARMY

"Don't Get Me Started…"
—Emma's Blog

Yellow Wahee Publishers
Printed in the USA
Available in print and e-book versions from Amazon

Also by Dan Chabot:
Godspeed: A Love Story
The Last Homecoming
Available at Amazon

Cover Design: SelfPubBookCovers.com/Island
End page photo by Luke Scicchitano from Stocksnap

To my grandchildren

May this magnificent country be forever preserved for you
and shower you with as many blessings as it has me.
You will never have to wonder where I stood.

PROLOGUE

Oct. 15, in a year not too far away

The D.C. cops couldn't remember the last time they had an 86-year-old grandmother in custody. On assault charges, no less.

Emma O'Doud's jump suit itched and was way too big besides, but at least it was pink instead of orange.

Even so, she was bearing up remarkably well. Through her cell bars she was drubbing the deputies in poker, trading earthy quips with her jailers, and charming them with salty stories about the old days. They were all laughing so much that she hoped her son wouldn't bail her out anytime soon. Emma was going to miss this place; she loved meeting new people, especially in such interesting circumstances.

"Emma, we might have to make up some bogus charges just to keep you around for awhile," said Sgt. O'Rourke, handing her the ice cream sundae he had bought from his own pocket.

Emma supposed she probably shouldn't have pushed that picketing, clueless kid into the Tidal Basin with the tip of her umbrella, especially right in front of the Jefferson Memorial with all those cops and tourists around, but he was asking for it, the way he was shoving that "Geezers Go Home!" sign in her face. And she had slapped another misguided young punk holding a sign saying, "Socialism Now!" on one side and "Silence Farting Cows!" on the other, and then she held off with a menacing pair of knitting needles his woke obliviot friend as he advanced on her, blathering about critical race theory and the evils of America.

It didn't help either when she got in the face of that idiot college professor in the Che Guevara shirt who was burning an American flag. She had to admit that it did take a long time for the medics to stem the bleeding from his nose. The worst part was the blood all over her new purse.

"Were you born this way or did you have to go to asshole school?" she had shouted at him as two burly young accomplices helped the professor up. They made a brief move toward her before thinking better of it when a vision of tonight's broadcast news ("Thugs Rough Up 86-Year-Old March Leader") flashed through their minds.

Some of Emma's marcher friends, watching this tableau unfold from beneath the huge statue of Jefferson inside the Memorial, swore they saw the corners of his mouth twitch.

ONE
Emma

So how did upright widowed grandmother Emma O'Doud, former schoolteacher, political naif, blue ribbon strawberry preserves champion at the Haviland County Fair, organist and choir director at St. Therese Catholic Church, newest resident of the ambitiously-named Serenity Senior Sanctuary & Rest Retreat, wind up leading a protest march of seniors?

It all started when Emma's son, Christopher, concluded that she should not be living on her own anymore, a decision hastened when she ran over two mailboxes and a neighbor's lawnmower, plus a fire hydrant and two defenseless birch saplings, while backing out of her driveway. Christopher had a good view of the proceedings, since he was in the passenger seat.

After inspecting the wreckage, he came to a reluctant conclusion.

"Mom, I am taking away your driver's license. You will not drive again," he suggested gently.

The boyish, blond policeman nodded enthusiastically from a point safely outside the range of the fire hydrant geyser.

Emma didn't object too much.

"My motor skills obviously are deteriorating," she muttered in a lame attempt to inject some humor into the situation.

It was time anyway, she had concluded, before she hurt something besides mailboxes, lawnmowers and saplings, maybe even herself. Her car was ten years old now anyway and needed repairs or replacement, her hip was acting up again, it was getting more and more difficult to maintain the big house, and besides, the mailbox/lawnmower incident was only the latest in a long string of episodes that included a fire department visit when she forgot that pan simmering away on the stove, and a repeat visit plus a ruined microwave when she set the timer for 90 minutes instead of 90 seconds.

Christopher became especially concerned when he learned that she had driven to Dandelion Corners, a town 40 miles away, and then returned because she couldn't remember why she had gone there. The clincher came when she misplaced her cell phone and keys and was incommunicado for several days while her son tried desperately to reach her. She finally found them in her freezer when she went after some ice cream.

"You could use my phone when you need to make your cold calls," she suggested sheepishly. Christopher was not amused.

Christopher and her grandson, Sebastian, 12, lived nearby, but Christopher was often away calling on customers and thus not always on hand to bail her out of her mounting predicaments. So now, without a car and transportation, even more of her independence had to be surrendered.

"Harry would want me to do this," she reasoned reluctantly, brushing away some stray gray hairs along her temples and wrinkling her nose at the paper in her hand, which spelled out the intricate code of conduct at the retirement home. Squinting through her vintage round reading glasses, she struggled with instructions that were as detailed as the rules for *Dungeons and Dragons*.

Emma was still fit and trim at 86, and in relatively good health, except for her hip, some arthritis, and minor osteoporosis. She was an attractive woman still, in a senior kind of way, and her soft, wavy bob, except for occasional color "adjustments," had not changed in 65 years. The long red hair of her youth was now just a memory. She was outspoken and feisty, and retained a healthy sense of humor and sarcasm. And she had the voice of an angel, especially when it came to Irish ballads and folk songs.

"Mom, your *Danny Boy* would make even Genghis Khan cry," Christopher once told her.

Emma's husband of 56 years had passed away a few years earlier, leaving her with a house, some investments, and life insurance proceeds that she hoped would be enough to help her live out her final days in relative comfort. But now she was resigned to giving up the house.

"Harry was so concerned I wouldn't be able to maintain this big place anymore," she told the real estate agent.

"He did so many nice things for people," Emma continued. "I think I fell in love with him the time I saw him sitting out under a campus tree with a student whose Marine father had been killed in Vietnam. I saw them out there every day for weeks. I asked him what he was doing. 'His mother is a basket case,' he said. 'The kid has nobody to talk to.'

"Oh, I wish you had known him longer," Emma said. "Your grandfather was big, 6-2, looked like a movie star, had all the other female teachers and even the students swooning over him. The first day I was there he came up to me and asked me out. We were engaged within a month."

The young marrieds eventually went back to college for advanced degrees, and then on to the state university, where Harry became chairman of the English Department and Emma taught American history until she became pregnant with Christopher.

"I liked those years being a young mother better than anything I ever did," she recalled wistfully. "Today, some people say marriage is a trap for women. Well, I loved being "trapped" in a loving, stable, family relationship."

Later, Emma wrote several successful historical novels, ran a book store, and taught creative writing to other aspiring novelists.

One of her novels was a time-travel tale, with Thomas Jefferson returning to present-day America and expressing amazement at what he saw.

"He wasn't surprised by phones or automobiles or television or even computers," she told Sebastian impishly. "He did think it was sort of silly for companies to pay people to sing their messages in sappy commercial jingles, though. But he was furious when he learned that the Electoral College was under attack, that there was a big anti-gun movement and that speakers were being shouted down on college campuses.

"And he found it hard to believe that people were willing to pay $3 just for a bottle of water, $6 for a cupcake, $12 for a cup of coffee, $20 for a glass of wine, that athletes were paid millions of dollars a year to play a game, and that some people took a bath and changed their underwear every day."

Sebastian, grinning, scrunched up a skeptical face.

"How did he feel about gender transitioning?"

"I don't think he had a position on that. But I know he was against kids spending too much time playing video games."

She looked sideways at him over her glasses.

"They didn't have video games then."

"They didn't have transgenders, either."

Emma also had written a fantastical historical fiction novel about a thriving, prosperous nation that had suddenly begun providing incomes and free food, housing, education and health care to everyone, thrown open its borders to an unvetted flood of immigrants, defunded its police, gutted its military, and taught its students that their country was evil and despicable, students who then over a generation or two turned a golden empire into a third-world cadaver that stronger powers overran and began to pick over, thus satisfying a theory subscribed to by some that the average age of all great empires was 250 years.

"But I couldn't find a publisher for that one; they considered the plot too outrageously far-fetched."

Emma and Harry led busy lives filled with university activities and community functions and travel. She was president of her Woman's Club and the Altar Guild at her church, den leader for Christopher's Cub Scout troop, and founded a funky civic club of women called the Bumbershoot Babes, who knitted sweaters for soldiers abroad and once a year marched in the big local Fourth of July parade in a precision drill where they folded and unfolded colorful umbrellas in unison.

"That sounds like fun," Sebastian said, looking at his grandmother with a newfound appreciation for her playful side.

"Oh, it was," Emma laughed. "One year it rained on the parade, and we were the only ones ready for it."

Harry was an early casualty of the emerging PC and culture wars in the country. He retired from the university in disgust after he was told he could no longer use certain classics in the English literature curriculum. It started with *Huckleberry Finn,* banned because of racial references and stereotypes, and *The Scarlett Letter,* for mistreatment of women. Then the culture warriors moved on to *The Last of the Mohicans* for misappropriation of indigenous peoples' cultures, and *The Iliad* for glorification of war. There also was a vicious leftist campaign against *To Kill a Mockingbird*, which ended only when the PC fanatics were reassured that no mockingbirds had been killed in the production of the novel.

'Don't Get Me Started'

The last straw came when the university banned a Doo-Wop quartet from the campus on grounds that the name was offensive to Italians.

Harry objected vociferously.

"What's next?" he fumed in his letter of resignation. "*Oliver Twist* promotes the exploitation of children? *The Hunchback of Notre Dame* shows no empathy for people with disabilities? Falstaff for body shaming? Will even poor Elmer Fudd be banned because his speech impediment is mocked?"

"The leftist-progressives are taking over the university," he told Emma. "This is just the beginning. There's no such thing as free speech there anymore. Students are being spoon-fed socialist dreck and drivel and traditional American values are scorned. These kids have no appreciation of their own glorious American history, which is constantly derided. Opposing voices are being squelched. Thomas Jefferson himself would not be allowed to speak there today. Too controversial."

Harry was quite prescient. Emma always believed that the resignation led to his depression and gradual decline.

After Harry died she lost interest in most things. Many of her friends were gone, too, and she was beginning to feel that a new, harsh, unfamiliar world was closing in around her, a world she did not recognize anymore. Christopher became concerned about her safety in living alone, that she needed to be circulating with other people to keep her mind active and her spirits from flagging.

Serenity Senior Sanctuary & Rest Retreat seemed to be the perfect place.

Emma preferred to call it Arthritis Acres.

TWO
Arthritis Acres

But Emma did not like Arthritis Acres very much. Harry would not have liked it either. The surroundings were pleasant enough – a spacious campus, comfortable rooms, regular meals that catered to everyone's modern restrictions – diabetes, vegetarianism, kosher, lactose intolerance, gluten free, allergies. Especially allergies – to nuts, peanut butter, green vegetables, shellfish, sugar, salt, pancake mix, pepper, red meat, poultry, vinegar, pollinated fruit, fish, the very smell of fish, rosemary, sage, thyme, paprika, even water and oxygen. Some residents were allergic to allergy medicine.

"It must be a nightmare to work in that kitchen" Emma mused.

Arthritis Acres, like much of the rest of the new America, had bought into the philosophy peddled by the new Ninnie Party that had seized control of the government on a platform of transforming, nationalizing and socializing the economy. Ninnie was short for the new party's pompous slogan, "Nurturing National Needs," or NNN. Opponents, largely old-line patriots like Emma, much preferred the shorter pejorative term they coined from the abbreviation.

Emma also maintained that Ninnie was a shortened form of Nincompoop.

A flood of clueless eager young socialists, newly minted by the universities and newly endowed with the vote, had helped thrust the Ninnies into power.

Officially, the new party was the Citizens Progressive Democratic Labor People's and Workers Action Alliance Front for Liberation, Freedom, Justice and Harmony – an amalgam created by a contentious 100-

member Ninnie party committee that was determined to avoid the term socialism but had fooled nobody.

There now were promises of federal job and wage guarantees, economic security for those unable and even unwilling to work, free housing, free health care, free higher education, free food, free clothing, free gasoline, free quinoa, tofu and kale, free everything for everybody. Even cupcakes were now to be free, which put an end to the high-end cupcake industry.

Emma was skeptical about letting the government run anything, especially health care.

"I can see it now," she told Sebastian. "You go in for a tonsillectomy and come out instead with a colonoscopy, proving once again that they don't know which end is which."

Nonetheless, large numbers of political lemmings were perfectly willing to follow the Ninnies off the cliff and into the sea of socialism.

"I heard they are even promising free salted caramel mocha Frappuccinos and cinnamon chai tea lattes to everybody," one breathless Arthritis Acres resident told Emma. She had already received her free voter registration card, another key Ninnie platform plank, even though she was an illegal alien, which now were to be referred to as "undocumented visitors" and showered with all the rights and benefits of citizenship.

In fact, ballots now were issued to everyone, whether they asked for them or not, sent out indiscriminately in bulk mailings, dumped in bundles on street corners like newspapers, dropped in the lobbies of apartment buildings, hotels and condos and from low-flying airplanes, given out in department store promotions and in swag bags at grand openings, thrust at passersby by street-corner hucksters who also might be touting the nudie show at the strip-tease theater just down the street. There even was a drive to include a ballot in every box of breakfast cereal, but that had to be abandoned when it became apparent that the boxes were not big enough to accommodate the myriad of choices offered on a complex city-state-national election ballot. Instead, you could write for your free ballot, or ballots, using the address provided on the box.

Promoters of the "everybody votes" scheme went after their quarry wherever they found them.

"Mama, what is this piece of paper I got in the mail?" wondered little Greta, 5, in Galveston.

When opponents protested this gross violation and abuse of a sacred American rite, they were told they should welcome this "enthusiastic, inclusionary embrace of participatory democracy."

A Ninnie congressional committee was working on ways to pay for all of its largess, and had been meeting around-the-clock, emerging only now and then to issue hyperbolic press releases, change their underwear and claim their congressional freebies. So far they had not accomplished much except to fall back on their traditional approach to every problem – raise taxes.

"And here we thought the Ninnies had already taxed everything that could possibly be taxed," Emma mocked. "How could we be so wrong? They have invented new levies that nobody else had thought of before."

Some of their new policies did not fare so well.

The air in tires was to be taxed. The Law of Unintended Consequences immediately took effect, human nature weighed in, and the bumbling Ninnies, already specialists at creating inflation, now had to turn their attention to an epidemic of deflation. Automobile fuel economy immediately deteriorated, which was heresy to the Ninnie save-the-planet credo.

"There is an upside," Emma pointed out. "This has been very good for the tire industry, which had to put on extra shifts to meet the sudden rush to replace worn, purposely underinflated tires."

Under the new regime,"bodyprints" were to be taxed. Similar to a carbon footprint, this was a calculation of the amount of space you took up on this earth; the more space you took up, the higher the tax.

A new book, "The Bodyprint Diet," became a runaway best-seller.

Larry, a notorious skinflint in the room next to Emma, had tried and failed for years to trim down from 290 pounds. He was at 260 within a month. In a surge of hypocrisy unmatched since *Elmer Gantry*, obese celebrities, journalists and even portly Ninnie politicians began to think about changing parties.

The Ninnies did not stop at taxing air and bodyprints, but inflicted their onerous policies on all manner of daily affairs. Now there were levies on family reunions (permits needed, bigger families penalized); on magazines, butcher paper, newspapers and anything else that came from downed trees, including toilet paper, a levy that particularly upset folks in areas where beans (Boston) were a popular commodity, or sauerkraut (Milwaukee) or bran (Nebraska). There also was a tariff on Bingo games, which further enraged legions of seniors who already were being squeezed on denture adhesives, liniment, and incontinence pads.

There even was an attempt to tax nostalgia, but not even the Ninnies could figure out how to police that one.

"The Ninnies don't like nostalgia because they preach that there is no such thing as the 'Good Old Days,'" Emma told Sebastian. "Before they took over, you see, the country was evil, unfair, racist, selfish, heartless, indifferent... Well, these certainly will never qualify as Good Old Days either."

In a burst of 'protect the environment' mania, the Ninnies also imposed, but then withdrew, a tax on excessive tail-wagging by dogs. They reasoned that if the butterfly effect could wreak weather havoc across the globe, then certainly countless unregulated dogs might indeed create a catastrophic climate tumult far greater than mere butterfly wings could generate, and set off cataclysmic typhoons in Japan, hurricanes in the Atlantic, cyclones in India and tornados in Kansas, maybe even all at the same time.

"But they had to abandon that when it became clear that a massive bureaucracy of inspectors would be required to police all of those wagging tails," Emma smirked. "The Ninnies certainly had nothing against big bureaucracies, worshipped them, as a matter of fact, but this prospect was too much even for them."

The new government was rapidly electrifying the whole transport system, financing renewable energy, controlling methane gas emissions, eliminating petroleum-powered cars and airliners, and overhauling every building to meet new energy efficiency standards.

"Speaking of dogs," Emma told Sebastian with a grim smile, "you'll be hard-pressed these days to find even a doghouse without a solar panel on the roof. And all of this energy efficiency must be done soon to prevent the world from ending, which, when it happens anyway, will be the sole fault of the selfish, polluting Americans, of course."

Fortunes were being made as wily investors, anticipating a world without airliners, poured money into the bridge-building industry, especially the firm that had the contract for the span from Miami to Lisbon, Portugal and the one from San Francisco to Honolulu. New power plants were being fueled by dandelions, lawn clippings, crabgrass, zucchini and other commodities of which there seemed to be an endless, inexhaustible supply. A Ninnie committee was working on how to sustain a battery-powered car on the 4,143-mile trip from Miami to Lisbon.

And there was even more to the Ninnie horror, Emma discovered.

"Hate speech" and offensive language were to be banned and penalized. The borders were now unenforced, re-education camps were established for anyone accused of a racist thought or attitude. Nations anywhere that had ever been offended by previous US policies of intervention, diplomacy and cultural misappropriation were to receive reparations.

"Starting with the French," Emma said. "We must now make apologies and payments for using words like French fries, French dressing, even French kisses. A new meaning for 'Excuse my French.'"

The management at Arthritis Acres, one of the first to espouse and adopt the Ninnie philosophy, jumped in with both feet.

"Under the new national policy, as a privileged American, part of your monthly fee will go toward the fund to reimburse Germany for the destruction the Allies wrought in bombing many of their cities into rubble during World War II," Emma was told by the home's administrator, Josef Stallingski, on her first day there.

"The Krauts started it," Emma pointed out.

Stallingski blanched.

"You can't use offensive, pejorative terms like that here."

"Okay. Jerries then, or Fritz, or Boche. And besides, we already did that."

"Did what?"

"Rebuild. And not just Germany. All of Western Europe. It was called the Marshall Plan."

"Yes, well. Then consider these belated punitive damages."

"Are you serious? I refuse to pay."

"Then life will be quite uncomfortable for you here. And besides, you have no choice. It is an automatic payment. And for your information, there are many other terms that are quite offensive and hurtful to certain groups, and thus are not acceptable here."

Stallingski waved in her face a list of forbidden terms. Emma caught a glimpse of a few of them – Cheesehead, Hillbilly, Redneck, Cracker, Oriental, Gypsy, Gringo, Eskimo, Trailer Trash, Okie, Jerk, Hick, Conservative.

14

Emma blanched. "Who decides what's hateful speech and offensive language, and what's racist and what isn't?" she asked. "And what's wrong with some beneficial US intervention when you're the biggest kid on the block and others come to you for protection?"

"We decide," said Stallingski. "And there is no such thing as beneficial intervention. The US has inserted itself into the affairs of other countries for far too long, with disastrous imperialistic effects."

"The US financed and built the Panama Canal," Emma pointed out indignantly, fixing Stallingski with a steely blue gaze. "And besides the Marshall Plan, have you not heard of the Peace Corps, or the Berlin Airlift?"

Stallingski, a bald, corpulent stub of a man in his mid-forties, turned away and ignored her, which was hard to do given Emma's feisty personality and her penchant for asserting her conservative views.

From her first day there, she was in constant pitched battle with the dictatorial management of Arthritis Acres, and often with some of her fellow residents. She suspected that management, as well as the new government, was spying on her somehow through the alarming swarm of strange-looking "labor saving" technical devices she found in her room.

Sometimes she felt like she was in one of Mao's confessional camps, where errant Communists were sent to be rehabilitated.

"You have been hoodwinked, Christopher," she scolded during one of his early visits. "Certainly we can do better than this stalag. How about a nice homeless shelter, or a tarpaper shack down by the railroad tracks, or even a manhole or a comfy culvert somewhere?"

Christopher had interviewed administrators of five senior homes in the area, and settled on Serenity Senior Sanctuary and Rest Retreat largely because of Stallingski's glowing description of the Golden Age retirement heaven that awaited his mother. It also was within a half-hour of his own house.

Emma was suspicious from the start.

"Everyone here is treated as if they were our own parents," Stallingski had said.

"Yeah, maybe if you're remembering how you had been shackled in the basement and fed gruel once a day," Emma muttered.

"Our residents enjoy a daily variety of recreational, educational and intellectual stimulation."

"Stimulation? They probably use a cattle prod to get them out of bed and up and running in the morning."

"Residents can partake of three hearty meals a day and unlimited snacks in between."

"Oliver Twist probably ate better than this."

But Stallingski succeeded in selling Arthritis Acres as Shangri-La for Seniors, and Emma soon was in hand-to-hand combat with the staff and other residents.

Stallingski explained the "rules" to her on her first day.

"You will find life here quite regimented," he said, looking out at her from beneath eyebrows the size of small hedges, "because all of you are quite old and ailing. We believe that humans in general are not capable of looking after themselves, and that is especially true of seniors. We, meaning the authorities, will control and live your life for you, because we feel you are not adept at independent thinking. Look at the mess your generation has made of things."

Emma glanced around, looking for the door. "Mess?" she mumbled under her breath. "I expect it has only just begun."

"What was that?"

"No matter. But whatever happened to that old-fashioned concept that all people are created equal?"

"Oh, certainly, yes," Stallingski replied. "Everyone is created equal, but we are more equal than you."

Emma began to protest, but he interrupted her.

"You do not make correct decisions. You will find that here in our senior utopia your diet will be nutritionally exact, there are no inefficient light bulbs or shower heads, no unnecessary oversized sodas, the water in the toilet tanks is exactly calibrated for efficiency, and you will be allowed a very precisely calculated carbon and bodyprint."

"How about my car? It's fueled by shredded cauliflower leaves. Can I keep it?"

Stallingski was immune to sarcasm.

"We have daily meetings of the residents, where everyone is free to express their opinion on anything, as long as it does not offend or hurt anyone or promote a view contrary to the views of the management and the government."

"I see. Can I say 'go screw yourself,' or call someone an asshole? I like those words. They are very direct and descriptive, very useful, even perfect, in some situations. Or must I say 'perform an act on yourself that is physically impossible,' or call you a 'posterior body cavity' instead?"

Like most Ninnies, Stallingski was humorless and dead to any sense that he was being mocked. He blanched.

"Oh, no. Our Hate Speech Committee would have to step in and discipline you. We would send everyone else to their Safe Space and you to Detention until you pledged to cease such horrific, hateful behavior. For residents who commonly use language like that, we will insist that they issue a Trigger Warning well in advance so people will have time to get to their Safe Space."

"I can think of another kind of trigger solution," Emma mused.

It probably was at this very early point in her confinement, Emma recalled later, that she began to plot her escape from this den of posterior body cavities.

THREE
Sebastian

Sebastian was the light of Emma's life, in more ways than one as it turned out. Her grandson was her most regular visitor. After his mother died in a car accident when he was 6, Emma became a primary caregiver and the most stable feminine influence in his life.

Christopher traveled and worked erratic hours as an IT specialist for a major corporation, so after Emma moved to the retirement home, Sebastian was in child care for long stretches and became accustomed to looking out for himself. After he began experimenting with the spare computer equipment his dad stored in the house, he became very proficient with the technology.

"You know, Thomas Edison's parents often were not home either," Emma told him one day to test his sense of humor. "He was pretty much left to his own devices."

She looked sharply at her 12-year-old grandson.

"Yeah, well, do you know why it took him so long to invent the light bulb?" he shot back. "Because he had been working so long in the dark."

Emma laughed and ruffled his hair. His sense of humor, obviously handed down from his grandmother, appeared to be intact.

Sebastian was lean and wiry, athletic, well on his way to becoming a six-footer. He hadn't discovered girls yet and was content to spend his spare time tinkering with his dad's computer leftovers.

He stopped by Arthritis Acres almost every day, sometimes by bike, sometimes by bus, and became such a fixture that the other elderly residents adopted him as the unofficial house grandchild. He was sensitive, polite, thoughtful, and one day surprised his grandmother with a lantern light contraption that he said would help them stay connected.

"Look, Grammy, here's how it works." He showed her a small vertical rectangular glass box that connected wirelessly to a computer and then beyond.

"I have the same box in my bedroom," he said, "and whenever I touch it, yours will light up, so you will know I am thinking about you. Then you can touch yours and mine will light up, too, so we're kind of connected through the ether."

Emma thought this was the most exceptional, thoughtful gift she had ever received. She hugged him fiercely. It wouldn't be long before she would put Sebastian's device to a very expedient use.

§§§

Sebastian was bright and inquisitive and loved listening as Emma, armed with 80-some years of memories about economic depressions and war, prosperous times and astonishing national achievements, schooled her grandson in the wonders and joys of America.

"This is one person, at least, I can influence before the Ninnies and progressives take their shot at him." As a former history teacher, she was well-prepped.

"We are so fortunate to be living in this glorious country," she told him. "For hundreds of years it has been a beacon of hope to oppressed and victimized people from all over the world. They came here legally to escape poverty and oppression and despair, and used their talents and ambition to live The American Dream. They *created* the American Dream.

"America has always been a land of rugged individualism, self-reliance and accountability. We have no patience for 'entitled' whiners and slackers, who expect something for nothing, who do nothing to help themselves, who always blame others for their abysmal economic circumstances."

Sebastian, patting down his stubborn blond cowlick, listened with interest. He didn't hear many ideas like this in his classrooms, which no longer taught archaic concepts like American exceptionalism and the great melting pot and the notion of legal immigration. They didn't teach cursive writing anymore either, which made Emma very sad to think that Sebastian might never be able to read the poignant letters that her mother and father had exchanged during World War II, when he was with the Marines in the Pacific and she was at home, writing him daily with news about the home front. The bundle of living-history letters was in a box under her bed now. Would they some day be incomprehensible to all but scholars?

She remembered one, especially, where her father entreated his wife to be strong amid the hardships and uncertainties she faced.

"This war will be over some day," he wrote from a far-off island battlefield. "We are all anxious to be done with this nasty business, but we all know, too, that it has to be done. To a man here, we feel we are helping pay our country back for the many blessings it has bestowed on us and our families."

Emma blinked back tears as thoughts of her father overwhelmed her. She had only dim memories of him before he left for the war; he did not come back.

"You know, you should try to learn cursive on your own, and I could help you," she said suddenly, only half-kidding, after telling Sebastian about the letters. "Then some day you could join us old geezers in the resistance, plotting a revolution against the Ninnies, and we could communicate in a secret cursive code that nobody else understands."

Emma was certain that some of the new ways were not really better than the old ones. She supposed that a lot of seniors probably felt that way. She believed in her heart, and was sure that a lot of others did, too, that the America she loved was under relentless attack by menacing agents of change.

"There are powerful, sinister forces out there determined to change this marvelous country, to turn it into something a lot of us don't want," Emma told her grandson. "They are consumed with the idea that America has not always been fair to all races and genders, that we should pay forever for the sins of our past, that we should all share everything, regardless of what some people might contribute.

"They call their utopia socialism, which means 'share the misery'. They resent capitalism, the economic engine that powers this marvelous country, and which means 'share the success and happiness and progress.' Socialism is mutual shared poverty. Everyone is equal, all right. Equally oppressed. Those who embrace socialism obviously have never lived in a country that practices it."

Sebastian was getting a different version of American history than his classmates back at Thomas Jefferson Junior High, which the Ninnies were trying to change to Fidel Castro Junior High.

"Americans are not a particular people from a particular place," Emma continued. "They are the embodiment of a stunning idea, a grand experiment where people govern themselves, a nation encompassing freedom- and liberty-loving people from everywhere – Greeks, Norwegians, Irish, Turks, English, French, Swedes, Africans, Asians, Arabs, whatever, whether Christian or Jewish or Muslim, or Buddhist or atheist or Rastafarian.

"We invented globalism before it was popular with the Ninnies, before it became a leftist buzzword. America is home to every nationality on the globe. This is the original brand of globalism, right here, in action, every day,

"They came here for opportunity, to make a comfortable life for themselves and their families, to stretch their wings, to reach for the stars, to make the most of their God-given talents and develop their full potential. Here is where they could hit the jackpot, reach for the brass ring. The Ninnies would deny them all that.

"All these people came here to be Americans, not hyphenated Americans. But these days there are, unfortunately, people who are AINOs – Americans in Name Only – who at their core do not believe in the America I believe in, who want to change the system that has brought us to global greatness, whose permanent allegiance remains pledged to another culture and philosophy, another way of life, maybe even another flag.

"So what the hell are they doing here?" she said, her voice rising, as it always did when she got worked up about her beloved country, forgetting for a moment that her audience was one 12-year-old boy. "This is America! If you prefer some other place, go there! After all, the border is open! So leave!"

Sebastian, alarmed that she was working herself into a lather again, interrupted her patriotic soliloquy. For a class project he had interviewed her and then written a biography, so he had heard her stories about hardships and heroes before, and he had an idea.

"Grammy, you feel so deeply about this, and tell such great stories, that you should share them with other people. I bet lots of them feel the way you do, don't like what's going on here these days."

21

"I know they do. But how do I go about reaching them?"

"Well, I've been thinking about that. You should write a blog."

"A blog? What's that?"

"Well, it's your own little space on the Internet. You write whatever you want, whatever you're thinking, like a diary or a letter to somebody, only it's seen by lots of people instead of just one."

"Oh dear. But they monitor everything we do here. The Thought Police would never allow my patriotic, capitalistic ramblings, otherwise known as the truth, to leave the building. Too subversive."

Sebastian thought about that for a moment.

"Well, I could help you. You type what you want to say on your computer and then I'll come over and scan it to my mobile phone or transfer it to a flash drive, and then go home and put it on the blog that I'll create for you.

"They'll think you're just ordering bran cereal and prune juice or hearing aids on the internet, as usual, or writing granny stuff like recipes, or letters to doctors, or to my teachers, telling them what a magnificent and intelligent grandson you have and insisting that I had no part in that unfortunate episode where peanut butter was smeared on all the door-knobs."

He waited for a reaction. But she was preoccupied with this idea.

"Well, just make sure you deserve a letter like that. But let me think about it. Sounds like something I might enjoy. If nothing else it might help me blow off steam and get my mind off of some of the horrid people I have to put up with here."

Sebastian had another suggestion.

"You could use the lantern light to signal me whenever you had something new."

And so Sebastian became the light of her life in a whole new way.

FOUR
Birth of a Blog

Emma was at war with Commandant Stallingski from her first day at Arthritis Acres Re-education Camp, when she was ushered to her room and found it already adorned with a cross-stitched plaque on one wall reading, "From each according to his ability, to each according to his need."

"How inspiring," Emma said, looking around at her new surroundings. She rummaged through her moving boxes, still stacked along one wall, and replaced the offensive adage with one of her own. A quote from Irving Berlin, it said:

> *The world would not be in such a snarl,*
> *had Marx been Groucho instead of Karl.*

She also would have preferred quotes by Patrick Henry or Thomas Paine, but, given the oppressive, dictatorial atmosphere of the place, knew she would have better luck asking for sayings by Vladimir Putin or Supreme Leader Kim jong-un.

It was a small, comfortable apartment, with a bedroom and bathroom, living area and small kitchen. The TV set in the cozy living area beamed only leftist/progressive channels, Emma discovered to her horror.

Arthritis Acres was divided into two wings – hers, which housed still-functioning senior citizens who needed a minimum of assistance, and another, separate nursing facility that was populated by the ailing and frail elderly, some of them on the edge of dementia or even past it. Emma avoided this part of the building; she did not like to be reminded of what might be in her own future – confined to a wheelchair, staring blankly into the distance, unable even to recognize Christopher and Sebastian.

The public rooms, such as the dining room, television room and activities room, bore plaques with familiar honorific names – each one a prominent Ninnie socialist or a dictator or a communist agitator.

"Where are the Chairman Mao toilets?" Emma wondered aloud. "Where's the Lenin torture chamber? The Hugo Chavez trash room?"

If all this wasn't warning enough, Emma began to suspect that she was confined to a special kind of Ninnie hell when the Commandant summoned everyone to a 'house meeting' to welcome Emma as the newest resident. She learned that each board member of the residents' association had been hand-picked by Stallingski because, as he put it, "We do not want to encourage any idea that the residents actually are competent enough to make intelligent voting decisions or have a hand in running the home."

"Just like outside," Emma seethed. "Lip service to democracy and elections, while making sure they win by any means necessary."

It was a vivid reminder for her of the changing world beyond the Arthritis Acres doors.

"It's come down to people who believe in a freely-elected government against those who do not believe in any government that is not controlled by them," she complained to Sebastian during one of his early visits. "They believe the American people cannot be trusted to elect the "right" people.

"And if some interloper happens to break into the sacred circle, they immediately connive, scheme and obstruct to get power back through courts, trickery, the bureaucracy, regulations, civil unrest, political correctness. They want their own Designer Constitution, their very own dictatorship. They don't really believe in a fair election process. And these people call themselves Americans?"

Emma saw in this attempt to turn her country into a socialist, one-world utopia, frightening parallels to some of the darkest periods in recent world history, nightmares of barbarism and cruelty.

"Are we headed for another era of knocks on the door in the middle of the night, when nonbelievers in the new utopia are hauled out of their homes and disappear?"

It was at this point that Emma decided a blog might be a very useful thing – not only as a release for her increasing hostility to what was going on around her, but also as a call to others who might share her frustrations about the slow betrayal and disintegration of their country.

She feared the nation was at a tipping point – where half the people wanted a free republic and the other half was being groomed to want free everything, where individual success was demonized to justify taking their possessions and money.

"Back on my old street, it seems half the people were on food stamps and disability," she told Sebastian. "And for many of them, both their need and their disability were questionable.

"Half of the people are going to say why work when they think the other half is going to provide them with everything they need."

Even Sebastian, at his tender age, could see where that might lead.

"So you study, work hard, get a job, then watch while your money is redistributed to somebody who didn't," he said.

"Exactly!"

"You should put all of this stuff in that blog. You would feel better."

Emma nodded. "Don't get me started. I might never stop."

Emma brooded about her first encounters with Arthritis Acres management, and the oppressive atmosphere that pervaded the place. She suspected that more ugly incidents and confrontations might lie ahead.

"Everything is racist or sexist or xenophobic or white privilege to them. Their minds are closed to any but their own fanatical beliefs. They only see what they want to see. If you disagree with them, you are racist and creating a 'climate of hate'.

"If you are proud of your country and its history, you are a white supremacist and a racist. If you are against unlimited illegal immigration, you are a racist. If you prefer white wedding gowns and contemporary white kitchens and white chocolate, you are racist. If you like milk and rice and vanilla ice cream you are racist. It never stops.

"Next they'll be protesting why bandages and toothpaste and marshmallows and flour can't come in some other colors. Is the day coming when we can't be seen in white clothes or a white car?"

Emma was on a roll, even if her audience again consisted of her 12-year-old sounding board.

"See, I warned you not to get me started," she said.

"The Ninnies tolerate, condone and even instigate much of the incivility, bad manners, rudeness, mocking of religion, and intolerance of other opinions that have become so common. Back in my day, if I can use that phrase without being branded a regressive relic, some of the language you hear on the street today, even from women and children, would get you a slap in the face or a punch in the nose.

"They want to tell you what to eat, what to wear, what to believe, they want to take your guns and cars, your crucifixes, tell you what words are acceptable, who to vote for. They will attack you for what you are wearing or for your choice of restaurants or shops and for daring to declare an opposite point of view.

"They have adapted the Nazi strategy, to make it so uncomfortable for people with opposite opinions – by shaming, embarrassment, beatings, vandalism, boycotts – that they become afraid to speak up against this woke oppression. And soon some of the browbeaten don't care anymore about creeping socialism or the American flag being burned or if Columbus statues are toppled.

"They want to control your life, even eliminate your right to be contrary. Talk about cancel culture: They want to cancel out everything that stands in their way.

"There was a time when you could say, 'Well, people are entitled to their own opinion.' Not anymore.

"As for guns, how does being stripped of your right to defend yourself make this country any more 'safe'? My understanding of the Second Amendment is that it guarantees your right to fight back.

"Instead of taking guns away from law-abiding citizens, why not take them from criminals? They want to take the guns away from the people who didn't do it."

Emma paused, aware that she was in the middle of a rant. But she couldn't help herself. Her country and her belief system were being abused.

"Oh, my, you certainly have got me started. But I fear for our country these days, and I never did before. When the Ninnies control things, their deplorable record of failure becomes obvious for anyone to see. Look at the places they have controlled, the neighborhoods they have allowed to become blemished and stained and trashed – Chicago, Seattle, Portland, San Francisco, Detroit, Baltimore… How dumb *are* people, anyway, to let this continue? These aren't shining cities anymore; parts of them are tarnished, slimed, disintegrating hulks, while their governments stand by and watch.

"I am trying hard not to lose my faith in the intelligence of the American people, the way they keep re-electing some of the same incompetent dolts to office, and keep getting the same disastrous results. Is the great American epoch going to end like Rome's, overrun by deluded socialist barbarians?"

Emma also felt it was time to school Sebastian in another critical aspect of the Ninnie makeup.

"You need to know something very important about the Ninnies, which makes them very different from the rest of us, and maybe helps to explain them. Most of them have no sense of humor. None. That's what makes them so pinch-faced and grumpy and perpetually angry – everything is potentially offensive to them. For those that do have a sense of humor, it often is the cruel and vindictive kind, aimed at hurting, belittling, ridiculing.

"Most of these people are so *serious*. I fear that under them, we are losing our national sense of humor. Tell a Ninnie a joke and they stare back with that 'I-don't-get-it' look. That's their problem, in a nutshell – they just don't get it.

"A sense of humor is one of the most valuable things a person – a country – can possess. Without one, the world is a grim, sad place, filled with grim, sad people. America has always been a place with an impish, playful, puckish national sense of humor. Promise me you will always hang on to yours. It makes life so much more pleasant."

Sebastian nodded and jumped in. "Did you hear the one about the Ninnie who walked into a bar with a talking dog under his arm? The dog says, 'Bartender, give us a couple of beers...'"

Emma bit, and raised her eyebrows questioningly.

"The bartender tells the dog, "Sorry, sir, but no Ninnies allowed in here."

FIVE
A Day in the Life

Anxious to see if she couldn't find *something* positive about her new surroundings, Emma explored the activities calendar, but was disappointed at the slender, restrictive offerings.

She dropped in first on a meeting of the Book Club, but left after perusing the day's list of recommended reading, top-heavy with anti-American tracts and such tomes as Chairman Mao's *Little Red Book* and Saul Alinsky's *Rules for Radicals.*

She leafed through a copy of *Marxism for Dummies.*, but soon dropped it.

"That's either an oxymoron or a paradox, I'm not sure which."

Two portly ladies were arguing over which book was more significant — Hitler's *Mein Kampf* or Marx's *Das Kapital.*

"What's there to argue about?" Emma wondered. "What a choice! Do I prefer a lethal injection or the electric chair?"

Then she tried joining a card game, but found it difficult to follow the new Ninnie-ized rules. For starters, the decks no longer had Kings or Queens ("demeaning, outdated images offensive to the working class"). The Queen had been replaced with a gender-neutral white birch icon and the King had given way to a Norway pine, but neither probably would last. The Swedes objected that the Norway pine was exclusionary, the Norwegians complained that it was blatant cultural misappropriation, and the white birch, well, that was so obviously racist.

"Have they considered a redwood or a black cherry?" Emma wondered helpfully.

There also was dissatisfaction with other prominent card faces. The feminists took issue with the Jack and said it should be replaced with a Jill, and while they were at it, renewed their old grievance about that nursery rhyme, complaining again that Jack always got to go up and down the hill first, while Jill always "came tumbling after."

In fact, Emma discovered that the PC people had even extended their reach to nursery rhymes. The culture warriors were quite sure there was something very offensively racist about "Baa, Baa Black Sheep," weren't quite sure what it was yet, but just give them time…

Emma shook her head when she noticed another popular tale had been relabeled "Three Sight-Disadvantaged Mice."

An influential cohort, led and financed by a prominent hardware store chain, objected to the use of the Ace as a playing card, arguing that it was unfair, hurtful and exclusionary to favor one chain over another with all of that free advertising.

In such matters, the nation had to turn to the new Ninnie Department of Universal Harmony (DUH) for a ruling. In. their bureaucratic frenzy, the Ninnies had set up a widespread net of new regulatory agencies, and there were bureaus now governing everything from aphid abatement to zinnia colors. There even was a bureau that oversaw all the other bureaus.

The compromise they came up with pleased nobody. The face cards would become Horse, Cow, Alligator, which set off a whole new round of squabbling among animal activists lobbying for and against the choices. Donkey advocates, mostly Democrats, were especially vocal and brayed loudly. The Ace was replaced with a Hamburger, so squabbling hardware chains then gave way to squabbling burger chains jockeying for position.

And while they were at it, in the name of political correctness, the Ninnies changed the suites as well. Spades (horrors, look it up) became Beets. Clubs (all those lily-white country clubs, you know) became Cucumbers. Diamonds (more white wealthy privilege) became Zucchinis. And Hearts, well, they had nothing against Hearts, but the multi-colored Watermelon (green and black on the outside, red and white with specks of black on the inside) was felt to be a perfect expression of diversity.

Emma collared the Social Director in the coffee room and complained that the new Ninnie lexicon had seeped even into the world of fun and games, and that some traditional retirement pastimes were missing.

"You don't even have a woodworking shop," she said. "Where are old guys supposed to build their birdhouses? And what happened to good old-fashioned fun like Monopoly and Scrabble and chess and even checkers?"

"They have all been deemed offensive for a variety of reasons," replied April Thistlewait, a chirpy young thing with multiple degrees in Leisure Studies, Storytelling, Popular Culture and Nannying.

"We did birdhouses for a while until some of our birdwatchers complained that it was unfair and discriminatory. All of them were designed for martins and sparrows and finches and wrens, and there was nothing for larger birds like eagles and herons and condors. We tried to explain that a condor house would need 800 board feet of lumber and a workshop the size of an airplane hangar, but we had to relent when they brought an avian equal-housing complaint against us. Luckily, there aren't any condors around here.

"As for Scrabble, well it's too difficult to police and prevent the use of ugly, horribly hurtful words, like 'freedom' and 'liberty' and 'ambition' and 'initiative' and 'conservative.' Monopoly, well, that just glorifies capitalism and the idea of private property, and we don't do that here. Chess and checkers, they have more of those horrid concepts like kings and queens and knights and bishops and such."

"What about bowling?"

"Oh, no. Not allowed. Sends a very unwelcome message, especially to children. Think about it: 'Throw a big, heavy, dangerous ball at some objects, see them all fall down, and then rejoice.' I'm sure you can see the harm in that."

Emma could not.

"I know you're going to ask about darts. Well, there's certainly a safety factor there. Goodenough Chambers, he's 94, you know, mistook the Wheel of Fortune wheel for the dartboard one night and threw a dart through the screen of our new 60-inch TV set. It's lucky Vanna didn't get hurt. We had to move the dartboard away from the TV."

Emma stared at Thistlewait, waiting for a smile or a wink. None was forthcoming.

Emma also noted the absence of common senior pursuits like shuffleboard and bridge.

"Outdoor shuffleboard can be quite controversial, because it has those disks of varying colors. We started with the traditional black and yellow ones, but then Dermot Soaring Eagle complained that there was no red. So we replaced yellow with red, and naturally Wo Tung-ting was offended and put up a stink. So we put yellow back and added white also to forestall complaints by right-wingers, of which there are few or none here anyway, you know. And as for bridge, well, there are some very hurtful terms there, like dummy."

"That's not what dummy means," Emma protested.

"And trump. Especially trump. But no matter. There are enough other games to keep our residents happy. Like bingo, and badminton and croquet."

"Oh, whoopee," Emma said.

"But we are not really very fond of any of those, either, because that means somebody is going to win and somebody is going to lose and somebody then is going to be hurt and resentful.

"Same for musical chairs, and piñatas. It is our duty here to protect residents, to shield them from hurtful activities. We prefer games where everybody wins, where everybody gets a trophy.

"Now dominoes, there is the perfect game. Blacks and whites together, in perfect harmony. And karaoke. Perfectly safe activity because everybody is so horribly, equally horrible at it."

Emma protested. "But these are adults, who have lived in the actual world for years, who have dealt with the hardships and realities of real life. I think they could manage the trauma of finishing second in a shuffleboard match."

Thistlewait smiled sweetly.

"We don't think so," she said, echoing the official Ninnie line. "They have made poor decisions all of their lives, and now we are making the decisions for them, because look at the state of the world they have left us. So now, in their declining years, we need to protect them from themselves, in the kinder, gentler world we have created."

Emma was incredulous.

"Girl, do you read the newspapers? Do you watch the news? I haven't noticed that terrorist attacks have become any kinder or gentler,

31

unless you mean they just slowly torture people to death now instead of beheading them.

"And there was a time when, if people disagreed, they would peacefully assemble, march for their cause, or petition the government. Now, they burn down cities and loot what's left."

Thistlewait, like all Ninnies, was uninsultable, immune to sarcasm or the truth. She took a sip of her black coffee.

"I hate black coffee," she said suddenly.

"Then why do you drink it that way?"

"Because it's symbolically insulting to add milk or cream to black coffee. It dilutes and disrespects the black experience, the black identity, the black heritage. Look at the terrible message it sends – 'This black is not suitable, we have to whiten it up a little.'"

Emma was momentarily speechless. By the time she recovered, Thistlewait had turned her attention to Saturday's costume party, where everybody usually came as themselves because any kind of costume usually was offensive or hurtful to somebody or other.

"Tell me about the costumes," Emma said. "This has got to be good."

"Well, Prudence Persimmons came last time as a lovely flower but then spent the entire evening fending off the advances of Hiram Hornblower, dressed as a bee and determined to pollinate her," Thistlewait said. "Ludwig Ledbetter spent a lot of money to look like an actual hot dog, complete with mustard and relish, but had to leave early, hounded out of the room by the home's vegetarian cohort.

"And everybody wondered what Clementine Cadwalader must have been thinking when she came as The Old Woman Who Lived in a Shoe. She left early too, sobbing, and should have known the Feminist Club members would gang up on her for extolling a woman Who Had So Many Children She Didn't Know What to Do."

Thistlewait frowned and shook her head in relating how the retirement home still had not recovered from the scandal of two years past, when Ephraim Hodgekiss had the audacity to come in blackface, and was immediately set upon by Comrade Stallingski, who excoriated him for demeaning an entire race.

"That's soot," Hodgekiss had said defensively. "Hard to pose as a chimney sweep without picking up some soot here and there."

Incredulous, Emma turned to go. Thistlewait called after her.

"We also have some wonderful outings and excursions you might be interested in. Next week we're going to a Ninnie museum where there's going to be a workshop on how to most effectively accuse your political opponents of the same despicable tactics that you yourself are using. There also will be a colorful display there of the flags of all 57 states.

"Then the week after that we're going to the shrine of Alejandro Hernandez from Honduras, to celebrate his 2001 milestone as the first person in the 21st century to successfully sneak over the border and enter our country illegally. Alejandro himself might show up. He comes out of hiding occasionally to claim his free benefits.

"We're also working on a visit to Ninnie headquarters, where we will learn the techniques they have perfected for transforming beautiful, efficient places like California into unaffordable, squalid calamities. It could be fun, unless you feel that it might be too depressing?"

"I've got to get out of here," Emma muttered.

Sebastian was waiting for her, back at her room.

"So show me how to do this blog thing," she said. "I'm like that guy in that movie. I'm as mad as hell and I'm not going to take this anymore!

"I just wish your grandfather was here, but maybe it's just as well that he isn't, because he couldn't stand what's going on any more than I can."

Emma became very quiet suddenly and looked off into the distance. Sebastian saw a tear run down her cheek, and then another.

"Oh, Sebastian! I miss him so much, even after all these years. We were young sweethearts, we had such a wonderful life in this wonderful country, we did so many things together, lots of them with your dad, went so many places. He was so smart, so witty. I miss him every day..."

Her voice faded away and she began to sob softly.

Sebastian had never seen his grandmother cry. She was always the rock, the glue that held the family together.

He wasn't sure what to do. So he did the instinctive thing. He put his arms around her and they cried together.

Grandmother and grandson stood there for a few moments, lost in their memories, until finally Sebastian stepped back.

"What do you want to call it?" he said.

"Call it? Oh, the blog. Oh, my. Do I have to call it something? I never thought of that. What do you think?"

"How about 'Grammy's Gripes,' or 'Fodder for Fogeys,' or 'The Geezer Gazette,' or 'Codgerly Quips'?"

Emma, dabbing at her eyes with a tissue, grinned and looked at her grandson suspiciously.

"You're having a lot of fun with this, aren't you?"

"Or, how about this?" he said. "'Don't Get Me Started'. You're always saying that."

After Sebastian left she began hammering away at her computer.

Soon, Sebastian's lantern lit up.

SIX

Don't Get Me Started...

Emma's Blog #1, Jan. 24, in a year not too far away...

If you have stumbled upon this blog, perhaps while looking for a recipe for chicken dumpling soup or advice on how to tell if your lover is cheating on you, welcome! You won't find either of those here, but you will find some definite opinions. Or rants. Take your pick.

If you are a sensitive, leftist, do-gooder Ninnie soul who is easily offended and needs a trigger warning to protect you from hurtful truths, you should probably look elsewhere for enlightenment. But if you decide to stick around, maybe it will do you some good.

My name is Emma. I am 86, a widowed grandmother, and a retired history teacher. I live in a retirement home managed and populated by a motley assortment of clueless Ninnie misfit nincompoops, in an environment too much like what's happening in our larger world today. You will meet some of them here.

My son, Christopher, arranged for a place for me here in the mistaken belief that this was a normal retirement residence. If this is normal, we are in big trouble. If this is the new normal, we are absolutely doomed. I might be mistaken, but maybe this is where *One Flew Over the Cuckoo's Nest* was filmed...

My grandson, Sebastian, is tired of listening to my rants and says I should write a blog as therapy, to blow off steam, to keep the demons of depression and despair at bay. So this blog will be mostly about me and my opinions about a vanishing America, and aimed at my fellow seniors and patriots who dearly miss the country they grew up in, but anyone is welcome to come along for the ride.

I am biding my time here while I plot an escape from this leftist lair of loonieness. My husband died some years ago, and I miss him terribly, so

I am treating this blog as a letter to him, to let him know what's been going on down here since he left. He wouldn't like it very much... I trust he has internet access where he is. They have everything up there, don't they?

§§§

Well, Harry, you won't believe where I am. I'm stuck in a retirement community run and inhabited by people who are not exactly compatible with my core beliefs. The management style here seems to be patterned after the one in East Germany back in the old Soviet puppet days. In fact, Congress is controlled by a new socialist political party that I like to call the Ninnies.

Christopher thought I would be better off in a retirement home, and maybe he's right. I've had several 'mishaps' lately, like trying to brush my teeth with a tube of hemorrhoid cream, and Sebastian is still kidding me about the time he found a mixing spoon in my fresh loaf of banana bread.

I seem to be forgetting a lot of things, lately. I've had so many memory lapses that I finally went to see a doctor. He insisted I pay him in advance.

I know, I know. That joke's so old that it first appeared in hieroglyphs.

Anyway, Sebastian says I should write a blog, which might help me connect with some likeminded people out there. So here's my first attempt. Maybe I can find some new friends – I really don't like the word 'comrades' – who think like I do about our country and what's happening to it.

Harry, it's an upside-down-world here now. The Ninnies have taken over. But maybe not for long. If you listen to them, the world is going to end in a few years anyway. In the meantime, I fear we are in for one helluva ride.

Remember when kids used to be terrified by weathermen who told them to head for the basement at every sign of a fresh breeze? Well, they still do, but now the Ninnies have added a new twist by terrifying them with endless warnings about the looming end of the world unless we mind our polluting ways.

One of the chief culprits is the cow. Yes, Harry, the cow.

'Don't Get Me Started'

The Ninnies have determined that methane gas from our bovines is contributing considerably to the pollution and decline of the planet. There is a huge and influential anti-agriculture lobbying group out there called 4F (like 4H, only instead of Head, Heart, Hands, Health, it stands for Final Freedom From Flatulence). Farmers are not very fond of the bureaucrats who come around regularly to police and measure the methane levels – the Flatulence Abatement Response Team, otherwise known as FART.

An enterprising young college student, to the horror of his anti-capitalist professors, has come up with a possible solution to the methane problem, at least as it applies to cows. He has invented what he calls a Flatulence Suppressor, which can be outfitted to our bovine friends to suppress and muffle their unwelcome eruptions. Don't ask me how it works. I don't want to know. He's making a mint. Ah, the sharp smell of capitalistic success!

And it's not just cows, and not just the US. A lot of people also are holding their noses over baked beans, cabbage, broccoli, legumes, onions, wheat, garlic, beer, whatever – the globalists want to ban anything that might create intestinal rumblings and unpleasant vapors. An Italian newspaper put it this way: "Arrivederci Aroma."

What's next? Will the noise police be accompanying the flatulence squads, wielding decibel meters to search out and measure our little aromatic thunderclaps? Take it from me, we here at Arthritis Acres are particularly vulnerable because some things are inevitable and universal, some questions have obvious answers: Is water wet? Is ice cold? Do old folks fart?

Well, if nothing else, our offices and living rooms should smell a lot better.

Cows as a whole are now quite out of favor. Remember, Harry, how you loved those steaks from the grill? Well, that's all they're going to be soon – a memory. In this new touchy-feely society, beef cuts are disappearing from the butcher case, not only because of the methane terror but because of the violence done to cows in the stockyards. Next, I suppose, we should expect to hear about cows having their own Ninnie-approved attorneys, from the American Cattle Litigation Union, no less.

Sheep and chickens and pigs will be targeted next. Sort of a "Moo, Too" movement, I suppose.

I probably need to get used to a plant-based diet. Can't wait to taste the new poison ivy burgers.

I heard a bubbly, clueless reporter on one of those Ninnie networks ask a politician why we have to kill all of those poor animals anyway. "Why can't we just buy the meat we need at the supermarket instead?" she said tearfully.

Give me a break.

The cow caper may be just the beginning of the Ninnie legacy. Remember when they came for our light bulbs? Then they came for our toilets. They came for our dishwashers. They came for our cars. They came for our shower heads. They came for our airline flights. Next they will be coming for our religion, our guns, our rights to free speech and assembly, and then for _us_....

Harry, remember when deranged folks used to stand on street corners holding signs saying, "Repent! The End is Near!"? Well, there's a new twist on that now. The Ninnies are insisting that the world is going to end soon in an environmental cataclysm, amid a cloud of methane and smog, rising seas, and sidewalks too hot to walk on. But they're also talking about free everything-for-everybody and unlimited immigration, so they really can't be too worried about the future.

More likely, with a flood of unvetted illegal immigrants, there's going to be a need for more homeless shelters, more courts and jails, more social services, which is just the way the Ninnies want it – a permanent class of poor wretches dependent on the Ninnie government for everything. To finance their free utopia they will tax the wealthy into oblivion, but once their prey disappears, how do the Ninnies pay for anything?

One thing they are good at is raising taxes. Tax everybody into poverty and unemployment, to provide free pie-in-the-sky social programs and environmental controls to save the world. That's what the Ninnies are all about: control.

They are bringing commerce to a standstill – no more drilling for oil, no more polluting cars, no more smokestacks, no more airlines, no more mines or lumber. They will have to build houses soon out of something else – maybe ice in the northern zones, except if you believe them, soon there will be no such thing as ice.

Look for construction to begin soon on that bridge to Europe, and another to Hawaii, first legs of a new trans-ocean route for electric cars. Imagine that. Pretty soon we'll be able to drive around the world. Poor

Mom and Dad. Aren't long car trips already bad enough? "Are we there yet? Are we there yet?"

Harry, the Ninnies seem to have divided themselves into four distinct groups, each of which is attacking American principles and values from a different direction. And each raises a lot of unanswerable questions.

First, we have the *Wuss Division*. These are the whining softies and snowflakes who are against violence to cows, need Trigger Warnings and Safe Spaces, are abolishing the cruel concepts of school homecoming queens and honor rolls, and insisting that everybody now will get a trophy. They dislike waterboarding and "enhanced interrogation," apparently on grounds that we should be nice to the people who want to kill us. They say we should peacefully co-exist with terrorists, socialists, criminals, illegals, rioters, looters, Chinese communists and anybody else devoted to eliminating us and our way of life. A lot of these reprehensibles have something in common – because of the great courage of their convictions, they like to hide behind masks and hoods – just like the KKK.

These buttercups also were against the US bombing of enemy airfields and hideouts because of "environmental concerns." If it's ever left to these people to defend us, I fear we might have to fight off an approaching enemy with water balloons, rubber swords, and bows with suction-cup arrows.

And do I care if terrorists who killed 3,000-plus of our friends and neighbors on 9/11, and joyfully continue a policy of bombings and beheadings, are made to feel a little uncomfortable when they choke on some noxious fumes sent their way by our military? Do I care if the little cave in which they are cowering, along with 13 surrounding scrub trees, are obliterated? When pigs fly, to purposely use an animal reference that they find revolting.

The wusses require "safe zones" to protect them from uncomfortable and unwelcome opinions. Well, *they* make *me* uncomfortable, so am I not entitled to my own safe zone, sheltered from their spineless and unwelcome philosophy?

Just saying.

Then there is the *Racism/Victimhood/Privilege Division*. Discrimination now is the defense given for a lot of plain old underachievement, and a handy excuse for a failure to advance and grow, whatever your color. And if you're white, you aren't allowed to be resentful that minorities are given privileges and preference in education, housing and whatever, at the expense of others just as deserving but the wrong color, because that means you are oblivious to your guilt over slavery and your unfair and undeserved white privilege.

Well, since I never owned any slaves, and you never picked any cotton, maybe the discussion should end right here.

Shouldn't we all be treated alike? What's fair about favoring one race/sex/religion over another? Whatever happened to *merit*? And what's so "undeserved" when you struggle up from hard times and create a good life for yourself and your family? And besides, if you ask me, racial preferences just encourage more separation and stereotypes and resentment. Affirmative action says you have been accepted because of your skin color, not because of your accomplishments and potential. It says you are a token. What does that do for self-esteem? And why is it that only whites can be racist? Why aren't black colleges and the NAACP and other black groups also tarred as racist?

Seems to me that 13% of the population seems to get a disproportionate share of empathy and attention. I would guess that at least 13% of the rest of the population find themselves in less than ideal circumstances...

Just saying.

The Ninnies are quite concerned with the fate of the minorities they pander to, maybe because they fear if enough of them rise up in disillusion and anger over the consequences of their mismanagement, they will once again be the minority themselves.

Then we also have the *Multicultural and Diversity Division*. These are the people obsessed with the idea of diversity, who can't or won't accept that the expansive American culture is one of the most creative, unique and, yes, the most diverse the world has ever seen. Encouraging autonomous, separate cultures within it is self-destructive. Keep your traditions, food, customs, yes, but your primary allegiance is to your unique American culture.

All cultures are not equal: Show me the Guatemalan spaceship or the Iranian cellphone inventor or the Somalian Jonas Salk. And the language of America is and always has been English. Too many languages just encourages division – look at the immigrant ghettos. It creates confusion – a teacher struggling with a class speaking five languages. It creates plain old annoyance and animosity – a manufacturer forced to print the instructions for his widget in nine languages. One common language has made it possible for us to do the marvelous things we have done.

Don't get me started. We invented diversity and inclusion – the American Dream, the idea of the melting pot, where many cultures come together and live in harmony as one bright new shining one, sharing the best of each other's identity.

"E pluribus unum!"

Best not to get too hung up on this diversity concept, methinks. As I recall, 'diversity' includes such marvelous customs as female genital mutilation, female suppression, cannibalism, slavery, child-selling and, by some, a stated policy to eliminate all infidels – meaning people who do not believe as they do.

This obsession with "diversity" only emphasizes our differences, instead of our similarities, connections and unity as one nation. My reading of history tells me that 'diverse' peoples around the world have been busy killing and hating each other for millennia.

Just saying.

Harry, they are following this diversity and inclusionary stuff right out the window. A lot of ads and commercials these days are so crowded with mandatory diverse "inclusionaries" that the message gets lost amid the political correctness. There seems to be a new rule that says all ads now have to include a black, a white, an Asian, a Native American, a Hispanic, a Pacific Islander, a Flat-Earther, a religious Serpent-Handler, and a mixed-race couple. Next, they'll be making room for transgenders, vaccine deniers, vegetarians and at least one alien from a galaxy outside of our own. If it gets too crowded, just drop the white guy.

Don't get me started, I said.

This tokenism farce is getting so bad, Harry, that one of our major symphonies is thinking of hiring an Inuit as its conductor. He doesn't know a thing about music, can't even play a kazoo, but he sure brings diversity to the podium in his caribou-hide parka and leggings, right?

If you ask me, and I realize nobody has – yet, at least – all this talk of diversity, or "accommodation," and "fairness" just lowers the standards for employment, education, and morality and thus hastens the deterioration of the entire nation. Let's just cater to the lowest common denominators, right, instead of raising them, and thus let's forget about that foolish, outdated idea of merit?

Just saying. Give me a break.

Finally, there is the *Politically Correct Division,* notable for its reluctance to offend anybody, even if you have to twist the language into a pretzel to do it, even if you offend someone else by not offending the party of the first part. Christians, for example, are persecuted in their own "Christian" country – they can't wear a cross or pray to God in their classrooms, inscribe the Ten Commandments on a public building, even hesitate to say "Merry Christmas," all because someone might be offended.

Christians can't erect public religious displays on their holy days, either, yet Muslims are allowed to pray in the public streets, even though some tenets of their religion offend a lot of people. Discrimination against Muslims is called racism or xenophobia, but Muslim discrimination against me is OK because it's their religion. Huh? I'm still waiting for the news story about the Muslim country that welcomed millions of Christians...

God is out of favor with the Ninnies, even though he is etched indelibly into the Declaration of Independence. To the Ninnies, to socialists, the Government is God, and God is Government.

They have no answers to anything, they only raise questions:

Why do they make such a fuss about foreigners interfering with our elections, but they're OK with illegal aliens voting? And why do they want to fine us for not having health insurance, but give it to illegals for free? Why do they want to count people who aren't Americans in the American census?

Why are they pro-choice, except when it comes to guns, smoking, schools, "climate change," health care, energy, union membership, light bulbs, plastic bags, sodas, straws, even how you should vote?

Why do they preach incessantly the gospel of diversity, but can't abide a diversity of views?

Why do they want background checks on gun owners but not on suspicious voters or illegal aliens?

Why do they scream for a higher minimum wage and then complain bitterly and ask for reduced working hours when it pushes them into a higher income bracket and jeopardizes their housing subsidy? Why do they scream for a higher minimum wage and then wonder why good entry-level jobs are disappearing?

Why are they against the 'unfair' Electoral College, but like the 'Super Delegate" rule at their conventions? They want to change the Constitution, change the Electoral College, because they oppose anything that doesn't always work in their favor.

Why are they so hung up on gender equality? They want us to be free to marry anyone we want, maybe even our Old English sheepdog or our potted Saguaro cactus.

Why is it that if you protest their brand of Ninnie Fascism you are an obstructionist or even a terrorist, but if you burn the flag or kneel during the national anthem you are just exercising your first amendment rights to protest social injustice? Why do they accuse conservatives of the very Nazi traits they are practicing themselves?

Why is it okay to pay billions to oil nations that hate us, rather than drill for our own vast and plentiful reserves? Some of those billions often just disappear into the swamp of corruption.

Why do they say children of immigrants who came here illegally should not have to pay for their parents' crime, but today's white people are supposed to pay forever for the behavior of 19th-century slaveholders?

Why do they disparage and want to defund the police, yet when their own city or neighborhood is threatened by thugs and rioters, they want to know why nobody does anything about crime? How do you stop crime by stopping policing? As for all those celebrities who are in favor of gun control or confiscation, let's take the guns away from their bodyguards and see how they feel then.

Why is it that the radicals and socialists here have things that people in other countries only dream about, yet they want the US to be more like those other countries? Europe takes a month off in the summer, after four-day weeks. Americans are always working, because it's in their DNA, an ethic that has put us on top and keeps us there, at least so far. America's success has been built on education, ambition, self-reliance and personal independence.

It seems to me that those coming here just for the free ride, who won't assimilate, are ensuring their own failure, because they don't have the basic elements of being an American – drive, ambition, the competitive nature, the ethics, the determination to succeed in any undertaking and the tremendous sense of self-satisfaction that comes with it. I don't like to think about the possible flip side of this – borders so porous that the great American national character will be diluted, unlike the days where newcomers had time to gradually assimilate into this grand new country, and share their marvelous customs and heritage.

A wise man once put it this way: Losers go home at quitting time, but winners go home when the work is done.

Harry, America's sacred work ethic built this country. Now it is being diluted by slackers and slouches who just want to live off of the system.

Just saying.

Well, maybe all of those questions have no answers, except in the minds of delusional progressive leftists. We should expect even more insoluble problems as time goes on, as the schools controlled by them continue to turn out more ignorant illiterates – ignorant in math, ignorant in civics, ignorant in literature, ignorant in history, especially their own glorious American history. The history they do get often is a twisted version written by socialists and communists.

Thanks to the Ninnies and their university comrades, Harry, many of the young people coming out of colleges now believe that socialism and even communism are the answers to injustice and inequality. Some of them are endowed with bizarre degrees in useless pursuits, with advanced degrees in Stupidity and Gullibility. Can you really make a living these days in Beatle Studies or White Privilege?

And I'm constantly amazed that so many of them are young women. Young women! You see them in diversity parades and "cultural awareness" rallies and race protests, screaming obscenities and appalling vulgarities in the faces of police officers. God help us if these embarrassments to womanhood are the ones bringing up our next generation.

Just saying.

Some of these bimbos are out to destroy the very system and privileged life that daddy's capitalism made possible for them.

If these people think the world is unfair now, wait until they let the socialists have a whack at it. And the next step up from there is communism, which means the government actually gets the power to take what you have at gunpoint.

Harry, the education system here is so screwed up in some places that there are people, believe it or not, who oppose the idea of teaching kids right from wrong! They say that's too judgmental. Judgmental? No wonder charter schools are popular; studies show they do a better job of educating kids, especially minorities, than some of our abysmal public schools.

Harry, in one state they even have decided that students will no longer have to demonstrate that they can read, write and do math at a high school level to graduate. Give me a break.

There seems to be an attitude out there nowadays that parents have no right to interfere with what happens in the schools, with what their kids are taught. They are discouraged from attending school board meetings. Hey, our kids do not belong to you. What is this, a return to Hitler Youth?

How long are we going to put up with this leftist crap, Harry? What's it going to take to wake up this generation? Another depression? Another war? How long will we continue to elect socialists to Congress, leftists as mayors?

Whatever happened to "Give me liberty or give me death?" Now it's, "Give me free college, free housing, free food, free health care..."

Wake up, Americans!" we are shouting.

What if they don't wake up, Harry? They are dozing while America burns.

§§§

Well folks, you can't say I didn't warn you not to get me started. You can see I definitely have some opinions. If you share them, let me know. Send me your own comments and observations. If you don't like my views, well, I feel sorry for you and will be doing everything I can to help push you back into that naive never-neverland swamp you crawled out of.

Now I have to end this first blog. Socialism is so wonderful that I'm anxious to join one of those caravans of US emigrants headed for Venezuela and Cuba. Damn, I hope they still have some room left...

§§§

"In this country you can sing and say what you want and as long as you behave yourself nobody will do anything to you. Here lives the free man."

–Danish immigrant to Iowa, 19th century

SEVEN
Sunflower and Simper

Early on during her uncomfortable tenure at Arthritis Acres, Emma tried to make the best of it and resolved to meet as many of her new neighbors as possible, maybe even make a few friends. Usually she came up empty.

Among the strange people she encountered was an unusual mother-son duo that to her, typified much of what was wrong with her disintegrating society.

Sunflower Squance was the unreconstructed daughter of 1960s hippies and grew up in a commune in San Francisco's Haight-Ashbury. She worked briefly as a waitress, sued the proprietor on trumped-up sexual harassment charges, and then lived comfortably when the award supplemented her occasional jobs first as a pole dancer and later as the manager of an escort service.

She also had income from worker's compensation after she slipped from her stripper's pole and broke an elbow, and then unemployment when the injury healed improperly and she could no longer hook her arm around the pole in a sufficiently provocative and seductive manner, and then disability benefits when she succeeded in making a case that her enticement, teasing and suggestiveness skills had been damaged to the point where she was unemployable in her chosen profession.

To Emma, a lot of the nation's present unrest could be traced to Sunflower's 1960s – the counterculture, drugs, the Vietnam War and disrespect for authority, loosening sexual standards, social tensions, and a growing generation gap.

Sunflower had spent her adult life sheltering Simper, her pampered, selfish, shiftless snowflake son, father unknown, from the winds and tides of life. She had been, and still was, a helicopter parent, hovering over his every move as if she could protect him from hurt feelings, hurt pride, and failure.

The once-platinum blonde, 63, was graying and stooped now, with a wheezy cough, tremors, sagging tattoos, chronic depression and an array of other disorders that she attributed to too many youthful years misspent on marijuana and bad LSD trips. She was spending her declining years, and her declining savings, on Arthritis Acres accommodations, and looking forward to becoming a ward of the taxpayers instead. Her son certainly would not be able to come to her rescue.

Simper Squance, 45, was short, plump and balding, with very large ears, a scruffy beard and a vague resemblance to Homer Simpson. His pasty, sallow complexion had been perfected in her basement, where he had lived ever since he graduated from Dinwiddie A&M 16 years earlier with a useless degree in Peace Studies. He wore a slightly dazed, dreamy look, and had spent too many years himself in a haze of marijuana smoke and experimenting with a cafeteria of drugs. He visited at Arthritis Acres often; it offered an escape from his drab, windowless, hermitic life.

"And I can get a decent meal," he told one of his mother's friends. "Several meals. Mommy works the dining room for doggy bags."

Simper had been living in basements so long that he had become quite accustomed to it, and even preferred it to the spacious upstairs available to him once his mother had moved to Arthritis Acres. Emma found it distracting to talk to him, not only because of his leftist political and social leanings but because he blinked constantly, as if he had just emerged from a mole hole into the light, which indeed he had.

He had a girlfriend once, for a day and a half, who backed out when she concluded that life in a damp basement with a noisy sump pump and mold on the walls was not for her.

Sunflower did not yet have the courage to tell her son that the day was approaching when she would be forced to sell the home because of her diminishing financial circumstances.

Simper ("It's a family name!" Sunflower always hissed quite defensively whenever she had to introduce him), was presently unemployed, although he had held several prestigious jobs over the years, including a stint as a bus boy at Fred's Steak and Shake, two months as a part-time school bus driver, and as an occasional cat sitter for his Aunt Pearl's ill-tempered American Shorthair, which accounted for the grotesque, vivid scar along his left cheek.

For 16 years now he had been working on his futuristic screenplay, about a teenager with superpowers who saves the world from an evil capitalist whose restaurant chain cooks with hydrogenated oils, pays only the minimum wage and defiantly insists on using plastic straws.

Simper was the product of a fawning parenting philosophy and a public education system that had allowed him to get through school with a minimum of reading, writing and reasoning skills, and then enabled him to coast through 12 unchallenging, leisurely years of college on his way to a bachelor's degree that took him as long to acquire as contemporaries who finished medical school, served a residency and were already treating patients with restless leg syndrome and hemorrhoids.

Mother and son shared several delusional beliefs: Simper was brilliant and perfect, a victim of a society that did not appreciate his talents and virtues; deserved to be president of some major corporation earning at least $500,000 a year; should have a big house and big car right out of the gate; and all of this without having to expend any energy of his own. It had never dawned on them that their naive expectations had only set them up for failure in the real world.

Both were eternally bitter that the rewards they so obviously deserved had not materialized, and made that quite clear to anyone who would listen. It was all the fault of society, the system, of unseen forces determined to keep him oppressed and in poverty. Indeed, Sunflower insisted for a time that the Russians were responsible.

"They're up there with those satellites," she said. "Who knows what they're doing, beaming down those sinister rays at him, interfering with his life?"

Emma listened, but only once. Simper had stopped by her room to return a book she had loaned, thinking it would be good for him. It was Ayn Rand's *Atlas Shrugged,* which Sebastian had smuggled in to her.

"Did you like it?" Emma asked.

"Thank you, but I didn't read it," Simper said with a smirk. "I saw a review and it seems to be a regurgitation of tired praise for capitalism and criticism of socialism. It promotes and endorses an oppressive economic system and an inequitable society where the playing field is not level and some people have to struggle not only to survive but to preserve their self-respect."

Emma knew enough about Simper to not be surprised. She was ready. She unloaded on him.

"Oh, is that right?" she hissed, ever the paragon of tact and discretion. "Is that what you learned in all those years of school? Well, listen, sonny, if I can call a 45-year-old that. You are a perfect example of the kind of pampered, entitled, disillusioned socialist misfit that our universities are turning out these days.

"The world does not owe you a living. It does not care about your wounded self-esteem. You owe the world, you owe yourself, the ambition to try to make it on your own out in a cold, cruel world that mommy cannot protect you from."

Simper tried to marshal a defense.

"Things would be a lot different under socialism," he said, stroking his comfort chicken, which he brought with him to Arthritis Acres whenever he feared that he might encounter something or someone that might hurt his feelings. "There would be no income inequality…"

Emma cut him off.

"Listen, you little twerp, most of what you enjoy in life, which would disappear under your so-called utopia, was made possible because of capitalism, the people you prefer to call profiteers."

"There would be no poor and homeless people…"

"Get a grip, kid. Life is not fair, and it never will be, even though you and your kind would like to create an entitled, coddled underclass of loafers and freeloaders used to free food, housing, education, phones, transportation and health care, with blind loyalty to the beneficent mother-state. Why should anyone work? Or maybe that's the point."

Simper plunged ahead anyway, stroking his chicken so briskly that it squawked.

"There would be no racism or economic and gender inequality, everybody would have guaranteed rights to…"

"Oh, give me a break. Everything is race, or victimhood, or oppression with some of you ignorant boobs. Some people never take responsibility for their own failures – crime, poverty, broken homes are always the fault of someone else – politicians, the system, somebody else should fix it. They prefer being professional victims. And you live in a dream world if you think 'free' education and 'free' college and 'free' health care will really be 'free.'

"Listen, I grew up in a mixed neighborhood where a lot of people were 'oppressed' – Irish, Poles, Italians, Jews, Asians, whatever. They had a hard time of it – discrimination, bias, bigotry, intolerance – but they didn't lie around whimpering and sniveling, burning down stores, pulling down statues. They did something about it, they went out and made something of themselves, showed the world that they were just as good as anybody else, and in doing so validated the American Dream."

Emma had to stop for a moment to catch her breath. "Watch your blood pressure," she told herself. Emma believed in her heart that the bias and bigotry her own family and other ethnic groups had faced in her childhood had lessened considerably over the years in a mellowing, more honorable America.

She was not done with Simper, now preoccupied with trying to comfort his stricken chicken.

"You gripe about economic equality? Most people have to *earn* their own economic equality, starting with a job and then moving on to something better, unless, like you, you're content to become a ward of the government and abandon your God-given American opportunity to strive for something better.

"Gender equality? Where are you going to find a country with a better record of opportunities for women? Saudi Arabia? Senegal, or some other oppressive Muslim nation, or maybe China, stuck in some stifling, boring, rote menial job in some stifling, boring factory where you are watched every minute?"

Simper tried to say something again, but he never had a chance.

"You should check out the lockstep lives in Cuba and China and Russia and see how the socialist utopia really works. I kinda like it if my ambition and smarts and gumption get me a better job and salary than a lazy schlump like you who wants everything for nothing. Your laziness is *your* problem, not mine or society's. And as for your 'guaranteed rights,' they start with a right to pursue a living and take care of yourself. And if you can't or won't take care of yourself, maybe you should give up your precious cell phone and $6 lattes."

Simper finally got another brief word in.

"Socialism works in places like Russia and North Korea and…"

"Are you kidding me? Is that what you want? To stand in line for hours hoping to get a loaf of bread or a potato or some precious meat before the supply runs out? Maybe you like Big Government looking over your shoulder and breathing down your neck in every area of your life.

"Socialism is just another name for tyranny – tyranny by the privileged few. The only people living well are those at the top. Under capitalism, even those climbing the ladder live better than people in a lot of other countries can ever dream of.

"You have a good chance to get to the top yourself, because of a system that encourages individual ambition, competition and accomplishment, provides an incentive to improve and excel, to imagine and soar. And then to reap the rewards of your efforts. Under this system, capitalism, you just set it in motion and then get out of the way, and just hope you don't drown in the prosperity."

Simper looked like he was going to cry. He just wanted to get away from this horrible woman who had no appreciation for his genius. But Emma was not finished.

"You demand freedom from 'unwelcome ideas.' Well, here's an unwelcome idea – grow up, sonny. The world does not have to protect you from unsettling ideas or information; you might even find that they are good for you. Just because *you* happen to feel that this idea or that idea is wrong or right does not make it so. There are things such as facts, you know.

"You are such a pansy that you need safe spaces, trigger warnings, emotional support animals."

Emma looked contemptuously at Simper's comfort chicken., which shrank back into his chest in alarm.

"You want the right not to be offended by politically incorrect language, the right to avoid offensive 'triggers' such as the idea that you should have to actually work for a living.

"You want grief counseling when your grades tank or when your roommate's parakeet dies or when your political candidate loses. You want protection from 'disrespectful speech.' Well, here's some: You are an ignorant, pampered, ungrateful snowflake. Posterior body cavity, even."

Simper turned for the door, stroking his chicken so fiercely this time that it laid an egg in his hand. He was so surprised that he dropped it.

"Your generation has ruined our planet," he said, shaking egg yolk from his shoe, in a guilt-edged parting shot that he hoped would finally shut her up.

"Listen, you ignoramus. Our generation and our parents invented recycling, and not necessarily because we wanted to. My mother mended clothes and darned socks so her kids could wear hand-me-downs. We returned milk and soda and beer bottles to the store. We walked, and rode our bikes because we didn't have a car. We hung our washed clothes, including reusable diapers, out to dry on clotheslines in the back yard. We pushed a lawnmower by hand. We refilled our pens with ink instead of throwing them away when they ran out.

"We used razor blades until they were dull and far past their useful life; your generation can just go out and buy a new 12-pack of disposables. And our parents were pioneers in recycling old magazines and newspapers. They kept them handy in the outhouse. Still not a bad idea; some of today's leftist newspapers aren't good for much else anyway.

"So don't give me that crap about the environment. You don't seem to mind having computers and cars and all kinds of other technical conveniences. Where do you think a lot of the power comes from to run all of that stuff? From sources you don't approve of, like fossil fuels. You're a hypocrite, like all the rest of your progressive friends. You bemoan oil and coal and preach environmental hysteria about ice caps and the ozone layer and acid rain while buying 12-packs of plastic water bottles, turning down the air conditioning and driving everywhere you can't fly to."

When Simper paused in the doorway to readjust his chicken, Emma fired one last volley.

"Some of you people never come out of your safe spaces, stay on welfare, can't face the world. Wake up and face reality. Our enemies are not worried about offending us. They are concerned with how best to defeat, cripple, humiliate, enslave and kill us, and if you stay in your basement without a whimper, that makes it all that much easier for them.

"You think you have a right to NOT be offended. The very heart of this country's matrix is that you DO have a right to be offended, and especially a right to offend people who you think deserve to be offended. It's called the free exchange of ideas, give-and-take. Didn't your mother ever tell you that?"

53

As if on cue, Sunflower picked that moment to come looking for her son, just in time to hear part of Emma's withering diatribe.

"You can't talk to my son like that."

"Oh, yes I can. Somebody should have talked to him like that a long time ago," Emma fumed, winding up for another dose of grandmotherly advice. The teacher in her emerged again, as if confronting an unruly classroom.

"This is what comes of your smothering, helicopter parenting, it's what happens when 'everybody gets a trophy'. You have robbed your coddled little cupcake here of the incentive to excel, to push the boundaries, to strive for excellence and exceptionalism. Your child now is so unexceptional he can't see the fallacy in his beloved socialism and where it is all going to end. He takes all he has, this very efficient system, for granted, and wants to dismantle it!

"He has been so unchallenged that he needs drugs to live a life. He has no respect for himself or his country. We need him, and all those others like him, but America suffers from his non-participation, his lethargy, his self-indulgence, his need for support. This is one of the ways our enemies can bring us down, by helping to create a listless, drug-dependent class incapable of intelligent, independent decisions, a class blind to America's historic, noble mission and role in the world."

Emma had to stop when Simper's comfort chicken slipped from his arms onto the floor, then squawked away down a hallway, with Simper in pursuit. She was out of breath anyway.

"Well, that's enough. I'm reluctant to get into a battle of wits with you two, because you appear to be unarmed. If Simper is the face of the future, God help us."

Sunflower reddened, and turned away.

"Come, dear. We don't have to listen to this."

Emma watched as they hurried down the hall after the chicken, Simper sobbing on his mother's shoulder. She took a deep breath and smiled. She had that old satisfying feeling, back in the classroom again, explaining to her students the tools they would need to survive when they left her charge.

But she felt a twinge of regret, too. Underneath, Simper was not really a bad "kid." Delusional, yes, and misled by a domineering mother and an appalling political creed.

'Don't Get Me Started'

Emma and the Squances did not spend much time together after this "frank and candid exchange of ideas."

That evening, Sebastian's lantern flickered.

EIGHT
Don't Get Me Started...
Emma's Blog #2: Feb.12, in a year not too far away…

I'm not sure this thing is going to work, Harry. It's been awhile and I haven't had a single reaction to my first blog attempt.

Oh, well. Maybe nobody's listening. There's so much stuff out there on the internet, how is one lonely little blog ever gonna get noticed?

Well, anyway, Harry, you will not believe what the Ninnies are up to now.

They are very big on this "Everybody gets a trophy" idea. There's a guy who visits his mother here who is a good example of what this philosophy gets you. He's been living in her basement for years and only emerges from his burrow once in a while to see if there's going to be six more weeks of unemployment benefits.

The concept of winners and losers apparently is offensive to the Ninnies – in their minds, it is the same as "bullying." Give me a friggin break.

Parents and schools are so determined to protect everybody, especially young people, from "hurtful" ideas, hurtful thoughts, hurtful concepts, from the very idea of disagreements and failure, that they are instead hurting, grievously wounding, an entire generation. What kind of preparation is that for life in the real world?

In my day it was the mission of schools to prepare students for what awaited them, to enter society as productive, cognizant citizens.

Apparently, we are raising instead a generation of duped narcissists. I saw a study that says there has been a dramatic rise in the number of students who believe they are 'gifted,' despite the fact that they are studying less and scoring lower on tests than students of years ago. The study concluded that they are setting themselves up for disappointment and depression later in life, when they discover they aren't so gifted and 'special' after all.

Duh.

And this is happening while other countries are eating our lunch in global education rankings.

So maybe what we have created is a soft, pampered, indulged, conceited generation that will just roll over before the Chinese or terrorist hordes that might be crouched outside our door some day soon?

Just saying.

Anyway, the first thing the school Ninnies decided was that the Honor Roll should not be published in the newspaper anymore. Apparently, it embarrasses the stupid, er, "intelligence-deprived" kids. More likely it embarrasses the intelligence-deprived parents. They put it this way: "Publishing honor rolls leads to heightened and unhealthy competition for students, as well as insecurity, shamefulness, anxiety and depression." They say they need to "lower the emotional and social stress levels" of their wusses, er, students.

Hey, suck it up, kids. Life is not easy, which you are going to find out soon enough.

So where is all this going? Don't get me started. Let's say Nancy gets all A's, but she is wary and embarrassed because she knows not everybody did as well, and it's so hurtful, of course, for others to know they didn't make the cut. (Maybe if they studied a little harder...) Anyway, now Nancy is a pariah because she dared to achieve. You can see how this is going to turn out.

Give me a break.

The next step on the Ninnie agenda is to substitute the whole hurtful concept of grades in favor of something kinder and gentler. ("Mom! Mom! Look at my report card! It says I 'attended!' Aren't you proud?") In some places now they already are doing away with tests and letting students choose their own grades, so the poor little cupcakes won't feel so stressed at finals time. That will make it fun for the college admissions people. Some schools already refuse to provide colleges with those hurtful class rankings.

So what happens when you do away with the measurements that let you assess prospective students? Very mechanical Eddie, let's say, is accepted at a college and then they find out, too late, that he has little aptitude for academics. He and others like him then drag down the whole academic experience for others. Maybe Eddie should be in trade school, learning how to be a welder, where he excels and starts his own business and soon turns it into a national franchise. The American Dream in action again...

Like I said, don't get me started.

If you ask me, and again, nobody has, getting rid of grades, rankings, even tests themselves, just allows educators and society to cover up their failure to do anything about pupil underachievement and unpreparedness. Shouldn't we by trying instead to actually attack the underlying problems? What if we used this ostrich solution on other issues? Burgeoning crime rate? Let's just not publish the statistics. Pandemic? Let's ignore it, and maybe it will go away.

Also up on the Ninnie chopping block is the tradition of prom and homecoming kings and queens, for the same "hurtful" reasons. This idea of "royalty" apparently makes everyone else feel like serfs and peasants and damages their self-esteem. So there will be no competition, because that means somebody is going to lose. Becoming a candidate also means you're ambitious, and want to be successful, and that's BAD.

There will be no more talent shows in the schools anymore, either. Chalk that one up to jealous parents and students who have absolutely no talent themselves. No writing competitions anymore, either, or debates, same reason, because the new standard is mediocrity.

Next, the Ninnies will be going after athletics because, after all, somebody is going to lose and the self-esteem of six-foot-three linemen who weigh 260 pounds will be irreparably damaged, and besides, don't athletics, too, lead to "heightened and unhealthy competition," as well as its byproducts of "insecurity, shamefulness, anxiety and depression?"

Athletics, and music and the other arts, too, have traditionally weeded out the wannabees and the also-rans from the talented and competent, in the interest of excellence. You either make the team or you don't in athletics, you're either good enough to play in the orchestra or you aren't. Just like life, where you might have to practice more, or maybe even turn to something you can do better. Must we now give every mediocrity a position, sabotaging the goal of excellence?

Just saying.

'Don't Get Me Started'

So where is this going? The scoreboard always reads 0-0, the thrill, challenge and excitement of competition are gone, but everyone's psyche is soothed and safe and they are totally unprepared for life.

Already in some places there are no hurtful student elections, because the losers' dignity and self-respect is terribly violated. Get it, Harry? Nobody is allowed to be better than anybody else, in anything. We're all the same, nobody deserves more than anybody else, so why put in any extra effort? Just like socialism. Power to the proletariat!

Harry, remember Eddie Jackson? Ran for the student council, lost, was irreparably damaged by the experience, dropped out of school, became a homeless juvenile delinquent druggie, served time for a string of armed robberies, shot up a school, wound up wasting his life because of a student council election. Remember, Harry?

Yeah, me neither.

How about a competition just for snowflakes instead? They all get a participation trophy in the form of a buttercup stalk with a cupcake at the top. There will be awards for non-participation and contests to see who can do the least. The last person in the class rankings, the traditional anchorman, will now be a hero, just like the valedictorians of yesterday, carried out of the graduation ceremony on the shoulders of other losers.

I warned you not to get me started.

How does this inspire exceptionalism? No winners or losers. What sad preparation for real life, this cultivation of a class of coddled, spoiled, sheltered, protected, sniveling whiners shielded from the real world. Is it any wonder that socialism appeals to some people – they won't have to do anything for themselves and somebody else will take care of them. They won't get "hurt." They have no idea that their "hurt'" will be of an entirely new socialist kind.

Listen to this, Harry: It's gotten so bad that when two Hispanic students somewhere failed their English tests, the other 28 in the class were forced to take Spanish lessons so the two wouldn't feel "culturally isolated." It was in the papers, I swear.

Give me a break.

You'll never believe this, either, Harry. I read the other day where some Midwest school hired a playground recess consultant to manage play for the youngsters. "Playground recess consultant"? My God, Harry, what's happening? Teachers used to do that. How many college degrees do you need to nail down such a plum job? I can already see what's coming next – nap attendant, hopscotch manager, hide-and-seek director...

On the other hand, playgrounds can be very dangerous places these days, and may soon disappear. Sebastian tells me of a kid who got smacked in the eye by a soccer ball and now his parents have sued the ball manufacturer, the school and the parents of the kid on the other end of the ball. The school is closed temporarily so all students can receive compulsory grief counseling over this traumatic incident, and while administrators consider a proposal that all athletic gear be banned from the grounds.

And that foolish teacher who tried to administer first aid to the kid! What was she thinking? She actually hugged him to try to make him feel better! Now she's being sued, too, for child molestation.

And the school fired her because that was only the latest in a long string of violations. A week earlier she had actually "placed herself in danger" by breaking up a playground fight and got the two boys to shake hands. Back in our day, chances are they would have gone on to become lifelong friends. These two were moved to separate schools and forced into anger management counseling. And another kid who offered the one with a black eye a baby aspirin has been suspended for bringing drugs to school.

At another school, a coach was fired because he had exhorted his young charges to greater effort, to reach their full potential, and then praised them for their achievements. He was charged with "excessive, aggressive, toxic positivity."

Harry, what the hell is happening out there? Give me a break.

Remember I told you once about Ozzie Philbrick, the hyperactive kid who was with me long ago back in the fourth grade? Miss Garrity gently just let him do his thing, within limits. Today he would be overmedicated into a stupor. Last I heard of Ozzie he was in comfortable retirement in Florida after a long career as a mechanical engineer and had patented 48 of his inventions.

Speaking of, I hear there are some parents today who medicate their kids just to get them to sleep, or to calm them down when they get too energetic. Active? Energetic? Ambitious? Animated? Enthusiastic? Here, there's a drug to cure that...

'Don't Get Me Started'

Just the other day, out in front of our building here, a little girl who was singing and skipping down the sidewalk on a jump rope was stopped by a Ninnie policeman who called her parents because he thought she was being "excessively exuberant" and there might be something wrong with her. Now the Ninnies won't even let you be a kid.

Remember when our Christopher broke the Simmons' picture window with a baseball and you spanked him? Today we would be accused of child abuse, Social Services would be called in and he might be taken away to a foster home where he would be smothered with indulgent, anything-goes helicoptering supervision and we might be lucky to get visiting privileges.

By the way, grief counseling is the hottest new industry these days. You can get a degree in it and set up shop just about anywhere where there are hurt feelings, anguish and disappointment. One guy has a franchised chain of these mobile centers, whose TV commercials feature the song, "I Want to Hold Your Hand."

He sets up outside Little League tryouts, theatrical auditions and job interview sites, and even athletic contests, where he administers to the losers and their followers. Made a ton of money with this totally capitalistic concept, again to the everlasting disappointment of his Ninnie professors, I'm sure, who now need some grief counseling themselves.

He used to do big business at schools, too, where you could be consoled after that pretty blonde you lusted after in your algebra class told you to buzz off, or when you lost out for the lead in the class play, or didn't make it onto the homecoming court, or finished dead last in the heated race for class treasurer.

But that has dwindled away some since they abolished honor rolls, homecoming royalty, talent shows, debates and elections. When they get around to abolishing athletics, he might have to find some other line of work, although there might still be a need for his services in counseling the duds at charades, jacks, marbles and trivia contests.

The trouble is, unlike our generation, most parents today and their children have never experienced real hardship or hard times. So what do they really know about life? They won the cosmic lottery by being born in America, in the Horn of Plenty, and so remain naive, ignorant, self-centered and unappreciative. Many young people have no memory even of the horrors of 9/11.

When the next national crisis comes along, another pandemic or natural disaster or major terrorist attack, disrupting every aspect of life, they will be tested as never before to handle real hardship, a drastic reordering of their comfortable lives. Will they be up to it?

Do they ever think of how this marvelous place called America came to be, and has been preserved for them? A lot of people died so today's kids can be free to play their video games and conduct their lives via cell phone. Have they ever been to the Tomb of the Unknown Soldier in Arlington? They should go. Do they even know what a Gold Star mother or wife is? Well, I do. Remember, Harry, when it seemed like there was at least one on every block?

Do they get chills when they look at the Statue of Liberty, or goosebumps when they see and hear a parade band coming at them playing *Stars and Stripes Forever*? Maybe they're not real Americans until they do, until they can answer JFK's question, "What can you do for your country?"

In 1944, 18-year-olds were storming European and Pacific beaches into possible death; now, they expect a trigger warning if their college application is rejected, and a safe space to hide in. What if it was them at Normandy or Bastogne or Iwo Jima? I don't even like to think about it. We will curse them from our graves if they fritter away this irreplaceable country that was handed on to them. We will haunt them if they neglect this precious diamond, fail to protect it.

If you ask me, how can we expect a generation that has been taught to dislike its own country to defend it? A lot of them not only have no faith in their country, they have no faith in a God, either. How can we expect them to fight for something they don't feel deeply about?

Just saying.

I fear they take all they have in this glorious country for granted. America is the greatest paradise since the Garden of Eden. Do they think it happened by accident – the flow of consumer goods, technology, personal comfort, the freedom to go where you will, do what you want?

I like that old Barry Switzer line that says some people were born on third base and go through life thinking they hit a triple.

I fear we have created an "entitled generation" that has no appreciation for the unprecedented gifts they have been given, and are in danger of following the Pied Piper of wistful, unrealistic socialism to their doom. They think their world will be better under socialism?

'Don't Get Me Started'

Give me a break.

They are living in a time of unprecedented, unimaginable prosperity. This is as good as it gets, so far. How can they claim otherwise, or say they are 'oppressed'? They have no life experience yet to show them how lucky they are. All they have to do is look around to see it.

Sure, we all want a more just and perfect world where there is no poverty or misfortune, no discrimination or hardship. But there is no such world, no government can protect everybody from everything. Bad stuff happens.

One cure for hardship is for the indolent and the "entitled," and others who can, to get off their butts and go to work. They might even find that work is good for them. It gives you a purpose in life, a sense of accomplishment and advancement, something to do other than shooting up aliens in a video game, or checking to see how much is left on your food stamp card.

Harry, don't take all this to mean that I am down on this generation. These are very smart kids. I am encouraged every day by signs that more and more of them see the fallacy in the socialistic concepts that are being foisted on them. I see growing pockets everywhere of young people who realize that this is not a free, painless ride, that you have to actually be a participant in this thing called democracy, that this idea called America is very much worth saving.

What's it going to take, Harry, to wake up the rest of them, to learn the lessons their grandparents learned the hard way, in depression, in war? They're not even in physical shape to fight one. I saw a Defense Department study the other day estimating that 75% of young adults would be disqualified from military service for medical, moral or mental reasons.

God help us.

There's nothing like the military to instill in you a sense of patriotism and loyalty and devotion to your country. You remember, Harry, you were there. But few of today's young adults have ever served in the military or performed any other kind of national service. They probably don't even know anyone who has been in the military. The Ninnies don't like the concept of creating more conservative patriots.

I was in a mall the other day, sitting on a bench, and watched two ginormous parents, trailed by two little fatlings, waddle into an ice cream shop and emerge with triple-scoop cones.

Just saying.

Well, that's my rant for today.

§§§

"Men fight for liberty and win it with hard knocks. Their children, brought up easy, let it slip away again, poor fools. And their grandchildren are once more slaves."

–D.H. Lawrence

"Freedom is never more than one generation away from extinction."
–Ronald Reagan

NINE
The Professor

Emma's distaste for Sunflower and Simper Squance was exceeded only by her intense dislike of Budleigh ("please don't call me Buddy") Salters.

The retired professor of Poetry and Philosophy was in Apartment 109, three doors down, and she held him responsible for helping to turn out a generation dragged down by too many snowflakes, cupcakes, socialists-in-training and apathetic, unappreciative citizens.

Salters was a haughty, angry and disillusioned '60s hippie, tall and extremely thin, bald except for a leftover gray ponytail that he sometimes alternated with a man-bob. He chewed gum constantly, and demanded he be addressed always as "professor."

Salters was in his eighties now, and still consumed with righteous anger over a litany of affronts that he took very personally – Christopher Columbus, slavery, capitalism, America's treatment of Indians and women, and unfair social outrages such as potato chip bags that were never quite filled to the top, the shrinking size of chewing gum sticks and toilet paper rolls, and white wine that was not chilled properly.

He had been a professional student at one time, spending 19 years altogether in college, taking a course here and another there, postponing as long as possible the day when he would actually have to support himself. He finally gravitated toward teaching when he could not find a job in his chosen fields of poetry and philosophy, with a minor in art history, although he did inquire once of a big Silicon Valley firm if they had any plans to create the position of Chief Company Philosopher.

They said no, so he tried again elsewhere with Chief Poet and got the same answer, and took that as justification to stop looking for any gainful employment whatsoever in the outside world. Like many other instructors at his college, he had no real-world experience in any of the areas he taught others about.

Salters the Marxist, the son of a successful factory owner and a real estate broker, like many other socialists was reaping the benefits of parents who had been able to indulge him because of their own success in the contemptible capitalism system.

Emma delighted in throwing him conservative bait, which he always lunged for eagerly. Whenever she needed some entertainment, she stopped by his apartment to goad him into a rage.

"Don't you think that delightful little story about George Washington chopping down that cherry tree is a marvelous example for today's youth? It shows what a principled and honest person he was. He could not tell a lie."

She knew full well that Salters had written his doctoral thesis, a generous 200 pages, on that very subject, in an attempt to debunk one of the favorite tales about Washington.

"Balderdash!" he coughed, unintentionally inhaling a puff of his Meerschaum pipe. "That is a fairy tale, a myth!" He began rummaging in a drawer for the thesis, which he had paid to have published professionally, 400 copies, and bound in embossed leather besides. He still had 398 left, and his sister had two.

"But it's such a charming little story," Emma said sweetly. "What harm is done if it's not 100 percent true? It tells you something about the man, and sends a wonderful message to children."

"Bah!" he said reproachfully, peering at her down his extremely sharp nose, sharp enough to puncture a balloon. "He did not throw that silver dollar across the Potomac, either."

"Indeed he did not," fired back Emma the former history teacher, leaping at a chance to challenge the expert in his own territory. "The river in question, you might recall, was the Rappahannock. And there weren't any silver dollars then. He probably threw a rock, if anything."

Salters reddened, coughed, and looked away quickly, nervously stroking the faux-leather elbow patches on his tweed jacket. "Of course. Whatever. That's what I meant to say."

He hoped earnestly that Emma did not know that for a published scholarly paper, Salters had spent two years trying to debunk the silver dollar incident. He had looked up 18th-century records on wind resistance, Potomac River currents and tides, chased down old weather data, calculated the weight of a silver dollar and the distance across the Potomac in those days. His published conclusions showed that it was not possible for a human being to throw a silver dollar that far across the Potomac, or the Rappahannock either for that matter, unless maybe you were Roberto Clemente or Willie Mays.

But Emma did know. "Too bad he had the wrong river," she smirked, relishing the image of a pompous, pretentious, revisionist researcher rushing headlong down the wrong trail.

What Emma did not know was that the episode ended Salters' teaching career, when his superiors discovered that the university's name was on an article based on embarrassingly erroneous suppositions.

Salters immediately changed the subject.

"And another thing. That fable and painting about him crossing the Delaware – an obvious fabrication. Any seafaring person will tell you it is foolhardy to stand up in a small boat."

Emma blinked and shook her head.

"Well, he was an Army guy, after all, not Navy. And what difference does it make anyway? You studied art history. Didn't they discuss 'artistic license'?"

The retired professor, ever the purist, was so obsessed with the "mythical" history of the United States that he was determined to expose and ridicule subjects ranging from Benjamin Franklin and his recklessness in flying a kite in an electrical storm, to John Quincy Adams' penchant for keeping an alligator in the White House bathtub.

He harbored a particular animus toward Columbus, denouncing him at every turn for blundering into an unknown continent while looking for a route to India and bringing with him all the evils of a corrupt, diseased Europe.

"Columbus was a monster," Salters snarled. "He's responsible for every single problem we have."

"I can see that," Emma said mockingly. "And if Erik the Red hadn't discovered Greenland, it wouldn't be so cold there today. Henry Ford is personally responsible for all those unhealthy drive-in burger joints and water-wasting car washes all over the place."

She waited for a reaction, but received none. Sarcasm was wasted on Salters.

"If it hadn't been Columbus, it would have been someone else," she pointed out, "maybe the Portuguese, or the Vikings. Or the Chinese from the other direction. What makes you think things would have been much different under Vikings or savage Mongol hordes?"

Salters saw an opening.

"Well, there you have it. The Vikings were here long before Columbus but did not leave such a sorry history behind. They were splendid explorers."

Emma disagreed.

"The Vikings were pillagers, looters, murderers, rapists, highway robbers, kidnappers, slave traders and maybe also dabbled in sexual perversions as well."

"Unsubstantiated accusations. But no matter. Columbus set in motion a chain of events that led to slavery, persecution of Indians, repression of women…"

"Repression of women? They didn't need any help from him in those days."

"Whatever. He was a fiend. Columbus, Ohio and the District of Columbia and all of the other places like that should change their names and pay reparations to Native Americans. Observe Columbus Day? Pshaw! That's like celebrating a Covid-19 Day."

Emma knew something about antiquity herself and pushed back.

"As I recall, some Indians before Columbus were not exactly saints. They were pretty good at cruelty, cannibalism, mass human sacrifice, slavery. What do you prefer those cities change to – something more suitable to your tastes? Leninapolis perhaps, or Marxton? I can't wait until you tell the Knights of Columbus they have to change their name to Knights of Geronimo."

Salters' needle nose twitched as he resumed the search for a copy of his thesis.

Emma learned that Salters also nursed a whole litany of other grudges against America, which he surely had passed along to his students. He was working on a scholarly exposé for a magazine, savaging the westward pioneers for their callous disregard of the environment. He was particularly upset because they had allowed their animals to trample and defecate unchecked all over the unspoiled Great Plains.

"Are you kidding me?" she said, astounded that anyone would devote any time to such an empty enterprise. "Have you never heard of buffalo herds? Shit happens, you know. So does fertilizer."

Salters was foolhardy enough to confide to Emma that he also was researching a project that he hoped would establish that America's real beginnings dated to 1607, and Peregrine Shufflebottom, whom he was promoting as the First Leftist in America. Shufflebottom had been the first member of the Jamestown colony to come ashore, and immediately began setting up helpful bureaucracies to show the natives how they had been doing everything wrong for 15,000 years – fishing, hunting, planting, weaving, war party tactics, teepee-building, drumming, sweat lodges and the like.

He even was incensed at their cavalier attitude toward the use of eagle feathers, even though in these early days they were 300-some years away from being endangered.

He also chided Chief Powhatan for the tribe's lack of diversity, but had to back away when he discovered there were no blacks, Asians or Hispanics in the Virginia Tidewater region then. No whites, either, so by Salters' reckoning Shufflebottom also became the first to introduce diversity into America.

Powhatan had countered that all of the explorers and colonists on Shufflebottom's ship were white Europeans, so who was he to talk?

"Two can play this game," thought the crafty Powhatan, picking up quickly on the ways of the privileged white man, and demanded through his daughter, Pocahontas, reparations for the ignominy, depredations and racism his people had suffered at the hands of the colonists, even though they had only been ashore for 37 minutes.

The whole dustup was smoothed over peaceably when Shufflebottom showed the indigenous people how to protect themselves against hate speech and hurtful language by setting up Safe Teepees, and trained the medicine men in the techniques of grief counseling. He also showed them how to prepare against the insensitive raids of unenlightened, hostile, neighboring tribes by establishing a system of Trigger Warnings.

"Of course, he didn't call them that," Salters said. "They were Bow-and-Arrow and Spear Warnings."

Salters also insisted to Emma that Pocahontas was an early leftist hero on several fronts.

"In aiding the first colonists, she became the first American multiculturalist; in saving John Smith from death, she was an early opponent of capital punishment; in traveling to England with her new husband, John Rolfe, she became the first American globalist. And as the first American to go abroad, she also became the first American tourist."

Emma rolled her eyes.

Salterton also hoped to show that she did not die in England of unknown causes, as was commonly thought, but perished when her digestive system rebelled at the drastic change in her diet – from seeds, nuts, corn and squash, to her sudden fondness for bangers and mash, Scotch eggs and black pudding.

"Pocahontas deserves a better fate than to have Salters for a chronicler," Emma grumbled.

She laughed out loud when she learned that his 1607 Project included a campaign to designate Shufflebottom as the real father of his country, and to rename the capital city for him.

"Kinda' catchy, but good luck with that." Emma said. "I can just see our allies overseas, in a high level security meeting, tittering when somebody says, 'Let's run that by Shufflebottom and see what they think...

"You might do better trying to change San Francisco to San Atarium. Say, wait now, let's think about that..."

"There you go with the hate speech again," said Salters, oblivious as usual that he was being played. "Making derisive, insensitive, hurtful comments at somebody else's expense."

But Emma soon realized it was futile to debate with Salters. He could only see centuries of American injustice, slavery and mistreatment of minorities, and had spent his career peddling his brand of hate and revisionism to gullible youths, misleading them toward his Shangri-La mirage of socialist pipedreams.

Emma knew that in one of his courses he had offered, for extra credit, a seminar on effective techniques for disrupting and shouting down visiting conservative speakers, and even students who held views out of step with those of the Ninnies and the university.

"Tomatoes are effective for throwing," his handbook said, but it added, "For maximum impact, ink balloons are much better. They leave a more lasting impression. And carry a megaphone to amplify your voice. Do not give them an opportunity to respond or you run the risk of having

70

them bring the entire crowd over to their side, in which case you might be fortunate to escape with your life."

The handbook also recommended that students suspected of harboring opposing views be ostracized and even bullied. "There is no place here for dangerous people espousing and clinging to dangerous ideas, like unrestricted free speech and unsupervised liberty and irresponsible, misinformed, foolish voting," it said.

There was a campus legend involving Salters, about a lone young conservative student who wound up in a Salters class only because he needed an extra credit. On the second day of class, already fed up with Salters' constant America-bashing, he got up from his seat, raised a middle finger at him, shouted "God Bless America!" and stalked out.

Campus lore has it that as he sat outside on the quad, thumbing through the class listings for a possible replacement, he felt a hand on his shoulder. It was the pretty blond he had seen seated a few rows away. "How about a coffee?" she said.

Emma, too, had had about all she could take of the professor. But she gave it one last try.

"So how does all of this square with a university's mission?" she demanded to know. "Isn't a university supposed to encourage the free flow of ideas, to expose bright, inquisitive, impressionable young people to concepts they might never have considered before, no matter how controversial, so they can make intelligent judgements about the good and the bad, the right and the wrong?"

Salters snorted. "That's a very old-fashioned way of thinking. In the first place, there is no such thing as right and wrong. It's whatever feels good to you. Many people, especially young people with formative minds, cannot handle or process dangerous, subversive, archaic ideas like those peddled by conservatives and libertarians, for example. Would you give a baby a lighted candle to play with?"

"Only if you're a demented. fanatical, irresponsible leftist," Emma said.

Salters smirked and ignored her.

"Some ideas, some concepts, are just so loathsome, so dangerous, that they should not be allowed to see the light of day," he said. "That's our job, to hold them underwater until they die, so to speak. We do not give mass murderers a pulpit to preach the techniques of their despicable, twisted 'craft.' We do not give a doctor permission to espouse here his revolting Chocolate Cake Diet. We do not encourage irresponsible behavior such as terrorism or riots or looting or tearing down statues or..."

He stopped suddenly, realizing that indeed they did. But he recovered quickly.

"Students must be disabused of the heretical notion that they are entitled to keep what they earn, control what they have created. That just gives them crazy ideas about ambition and free will and spreading their wings and reaching for excellence and that kind of nonsense.

"We do not provide a platform for people who believe masses of misguided, misinformed, deplorable people are capable of choosing who governs them. Indeed, to protect them from themselves, we must control the levers of the ballot process. They need guidance, they need direction, they need the wisdom of a wiser, guiding hand!"

"Like yours?" Emma said.

"Of course."

"Who anointed you and your kind to be king of the universe?" Emma retorted. "You make a mockery of the concept of a free flow of ideas, free elections. You dismiss the idea that people can make up their own minds about things."

"Someone has to do it," Salters replied, "to protect us from masses of unqualified people being allowed to decide crucial questions like who runs the government. We have a long history of sometimes electing the wrong people. As educators, it is our duty to warn students about what can happen when the wrong people are in charge."

"Such as?"

"Well, take those so-called Founding Fathers. They were not the noble, selfless saints they are commonly portrayed as. They were in it for the money. They were wealthy landowners, they financed the Revolution, and when it was over they wanted their money back through taxes."

"I see," Emma said. "You go the Nazis one better. You don't burn books, you just rewrite them."

Emma was feeling ill in the face of such deceit and deception. She thought about responding, to point out that the Founding Fathers were not the bunch of doddering old white men that the revisionists liked to portray them as, that most were virile young men in the prime of life.

Instead, she headed for the door and unloaded one last barrage.

"I cannot tell a lie either. You are a delusional idiot. You see only treachery and evil in the most noble undertaking that man has ever devised. You prefer to ignore all the magnificent things America has done, concentrating instead on missteps made along the way. For starters, we forged an ingenious new form of government where everyone was equal, free to speak, free to practice whatever religion appealed to them, as long as they didn't insist on shoving it down the throats of everybody else.

"We saved the world from brutal dictators and evil dogmas, more than once. We encouraged democracy, liberty, freedom and intellectual experimentation all over the globe. We urged people and nations to loose their human imaginations and let their creativity soar. You and your kind would destroy all of that."

Salters, lost in his own biases and prejudices, declined to answer.

He had finally found a copy of his George Washington thesis.

"Maybe you can learn something from this," he harrumphed, thrusting it at her.

Back in her apartment, Emma thumbed through the treatise.

She almost quit reading after a lengthy section on Virginia horticulture in the 18th century, which strained mightily, on hazy evidence from the memoirs of Washington's gardener and crumbling survey maps, to prove incontrovertibly that the Washington family cherry trees had been obliterated by a blight quite some years before the Father of his Country was born.

A section on Washington's personality and appearance made her laugh out loud. Salters' "research" had led him to conclude that since portraits of Washington seldom showed him with a smile, he must have been a grim, humorless man, no doubt because of an unhappy marriage to Martha, depicted by Salters as a hen-pecking, critical, sarcastic shrew who gave the great warrior no peace at home.

Emma knew that the first president had been plagued with dental miseries all of his life, and suffered from ill-fitting, uncomfortable dentures.

"I'd be grim, humorless and unhappy too if my teeth always hurt," she mused.

Emma gave it up for good when she came across a page of diagrams, measurements and calculations that appeared to demonstrate that it would not be possible to cut down a healthy, mature cherry tree with a mere hatchet, especially if you were a little boy.

"What a waste of research time," she muttered. "No wonder we're still looking for a cure for cancer and Alzheimer's, and even the common cold."

Emma concluded that Salters was another good reason why college is not a good idea or even necessary for everyone, and told Sebastian as much when he dropped by.

"In the first place, who can afford it? Tuition and salaries go up, up, up, along with unmanageable student debt. More money is devoted to bloated university bureaucracies than to teaching. Students don't get much from their college education except huge debt, disrespect for America and a truckload of communist ideas, not very useful in a capitalist system."

Since Sebastian was already there, she didn't have to use the magic lantern this time.

TEN
Don't Get Me Started...

G uess what Harry! I have a reader! Her name is Tillie and she's from Topeka and she says she stumbled across my blog while looking for a way to make easy-to-peel hard-boiled eggs. She must have Googled hard-boiled and got me... She says she likes my attitude!

I guess it is hard-boiled. But when I look around at what's happening here, I am concerned for my country.

Harry, I don't know how much longer I can take what's going on down here.

There's this retired professor down the hall, he's typical of what the Ninnies are up to these days. They are determined to rewrite history, make today's America suffer forever for the sins of the past, blow up some of our cherished stories and traditions, and paint our favorite historical figures in the blackest hues. They even want to pay reparations to people who have been "offended" by us down through our history.

Give me a break.

Remember the delightful tale about how little Abe Lincoln used a piece of coal to do his arithmetic homework on the back of a shovel? Another college researcher is trying to prove his theory that Tom Lincoln and Nancy Hanks didn't even have a shovel and that their little cabin was heated with wood, besides. It's a great story about a great man. At this point, who cares if it's true or not? I'd like to shovel this nut-job's ass into a snowdrift.

Don't get me started.

I don't care if they find out that Johnny Appleseed was tipsy most of the time from apple wine and joined Alcoholics Anonymous. I don't care if Rip Van Winkle slept so much because he smoked something suspicious that he grew in his own garden. I don't care if Davey Crockett really never killed a bear when he was only three. I don't care if it turns out that Casey Jones was drinking at the throttle, or even if Paul Bunyan didn't give a whit about responsible and sustainable forest management. I don't want to know that Pecos Bill was gay or that John Henry was on steroids.

Can't they just leave our legends and folklore alone? Don't these people have anything better to do?

These so-called "educators," aided and abetted by the media, are leading the drive to tear down old statues and eliminate traces of anything else that "offends" them. It started with Confederate generals, and now there are people who find even the Statue of Liberty offensive, because the inscription at the base doesn't say anything about Latinos or gays or transgenders or the Navajos or Creoles or the Benevolent and Protective Order of Elks.

Some of these idiots even tore down a statue of William Wallace, the Scottish hero Braveheart, in Baltimore. They thought it was George Wallace. How dumb can you get?

And "educators" are feeding this tripe to a generation of gullible underachievers, many of whom are reached only by people like my "friend" – leftist, communist college professors. These supposed stalwarts of reason and the free exchange of ideas are part of a closed Ninnie system where opposing ideas are banned and scorned. Impressionable youths are being spoon-fed class and gender agendas, nonsense like critical race theory, steered away from patriotism and toward a socialist ideology.

I, for one, am highly critical of critical race theory, which has oozed now into lower grades as well. The dolts promoting it want to replace the traditional American idea of equal rights with one centered on unequal rights that depend on which "persecuted" group you belong to.

A lot of colleges these days are pushing anti-western, anti-white, "evil-America" collective guilt, all cloaked in a smothering, surrendering shroud of political correctness. And it's not just the colleges that are trumpeting this evil, 'unfair America' tripe. Add in some of the feminists, gays and lesbians, transgenders, Hollywood, media, climate extremists, unionists and a growing tribe of shiftless slouches who prefer not to work.

But in all fairness, the state of our education system is not entirely the fault of schools. There are some parents who should be sent back to school for instruction on how to raise responsible children who are proud of their country.

Public-school teachers often are given already damaged kids and then expected to educate and make good citizens out of a bunch of unruly, disrespectful, spoiled brats. You can bet this is not happening in China or Russia.

Just saying.

When they are given this blob of naive raw material, the Ninnie universities and the PC thugs immediately start shaping this pliable, malleable human dough into good little leftists – hollow, disconnected, ill-educated, uninformed or misinformed citizens incapable of making good decisions or electing responsible governments. These unrealistic idealists will help them create their socialist utopia. Many emerge from schools with a twisted value system that is the antithesis of this nation's basic principles.

Give me a break.

They are taught to be careful, lest they succeed in life and become one of the hated, vilified, despicable 'wealthy'. And be careful your college admissions 'adversity' test score doesn't dip you into dangerous 'white privilege' territory, which could doom your college chances.

Some of these people have no idea of what awaits them out in real life – demanding jobs, laws, bills and responsibilities, and a tradition, so far at least, that you are expected to make your own way.

University graduation, in some places, has become an annual rite where the institute takes a deep breath and coughs, and then belches out into our faces a fetid clump of new Ninnie sputum, and we turn our heads away as the stench overwhelms us.

I told you not to get me started.

And don't get me wrong. I am not criticizing an entire generation here, just that misguided, disillusioned faction that graduates with no jobs, no goals, no ambition, no patriotism. They are the U-generation – Ungrateful, Unrealistic, Unaware, Uninvolved. They are so unlike the other, realistic students, of both today and yesterday, who want to learn skills that will help them succeed in the real world. Thankfully, there still are large pockets of sensible youths out there who are not buying into this soiled bill of socialist goods. God bless them.

Harry, as a former history teacher, I don't recognize what they're peddling nowadays. Columbus is a villain. Columbus! A guy who had the qualities America used to admire – a sense of individualism, adventure, daring, a yearning to see what's over the next hill. Thomas Jefferson is a despicable character. We had it coming on 9/11. The western explorers and pioneers were loathsome despoilers of the environment. They are trying to hold historical figures to standards of behavior and political correctness that didn't exist then.

They whine that there weren't enough blacks and women and transgenders among our early historical figures. I feel like telling them, 'Well, that's because there weren't many. It was a different time, after all. So why don't you just make some up if it will make you feel better? You're already rewriting our history anyway.

How about this: Ludmilla Ledbetter really wrote the *Star-Spangled Banner* at Fort McHenry in Baltimore, but then Francis Scott Key stole her papers and took credit for it because she was "just a woman." Or this: Cosmo Coriander was the real hero of Paul Revere's ride. He rode the first 15 miles, but then Revere took over for the final mile so a black man would not get the credit. Or maybe this: Endeavor Chichester was an early pioneer in the trans-gender movement; it was he who first devised the system of separate outhouses for men, women and "other."

Harry, the PC people have taken over some of the schools. Any mention of the Holocaust is controversial now, because it seems to offend some Muslims, who deny it ever happened. Well, I can think of six million people who would be offended by their anti-Semitic religion if they were still here to speak.

Where is this going to stop? World War II history offends Germans and Japanese, so that can't be studied anymore either, even though "some people did something" at Auschwitz and Pearl Harbor?

Everybody is so sensitive these days, Harry. Indians are offended by cowboy movies. Real cowboys are offended by dude ranch sissies. Christians are offended by agnostics. Agnostics are offended by airlines that claim their flight was cancelled because of an Act of God. The Irish don't like to think about the potato famine. Potatoes are offended by being linked to people who just sit on a couch all day. Atheists are offended by Texas Christian University. Texas Christian University is offended by atheists.

'Don't Get Me Started'

Rensselaer Polytechnic Institute offends people who think the name is too long and who have a hard time spelling it besides. And Rensselaer is offended by poor spellers who could profit from a decent college education.

There even are people who are offended by the name of the New York University athletic teams, the Violets, on grounds that it's not an appropriately "vigorous" mascot for an athletic team. The Violets are offended by these Pansies

You can see where this is going.

Personally, I am offended by all of this.

The revisionist history books are being purged of positive mentions of white explorers, white patriots, white statesmen. As I recall, it was mostly white Europeans who launched this marvelous country and its unique system of government. Later, thousands of them charged into the South to free blacks from the evils of slavery, and these same oppressive white men are the ones who long ago acknowledged that women are equal, have a right to vote and be recognized as more than domestics.

This revisionist claptrap is what's being taught in our schools these days, Harry. What can you expect from some of the people who call themselves "teachers," and the gullible kids who absorb their nonsense? One teacher was in the news for referring to World War Eleven. *World War Eleven*? This ignoramus thought that's what WWII meant. These people are alive and among us, and voting. And teaching kids.

Where does it end? There will be no history taught anymore, except the history of those who see themselves as victims of something or other, and history that is politically correct.

Students in this new Ninnie PC era are now protesting the use of white to stand for purity – too judgmentally symbolic. They object to the term white noise – "Why not black noise"? Same for the White Pages. Well, they are disappearing anyway without any help from the Ninnies. Blacks aren't safe, either. Don't get caught wearing a white T-shirt or driving a white car. Where does this end?

Just saying.

Dumbed-down schools embrace the lowest common denominators. Students at one of our major universities freely signed a petition to repeal the First Amendment – the one guaranteeing freedom of religion, speech, press, the right to assemble peaceably. It's the <u>first</u> amendment for a good reason!

One survey showed that 10% of college grads think Judge Judy is on the Supreme Court. What's next? J. Edgar Hoover built a vacuum cleaner empire? Abraham Lincoln designed luxury automobiles? General Electric led U.S. troops in World War Eleven?

Don't get me started.

All of this really is starting to burn my butt, Harry. Some of these so-called educators are really leftist saboteurs, determined to turn out 'hate America' students ashamed of their country. After this is all over, which I hope will be soon, I hope these traitors will meet the same fate that befell collaborators in the countries under Nazi control, paraded through the streets with shaved heads.

I swear, Harry, I wonder what some of these kids today are learning. Back in our day there might be simple math questions like this: "If the tide comes in at the rate of 1.25 feet every hour, how long will it take to crest a five-foot seawall?" In today's dumbed-down 'woke' environment you might get, "Are tides a feature of the land, the air or the sea? And do you agree that mankind's irresponsible pollution, especially America's, will lead to the seas overwhelming the earth in a few years?"

An alarming 65% of students in one survey think "From each according to his ability, to each according to his needs" is in the Constitution. I'd give all of them failing Marx on that one.

Another survey says a lot of Americans couldn't pass a basic citizenship test. And you have to look hard to find a college that mandates even a semester course in Western Civilization anymore, the civilization that brought us ideas like democracy, gender equality, equal rights, free markets, scientific inquiry, trial by jury...

More and more young people are looking favorably on socialism. Can you imagine that, Harry? In some parts of the oppressed socialist world, kids are in the streets demanding freedom and liberty. Here, there are misinformed obliviots demonstrating in the streets for socialism.

I told you not to get me started.

And another thing: Sometimes more Americans vote for contestants on inconsequential TV shows than in legitimate, important elections. True, some of them vote more than once. So? Some of our elections aren't exactly pure either. In Chicago, the late vote coming in from cemeteries can tip the result.

'Don't Get Me Started'

The Ninnies control the school systems, so they can continue to churn out more ignorant, uneducated, uninvolved welfare "citizens" dependent on government for survival, to augment all the illegal aliens they want to enfranchise with a vote. You have to wonder sometimes what the teachers' unions care about most – their wallets, protecting incompetent teachers, or educating kids.

If you want to scare the bejesus out of a teachers' union official, sneak up behind him and whisper "charter schools" in his ear.

Seems to me that schools should be putting more emphasis on useful stuff, like how to choose a career, about credit and debt, budgeting, investing, buying a house, citizenship, filing your taxes, plus intelligent reasoning skills, like, "Should I take that free-ride scholarship from Stanford, or pay big bucks to go to the McGillicuddy Institute of Horseshoeing...."

And if socialism is so wonderful, why don't they try it in their own classrooms? All grades will be averaged. Those who studied get upset, decide not to study anymore. Shirkers are happy, get a decent grade for doing nothing, so on the next test, average grades plummet. In the end, they all fail. Incentive has been removed and the great leveler of socialism suppresses everybody into mediocrity.

Now the Ninnies even want to teach grade school kids about sex orientation, gender identity and "gender transitioning." There's a picture book for toddlers about a boy who transitions, medically and surgically, from a boy to a girl. They've got their nose in everywhere, even down to private family business. Didn't some people used to claim that there's no place for the government in the bedrooms of a nation? How about in classrooms?

The Ninnies even want history classes to discuss the sexual preferences of historical figures. Can't wait to ask Sebastian what he's learned about Alexander the Great's private life: Did he like to wear his wife's underwear? Did Genghis Khan lead Gay Pride processions through the towns of Mongolia? Did Noah get it on with any of his animals?

Give me a break.

The Ninnies also are crusading that since American history is a story of oppression, we should pay reparations to people we have offended and slighted and discriminated against over the years. You know – blacks, Indians, Eskimos, left-handed people (trouble with scissors, trouser zips),

81

short people (elevator buttons too high), tall people (ceilings in public buildings too low), gays, blondes (all those jokes). That sort of thing.

They also are offended because there were no women on the first Wright Brothers' flight, no black Pilgrims, and that Jonas Salk developed a polio vaccine without any input from transgender people.

This is the kind of preposterous stuff that's going on down here these days, Harry.

If this catches on, it could become interesting. Maybe the French will pay reparations to descendants of guillotine victims. The Scandinavians will have to pay up for all those villages the Vikings pillaged. The Muslims, and Christians, for that matter, should have to even it up for all the heathens and pagans and non-believers they have slaughtered over the centuries.

Maybe the Ninnies should have to pay reparations for all the beautiful city neighborhoods their policies and politicians have defiled, blighted and slimed – Baltimore, Chicago, San Francisco, Detroit, Seattle, Portland, Los Angeles – and to all the kids who were deprived of a decent education in some of their miserable public schools.

Imagine the possibilities. States of the old Confederacy have never really properly atoned for their sins. Let's cut their federal revenues, curtail their college appearances in bowl games (riots in Alabama!), reduce congressional seats, maybe even get a Scarlet Letter on their license plates.

Harry, you were downsized, passed over, discriminated against because of your age by that college you worked at for 30 years. We certainly were offended by that. Maybe there's some money in this for me...

And Christopher, with our help, has paid back all of his student loans. Now the Ninnies want to forgive today's student debts. Shouldn't they have to pay Christopher back, too, plus all the others who honored their obligations? Then: Borrow some money, pay it back honestly; Now: Borrow some money, wait for a Ninnie-controlled government that will forgive your loans.

Come to think of it, why should the US ask citizens to pay back student loans at all if illegals can get an education for free?

And now they want to provide money even to people who prefer not to work. Well, I am mightily offended by that, as well as by all of the able-bodied welfare cheats, disability manipulators, druggies, slugs, loafers and parasites who are content to just live off of the rest of us. Let's have them start paying reparations. To us!

If you work hard and succeed, you pay a fine – taxes to the IRS. If you loaf and fail, you are rewarded with "entitlements". Give me a break.

What's happening, Harry? So many people are angry or upset about something. They're starting to make me angry and upset that they're so angry and upset.

§§§

"We are called the nation of inventors. And we are. We could still claim that title and wear its loftiest honors if we had stopped with the first thing we ever invented, which was liberty."

–Mark Twain

ELEVEN
The Immigrant

Emma had few allies in her nest of Ninnieness, but one of them was from an unlikely and surprising quarter.

Deuteronomy Diaz was the Arthritis Acres building engineer and maintenance man. His parents had emigrated from Mexico many years earlier, took jobs as landscapers and house cleaners, raised a big family, eventually ran their own companies.

And he was extremely incensed at the shambles of the American immigration system.

Emma met him the first day, when he came in to introduce himself and see if she needed anything.

"That's an unusual name," Emma said.

"It certainly is," Deuteronomy replied with a grin and the exasperated air of someone who had answered the question too many times. "I have never forgiven my very religious parents for this. Neither have my brothers and sister."

Emma looked at him closely. He was about 40, with extreme Latin good looks, close-cropped, jet-black hair flecked with gray, and a matching mustache. She could tell by his vocabulary, demeanor and appearance that this was no ordinary 'janitor.'

"Why?"

"They carried this religious stuff too far. I have six brothers – Genesis, Exodus, Leviticus, Numbers, Joshua and Judges, and a sister, Ruth."

"I see," Emma said, trying to suppress a smile. "The first eight books of the Bible."

"Yes. I'm glad they stopped having kids when they did or I might also have siblings named Nehemiah, Ezra, Ezekiel, Obadiah, Micah and God knows who else.

"By the way, you can just call me Deuter."

Emma liked him instinctively. He was educated, smart, principled, glib, and had a sardonic sense of humor that matched her own. And above all, he had a deep and abiding love for his country. He was never without his American flag lapel pin, and below a colorful eagle tattoo on his left bicep was the legend, "Give me liberty or give me death."

Over time, the two of them would spend hours together in long conversations about the wonders of America; there weren't many other people at Arthritis Acres who shared their views.

Deuter knew his history, and it didn't take much to set him off.

"My parents came here legally, from a place of poverty and deprivation and not much chance to ever see anything different," he told Emma one day when he came around to adjust her air conditioning. "But they managed to leave all that behind, worked hard here to build a new life, raise and educate their children, become productive citizens. They never looked back.

"That's the way it was then, even going back to the first immigrants. They landed here after weeks at sea in leaky ships, carved out settlements and new lives from a wilderness. Later pioneers headed west in covered wagons across an intimidating prairie and mountains, filled in a new country from coast to coast.

"Some of today's 'gimmigrants' scale or dig under a wall, or hide in trucks, or float across a river, into a civilized, extremely developed, prosperous land, and then live off of the government, expecting free food, health care, education and maybe even an income. People who try to compare them to my parents will have a fight on their hands.

"And so will people who call me Mexican-American, or Chicano. I am an American, period."

Emma smiled broadly and gave him a high-five. The little girl who long ago had bristled at being called an alternate name for Irish-Americans had found a soulmate.

Deuter took the immigration issue personally.

"Yes, we are a nation of immigrants," he said. "But what's happening now is madness, insane. The whole thing has been turned on its head.

85

This is not immigration, it's an invasion. Remember 'Give me your tired, your poor, your huddled masses yearning to breathe free'? Today it's 'Give me free housing, a driver's license, a free education, health care, the right to vote...'

"What's happening today is obscene, an insult to all of those like my parents who followed the rules to come here. The Ninnies do little to encourage a regulated flow of legal, vetted immigrants, but are willing to open the doors wide to illegal aliens of questionable backgrounds, some of whom come from trouble spots around the world and are not here to look for anything but more trouble.

"Why is it that some of the same people who don't want us to be the world's policeman, insist that we be the world's orphanage, the world's asylum center, the world's nursery and refugee camp?

"They flood in here unchecked from depressed, backwater places where they are not allowed to speak freely, worship freely, live freely, and then they prosper and thrive, often with government – meaning tax-payer – help. And yet some of them retreat into enclaves and want to change their new place into a pigsty just like the one they left."

"You say it better than I could," Emma marveled. She came to learn that whenever Deuter launched into one of his patriotic tirades, it was best to just step aside and let him roll.

"Yesterday's immigrants like my parents came here with papers, and were assimilated," Deuter said. "They stood in long lines to be documented. They pledged their allegiance to their new country. They fought in our wars, sometimes against the very countries they fled from.

"They did not insist that we provide them with interpreters: some even changed their names to speed up the assimilation. All they had were their skills and their ambition, hoping to trade that for a piece of the American Dream."

Deuter's eyes were moist, his voice catching, as he relived his parents' journey to the promised land. He stopped suddenly and looked over his shoulder.

"As you can imagine, my views are somewhat out of sync with the management of this place, and the new government. Stallingski is everywhere with his spies. The feminists have already reported me for daring to refer to 'male and female' electrical plugs, and for calling my car 'she.' And I was reprimanded for referring to the residents as 'seniors' and 'elderly.' Apparently the correct term is 'life-experienced.' Good thing I didn't say geezer or fogey."

He paused and shook his head.

"I might not be here much longer."

Emma snorted and reached out to shake his hand.

"Me neither. People like us have been forced to go underground. We're like the resistance fighters in World War II. We might have to do what they did. Derail some trains and blow up some bridges and ammunition dumps."

Deuter grinned and nodded at Emma's joke.

"The American Dream. What a concept. My parents lived it, I'm living it, so did millions and millions of others. It worked. It still works! Look at the remarkable success stories of so many people, in so many walks of life.

"Irving Berlin, a Russian. Andrew Carnegie, Scotland. Albert Einstein, John Jacob Astor, Joseph Pulitzer, Henry Kissinger, Maureen O'Hara, Gloria Estefan... Such a long list.

"You don't even have to go back very far. The founders of some of our biggest tech companies are all immigrants. So were Nikola Tesla, Bob Marley, Maria Navratilova plus lots of others."

Emma wanted to know more about this well-spoken son of immigrants.

"What was your family like?"

"My father started as a landscaper, working for somebody else. When the owner decided to retire, he sold the business to him, knowing that it would be in safe, caring, responsible hands. Now it's a chain, the biggest landscaping and garden center in the state.

"My mother, same thing. Started out cleaning houses, working for somebody else, and then founded her own business. They sent all eight of us to college. This was supposed to be her ticket to heaven, eight kids with Biblical names.

"My mother went to Mass every day. Sometimes twice. I think she probably was disappointed when none of us chose a religious life."

"I'm sure she got over it," Emma said, laughing. "She'll be proud when we bust out of this place and organize the resistance. We'll be doing God's work."

Emma wondered how Deuter's siblings fared out in the world with such unusual names.

"What do the rest of them do?"

"Well, besides me, one runs the family garden center business, one is a doctor, one is a lawyer, one a successful novelist, another is a physicist, and sister Ruth is a classical musician directing a major symphony."

"That's only seven."

"Yeah, well, we don't talk much about Leviticus. He went rogue and teaches art history at one of those top liberal universities." Deuter grinned, winking. "We all vote every year on whether he should be allowed to come to the family reunion. It's usually pretty close. Sometimes he can come, sometimes he can't."

Emma wondered why Deuter was at Arthritis Acres.

"History repeats. I'm an engineer working for a building maintenance firm. Hope to create my own company some day."

Deuter's background gave him a first-hand, realistic take on immigrant lives.

"Immigrants are more likely than native-borns to start a business. They know all about oppression and disadvantage and stifled opportunity. That's why they're coming here! How do we know how much genius and ambition is hidden among us right now, among the new, illegal people who have come in? What a shame if they have to stay in hiding because of their status, fearful of being discovered, and will never know what they could have become. And neither will we. What a loss.

"If you ask me, the politicians who think unlimited immigration will let them turn the newcomers into docile pawns who will do their bidding are playing with fire. They even want to give them the right to vote, thinking that this will cement their hold on power, that they will all vote in lockstep for the Ninnies because of their "everything-for-nothing" policy – free money, health care, education, shelter, whatever. But what if the new arrivals become a powerful voting bloc and turn away, to a party that champions their ambition and achievement and self-sufficiency?"

Emma grinned at the thought of the Ninnies being turned out of power by the very people they envisioned would give them a permanent lock on the reins of government.

"A lot of these new arrivals are very intelligent people, striving for a taste of freedom," Deuter continued. "Do they really want to escape their harsh, repressive past and just trade it for the new socialist oppression that the Ninnies want to impose on everybody? They'd be trading one kind of poverty for another.

"If the Ninnies aren't careful, they might inadvertently solve the immigration problem all by themselves. With their history of high taxes and their soak-the-wealthy mania, they are discouraging ambitious people from even coming here. And they want to throw the doors wide open to unvetted aliens, inviting more lawlessness and strain on our social network. They're going to create a country that nobody is going to want to come to anymore anyway."

Deuter looked around again cautiously. He was enjoying this rare appreciative audience, a chance to unload on a compatriot. He couldn't talk like this before most of the other Arthritis Acres staff and residents.

"A lot of these new people come from countries that have no idea, no history, of the rule of law, so what can you expect?" he said. "They don't understand a country where people are expected to obey the law. So some of them commit dumb crimes.

"Some of the others want everything for nothing, to be able to barge right in and sit at the table, free. But whose fault is that? We offered them all of this, and now they expect it.

"Each of us pays taxes, part of which goes to support illegal immigrant programs. How is it that some of them who are working manage to send big sums back "home" every year, but they get free stuff here?

"I have an answer for the people who want to throw the doors open. Let's send an illegal immigrant home with each one of them."

Emma grinned, knowing that when it came time to escape, she would have an ally.

Sebastian's lantern lit up again late that night.

TWELVE
Don't Get Me Started...

Harry! I got another "hit!" That's blogtalk, meaning somebody found my blog and left a comment! All she said was, "You go, girl!" I guess she likes what I say. Maybe this is going to work after all!

And Harry, you'll really like this! Sex is going political, and our side is on top, er, so to speak.

Surveys say the US birth rate is in an alarming decline. Not only that, there are declines in Europe and elsewhere, except for Muslim populations, whose strategy seems to be to have as many children as possible with your multiple wives and eventually just overrun the world.

So we might be outnumbered soon from lack of new children, and, well, you know the best way to cure *that* situation. It seems that the Ninnie solution to our dwindling population problem is to import limitless unvetted illegal immigrants, people who, they hope, would then become loyal little Ninnies themselves.

Conservatives, on the other hand, think immigration should be controlled, that we should mostly repopulate the country the old-fashioned, tried-and-true way, the way that's much more fun, besides, if you get my drift. So now we have become the only major party pushing sex! Lots and lots of sex!

What a platform plank! It is your patriotic duty to go to bed right now and, well, you know... Tomorrow, too, and the next day... Maybe twice! What a great side of the issue to be on! The Ninnies don't have a chance! How do they explain that they're against sex? They're too dour and serious to enjoy it anyway.

Seriously, Harry, maybe there wouldn't be a population decline problem if there weren't so many unjustified and casual and late term abortions. I guess I side with the people who say a nation that kills its own children has lost its soul.

Just saying.

Once that becomes acceptable, who's next? Violence and disregard for life of all kinds becomes tolerable. Let's get rid of all those senior citizens who are such a drain on the health care system?

I fear we might look back some day and regret aborting all those lives, among whom were countless genius scientists, artists, thinkers, healers, innovators, patriots. Kill the unborns, but keep convicted monstrous thugs alive and in comfort at taxpayer expense?

How come a "child" needs permission of parents to go on a field trip or bring a medication to school, but in some places not to get an abortion?

Just saying.

Well, anyway, back to the illegals situation. Oh, excuse me, don't call them illegal aliens: In the mandated Ninnie doubletalk they now are "undocumented," or "out-of-status," or "unenfranchised." Their illegal "unaccompanied minors" often are grown, bearded "out-of-status" teenage thugs. A skilled Polish doctor or an erudite Swiss author is rigorously vetted in the immigration application process, but a common hoodlum can just scale a fence and walk right in?

A good friend of mine here is from an immigrant family that entered legally. And he is adamantly against the Ninnie open border concept that would let anybody and everybody in. He has no problem with oddballs who binge-watch reruns of *The Jerry Springer Show,* or listen to nothing but gospel music played on tubas – hey, we need a lot of loveable kooks and eccentrics to add some spice to our melting pot, right? But he draws the line at human traffickers, drug pushers. bomb-making anarchists and the like. He considers them an insult to his family.

He's a smart, educated guy, and has some definite opinions about what's happening at our borders.

"Give us your tired, your poor, yes, but don't make the US tireder and poorer in the process," he says. "Don't let them batter down that Golden Door. Make them come legally, and within realistic limits, or we will be overrun with 'wretched refuse,' refugees straining a generous, beleaguered nation in danger of becoming no better than those dumps they left behind."

That's an interesting comment, coming from an immigrant family. If there are no limits, no screens against the unwelcome, no standards for admittance, eventually our great melting pot of exceptionalism, genius and love of liberty will be diluted to a point where there is no universal loyalty to one America, one home, anymore.

As an empathetic nation, it should be our national mission, the mission of the world, really, to help improve those pathetic other places, to turn them into livable, enviable nations of their own. But it won't happen while they are controlled by corrupt, on-the-take governments.

The Ninnies seem to prize the bestowal of sacred citizenship no more highly than throwing candy to children from a firetruck during the Fourth of July parade. American citizenship is a diamond, not to be dispensed so casually.

Some immigrants now are already here in such numbers that they can stay in their separate enclaves, elect officials, defy authority and influence laws. They do not want to assimilate, put down roots, make wide attachments – the American Way. They, too, are AINOs, and want to stay that way.

I'm told you seldom see American flags flying in Los Angeles and elsewhere in Mexifornia anymore, but it's common to see immigrants waving Mexican flags, Somalia flags, others.

Here we go with the questions again. How come our flag and culture offend some of them, but our free benefits don't? Why do they wave the flag of their "country" but are terrified that they might be sent back there?

Why is there money for refugee resettlement programs here and abroad and not enough for our own veterans, homeless and poverty-stricken?

What's fair when refugees can get generous federal assistance and live better on their handouts than some citizen families?

Harry, we have to convince people that there are sinister forces out there who are trying to destroy our America from within.

Did you ever wonder how these vast illegal immigrant traffic routes are funded and organized? I suspect there is a lot of hate-America money behind those elaborate caravans, which require an expensive support network all along the way.

I think this invasion is funded and stoked by forces – meaning both people and countries –who intend to destroy us by flooding us with illegals, drugs, disease, human and sex trafficking, all aimed at sowing discord, dividing the nation, overloading the stressed social systems set up to care for people in legitimate need. They intend to fracture the country by pitting us against each other.

They hope to undermine our morals and our ethics and our pride in our country, partly by fostering a sector of drug-dependent, ignorant slackers who have no respect for themselves or their nation, by perverting an education system into one that has no regard anymore for basic notions like the value of life, or patriotism, or right versus wrong, or a Supreme Being.

Just saying.

I told this to our friend the liberal professor at Arthritis Acres, and he says I am paranoid and delusional. Well, he's been living in his own little socialist cocoon for so long that he will never be able to recognize or admit that he is part of the sinister forces that I am talking about.

These are people who have no respect for our traditions, our history, or for this grand experiment called democracy. They are pushing us toward socialism, a dismal system of government that has failed miserably everywhere it has been tried.

They are preaching free incomes, free food, free education, free housing, free everything, with no regard for how this would be paid for, no regard for the consequences. They are bound and determined to save the planet by banning all energy sources that are not totally renewable, stopping airline flights, and even putting cows out to permanent pasture.

They are dreamers of the worst sort – dreamers who have no grasp on reality or practicality. To them, our views are extremist. *They* are the extremists. They are opposed to everything that America stands for.

They are infiltrating our legislative, judicial and educational systems. Education system? It's more like an indoctrination system by leftist colleges and professors, maybe even more like an infection. We need a vaccination and herd immunity. These saboteurs are not going to go away unless we make them go away.

Just saying.

Harry, there's another favorite Ninnie concept down here, the sanctuary city and sanctuary state, where the illegals are safe from the arm of the law. How can that be allowed, for states to defy the law of the land? Isn't that how our Civil War started? And we all know how that turned out, don't we?

It's getting so bad that residents of sanctuary cities and states, disgusted with the sanitary and high-tax and crime conditions there, are bolting to safer havens in other states. Imagine that. Some of the sanctuary zealots are fleeing in panic from the very thing they have created.

Same thing with Ninnie-run cities that allow riots, looting and anti-police sentiment to run amok. I fear that if too many of the Ninnies flee what they have wrought, they will turn their new once-flourishing shelters, such as Texas, into the same kind of viper pits they left behind.

There's a pattern here: Just like a wave of illegal immigrants fleeing one stinking swamp of a country and trying to create another one here.

Well, how about some sanctuary relief for all of us taxpayers who are shouldering the burden of this illegal immigrant support network? I might declare myself an anti-sanctuary person and refuse to help pay to support it. And if they come after me, my lawyers will point out that what the sanctuary cities are doing is illegal, and they suffer no consequences, so leave me alone, too, buster.

Just saying.

I propose that conservative states and cities should declare themselves "illegal-immigrant-free-zones." The Ninnies will then howl that it's unconstitutional and a defiance of federal powers. Hypocrites.

Harry, when it comes to illegal immigrants, and the terrorists and drug mules hiding among them, I have a whole lot more questions that don't seem to have answers:

How come in some countries if you enter illegally you are imprisoned, tortured or maybe even shot? Or just "disappear." In America you are showered with free benefits, everything is printed or said in your native language, and you have the right to carry your homeland's flag in protest demonstrations saying that you are being treated unfairly!

If outlawing guns is worthwhile if it saves just one life, then why isn't deporting all illegals worthwhile if it saves one life?

Why, when a jihadist terrorist mows down innocent people in an office building, does the media call it "workplace violence?"

Why do they call them "Lone Wolf" terrorist attacks? You add them all up and it's not so "lone" anymore.

'Don't Get Me Started'

Lawsuits protest that some Muslims are offended by our culture, that they cannot obey laws that conflict with Sharia law. Then why are they here anyway? And where are the lawsuits protesting that we are offended by their culture?

Just saying.

They specialize in using our own laws against us. In the US, a basic tenet is freedom of religion. That also means freedom FROM religion, freedom from some of their dogma and menacing, brutal laws.

And we are not supposed to blame all Muslims for 9/11, and rightly so. But we are told all of today's whites must share the blame for yesterday's slavery?

Is not Islam, as preached by hardliners and terrorists, in many ways opposed to the American way of life, its basic beliefs, everything it stands for? Radical Islam deals in racism and bigoty and oppression.

It is part of their coda to kill Christians and Jews, anyone opposed to their barbarism, to oppress women. How do you explain those verses in the Koran preaching hate, murder, terrorism against all who refuse to submit or convert?

We'll respect the Koran when they respect the Bible, recognize their holidays when they recognize ours. We should allow them the same rights here they allow Christians in their home countries.

We are warned that in Europe there already are places with parallel fanatic Islamic subcultures bent on becoming the majority, meaning rule, meaning domination and submission.

They do not come to assimilate; they come to assimilate everyone else into a seventh-century culture that rejects ideas of freedom and liberty.

Can you imagine a Europe once saved by American troops, where the lights have gone out again, a return to barbarism, intellectual and economic bleakness, with no America to bail them out this time?

§§§

"It is the flag just as much of the man who was naturalized yesterday as of the men whose people have been here many generations."

--Henry Cabot Lodge

THIRTEEN
The Journalist

Emma ran afoul of Slant Greeley, editor of the Arthritis Acres *Reporter*, on her first day there, when she was featured on the front page as the newest resident.

She did not recognize herself.

"Mrs. O'Doud devoted her working life to a long series of liberal causes, most notably the drive to extend the vote to 6-year-olds," the story said. "She also demonstrated against such unfair corporate hiring practices as the one where applicants who showed competency for the position were chosen over those with no skills but from an approved minority group. She also led a successful drive to abolish the concept of stolen bases in baseball, on grounds that this 'allowable dishonesty' sent a permissive message to impressionable children."

"WHAT?" Emma sputtered incoherently. She read on with some difficulty, because the paper was quite damp from her spittle and the type had smeared.

"Mrs. O'Doud also espouses Medicare for pets, limo rides across the border for illegal immigrants, letting children assign their own academic grades, and defunding the country's defense apparatus. She has 12 children; her husband, an electrician, died in prison in 1998 while serving a life sentence for the deaths of six people who perished from electrocution in a home he had wired."

"WHAT?" Emma shouted again. "WHAT!!!?"

She hunted Greeley down and demanded an explanation. He was in his office, adjusting the green eyeshade he wore as an affectation, writing a story about another resident who had just won seven medals in the Senior Olympics. It wasn't true, "but it will make her feel so good."

"What is this? None of this is true!" Emma thundered, crumpling the page in her fist and flinging it at him. "Where did you get this information?"

"Of course it's not true," Greeley said nonchalantly, shifting his portly frame in the chair. "We are just following here in the best traditions of today's journalism. It's all about entertainment, shock value, titillation. Often we just make it up, especially if it's more interesting than what really happened."

"But, but..." Emma stammered, at a loss for words for maybe the first time in her life.

"That's the way it is these days." Greeley elaborated. "Speculation on what might have happened, or sometimes just wishful thinking on what really should have happened, or sometimes just revising things so the news fits better with our own political agenda and personal prejudices, especially if we can make those deplorable conservatives look bad. We don't have enough staff, you know, to chase down every single fact, so sometimes we have to create our own facts. You must agree that your new life is almost certainly more colorful than your old, drab one."

Emma sputtered again incoherently at this stark, dishonest violation of her privacy, and of this distorted view of journalism. Greeley, whose real first name was Titus, smiled benignly. In college he had been nicknamed "Scoop," but once out in the working world he decided "Slant" was much more descriptive of what he really did.

Emma glanced through the pages of another issue and was startled by some of the headlines.

"Right-Wing Views Cause Cancer," said one, over a story about a woman found dead next to a radio tuned to a conservative talk show.

"Study Shows Most Cows are Republican," said another. The story quoted a professional "cow whisperer" explaining that that's why cows had such a cavalier attitude toward despoiling the planet.

"Duped Voters Pick GOP Candidate"

Greeley chuckled.

"We wanted to say 'Idiot Voters' but they wouldn't let us. 'Idiot' is too disrespectful to the mentally impaired, you know."

Emma was aghast.

"Who's 'they'?"

"New agency that polices all media for appropriate and approved language. It's official name is the Governmental Accountability Group, or GAG. There are a lot of words you're not allowed to use anymore."

Emma's eyes widened. She had noticed herself that her word processing program would not recognize, would not let her type, favorite words and phrases that she had used often, such as "leftist kooks" and "liberal bilge" and "Bill of Rights." She suspected "idiot" was banned because it hit too close to home, was used too often by Ninnie critics. Uncomfortable. Hurtful, even.

She could not believe what passed for journalism in this place.

"You can't be serious about this," she told Greeley, waving a paper under his nose, nearly knocking the green eyeshade from his head. "Supermarket tabloids are more reliable than this."

"Of course," Greeley said. "That's the new normal. The press is no longer under any obligation to tell the truth. That's so old school. We're free to make it up now, just peddle our own opinions, which these days are all pretty much the same anyway.

"All those mysterious, unidentified people who used to make a living as "reliable sources" are out of work now, but they'll be all right. They can still probably make a good living as anonymous whistleblowers instead.

"We deal now mostly in unreliable sources and unsubstantiated opinion. You must admit that it's a lot more entertaining this way. Better than some stuffy old Planning Commission meeting or boring election for Third District alderman."

Emma shook her head in disbelief.

"Whatever happened to real journalism, where you presented both sides of the story, reported all the facts, and let people make up their own minds, served as a watchdog on corrupt politicians and protected the public trust?"

"Aw, nobody does that anymore. Pretty old-fashioned. Ordinary people can't be trusted to make important decisions anyway. In fact, if we don't approve of somebody these days we just work with the Ninnies to get rid of them."

Emma was stunned

"Whoever said it was up to you to decide such things?"

Greeley ignored her and turned his attention back to the front page editorial he was composing, one calling for free, four-bedroom suburban homes and lifetime incomes for illegal immigrants.

"Oh, another thing," he said. "In this kinder, gentler nation we are creating, newspapers now warn our readers on the front page that some of the stories they will find in the paper might have hurtful, upsetting content – you know, wars and traffic accidents and natural disasters and suicides and such, maybe even a horrific account of a conservative winning an election here and there."

Emma muttered something incomprehensible.

She looked around his office, plucking some older copies at random from a bin, and was surprised and then appalled to learn what was happening in her country. Because residents' access to outside news sources was severely restricted, they only knew what the Ninnies wanted them to know through the *Reporter* and approved leftist news outlets. Emma discovered to her horror that in the news columns, only carefully-screened actual stories were allowed to join the invented fabrications.

"White House to be Repainted," headlined one story. It quoted a government decorator as saying the palette had not yet been chosen, but that, "Out of deference to a diverse population, it would be some color other than white. Perhaps even stripes. Or maybe polka dots – black, brown, red, yellow, white, something like that, something very inclusionary."

A front-page photo in another edition showed deliriously happy people emerging from the new government office called FREE (Federal Relief and Entitlements for Everyone), holding up chits for free houses, cars, education, country club memberships, water, electricity, food, dental floss, tick powder for pets, zit cream for teenagers, incontinence pads for seniors.

"Look! Free Jehovah's Witnesses pamphlets!" said one excited, confused shopper.

Emma fumed. How are they going to pay for all of this?

Another story explained it all, a lesson in basic Ninnie philosophy: The wealthy were to turn over all of their extravagances, such as private airplanes, antique auto collections, second homes, country club memberships, private islands, opera tickets, hobby farms, gold toothpicks, monocles, race horses, caviar farms, sterling silver paper clips, luxury doghouses, colored toilet paper and the like, to be shared by all.

Emma wondered aloud how a mechanic with four children, say, making $40,000, was going to get to his new private island, or to enjoy the opera, since the only Rigoletto and Carmen he had ever heard of were that weird couple across the street who ate at their favorite *trattoria* every Tuesday and Friday and always ordered the spaghetti Bolognese.

"Well, no matter," she smirked. "I wonder how I'd look in a monocle. Maybe even a pince-nez."

Another edition of the *Reporter* detailed how the new Ninnie policy of total, absolute tolerance was working beautifully. Most crimes now went unpunished, because there was no such thing as crime in the perfect Ninnie world, and thus no need for police. All "infractions" were now assessed an economic value, and if the amount of the damage or loss was deemed to be less than $500,000, the scoundrel was home free.

"It is so unfair to penalize a purported lawbreaker for his transgressions when it really is the fault of bad parents, bad neighborhoods, bad companions, bad air, bad diets, bad weather, bad roads, society in general," said a government social scientist outside a now-empty prison. She didn't seem to mind that one of the freed inmates had stolen her car and purse while she was interviewing another.

Burglars and hoodlums could now just move into their target homes without the bother of actually having to burgle them. "You didn't build this anyway," was the usual justification. This was an outgrowth of a longtime Ninnie policy goal now written into law – thieves were now entitled to openly sell things they stole if it was determined that they needed the money to live comfortably. Hoodlums now also were entitled to camp out on and even take over private property if it was deemed that they otherwise had inadequate shelter.

This also was a quite effective way of satisfying another longtime Ninnie goal – redistributing the wealth.

Illegal aliens now were routinely released after committing even the most horrendous of crimes. One of them was found not guilty by a leftist jury after his lawyer argued that his rape victim had "dressed provocatively" by showing an ankle, and besides, brutal rapes were quite common where he came from, so he could not be expected to be familiar with the stricter rules in his new, civilized country.

Police forces had long since been abolished, ever since the Great Appeasement of 2020, when the Ninnie leaders of some cities decided that riots, looting, fires and the destruction of entire city blocks were not only permissible but a quite justified, useful and legitimate means of urban renewal, even if sometimes premature.

The most familiar image of the times, destined to become as famous as the flag-raising photo at Iwo Jima or the sailor kissing the nurse in Times Square as World War II ended, was of a solemn leftist TV reporter reassuring viewers that the street demonstration and protest he was covering was quite orderly and peaceful, even as burning buildings behind him collapsed into rubble and black-hooded rioters danced tauntingly in front of the camera, shouting vulgarities and brandishing middle fingers. His report ended abruptly when he was hit with a brick.

If you had problems these days, you called a social worker, who was likely to recommend breathing exercises to ease your anxiety at having been mugged, say, during church services. If you were a business owner, distressed because your establishment had been looted and burned down by peaceful protesters, your life's savings and work obliterated, you might be directed to agencies that could help you manage your anger and frustration. Aromatherapy was a favorite recommended remedy.

In extreme cases, say your elderly parents were brutally assaulted in a supermarket parking lot and their car, purse and wallet stolen, free classes in Gentle Yoga were offered, while your parents would be eligible for healing massage therapy at a pain clinic if their nine-page application was approved.

Theft and sale of identities was tolerated because it turned out that many people, not just the criminals, were much happier with their new identities than with their old, boring ones, especially if their new credit card debt was lower. Shoplifting was sanctioned and epidemic, because it now was deemed unfair that some people could afford $90 bottles of wine while others had to settle for the one-dollar gallon jugs on the bottom shelf.

Consumer protection laws were becoming more and more stringent as the Ninnies ramped up their policy of protecting everybody from everything. This led to rampant black market bootlegging of cheap, inferior products. Sales of one "bargain" beer brand plummeted when word leaked that a suspicious bartender had sent a sample to a testing laboratory and got back a reply saying, "We regret to inform you that your horse has diabetes."

Prime tickets to athletic events and popular concerts did not go exclusively to the well-heeled and celebrities anymore, either. Promoters were required to hand out a percentage free to street people, line-jumpers and welfare loafers. Late arrivals often were shepherded to the front of the line in the interest of fairness and equality.

"Not that we subscribe to his teachings, mind you," explained an official at the government information office. "But did not Jesus say that, 'The first will be last, and the last will be first'?"

Church officials protested, to no avail.

"Now the press is even misquoting Jesus, taking him out of context," complained an Episcopal bishop.

§§§

Emma discovered in talking to Deuteronomy Diaz and others that Greeley came out of college in the '60s brimming with idealistic leftist fantasies, planted by his professors, expecting that he would be able to change and reform the world and its evil ways. But then reality set in and he confronted human nature and frailty head-on, and had to concede that he would not be able to end wars and poverty and injustice after all, whether by himself or with other dreamers.

He was going on 75 now, still sulking that the world had rebuffed him, graying, overweight and lame from a bad knee, and ignoring his high blood pressure and diabetes. But he remained convinced of his mission: persuade as many people as possible that government and socialism were the answer to all of the world's injustices and that conservatives, the business world and the military were evil, because his professors and the Ninnie party had told him so.

Deuter knew him well and was familiar with his career.

Greeley had settled in after college as a reporter at a small daily newspaper in Tennessee, covering small-town government and politics.

"Apparently he learned there to his bitter disappointment that he was never going to uncover the scandal of the century at the Piedmont County Sewerage Commission, write best-selling books as a result, become a talking head on prestigious network news shows, or be a shaper of public opinion," Deuter told Emma.

Greeley moved around to other papers, but his older, wiser, conservative editors, taught by their old-line journalism professors to be objective, impartial, unbiased and evenhanded, and who lived in the real world, saw to it that his fanatical leftist views never slanted what appeared in the paper.

But time wore on, and as the older editors retired and died, the leftist hippies like Greeley took over the editor slots.

"That was the beginning of the end," Diaz said.

Now they were part of a deadly, lethal combination – they were directing and supervising the new leftist reporters pouring out of the colleges, all with a mission to stamp out and obliterate from history any trace of conservative thought or the idea of an exceptional country called America.

Soon they were preaching only to the choir, as sensible people abandoned newspapers as reliable purveyors of news and the truth and turned elsewhere, although elsewhere was just as desolate and bereft of open-minded reporting.

So after he and his dogmatic contemporaries shredded and demolished a once-honorable profession, they were left with declining readership, declining advertisers and declining respect. The number of newspapers began to decline drastically as well. The word "impartial" had ceased to be a word, at least in most big-newspaper stylebooks.

"And who needed newspapers anymore anyway?" Diaz said. "The truth now resided on the internet, where anybody with an opinion could set up shop as a pundit. Remember the old saying, 'It must be true, I read it in the newspaper'? Hah! Nobody can say that about the internet."

"Nobody can say that about newspapers anymore either," Emma added.

So now, disillusioned and bitter in his retirement, having realized none of his youthful idealistic dreams, Greeley was reduced to publishing a daily dose of fake news and peddling the Ninnie line to geezers at the Arthritis Acres Nursing Home. He did relish, however, the title Stallingski had bestowed on him: Minister of Propaganda.

"Aren't you ashamed of what you're doing?" Emma asked finally, crumpling up another edition of the *Reporter* and throwing it into a nearby waste basket. "I wouldn't even put this on the bottom of a bird cage. You are insulting a once-noble profession, betraying its mission and ethics."

Before Greeley could muster a reply, Stallingski came into the room with a story he wanted published in the next edition.

"The big annual picnic is next week," he said. "Everyone is expected to pitch in on getting the place ready, setting up chairs and tables and decorating the place and that sort of thing. Unless they don't want to, of course, and if they don't want to, well, that's perfectly all right and they will still get their cake and ice cream anyway."

Emma was outraged.

"You mean if that lazy lout Salters declines to participate, as usual, he gets to enjoy the fruits of everyone else's labors anyway?"

Stallingski nodded.

"From each according to his ability, to each according to his needs," he said comfortingly.

Emma's thoughts drifted back to a time in her youth when her 45 rpm record player needle got stuck on Perry Como's "Bibbidi-Bobbidi-Boo" for an hour.

But at least it was somewhat comforting to know that Salters had no abilities to share.

Emma stopped by Greeley's office again the next day to pick up the latest issue, not that she expected to find much actual real news.

The main story was about the continuing ravages of climate change and rising sea levels, complete with a doctored photo of water up to the third and fourth floors of office buildings in Lincoln, Nebraska, and an enormous cruise ship tied up to a balcony at the state capitol building there.

"This can't be true," Emma protested. "In Nebraska? That would mean almost everything else between the coasts was underwater, too."

"Well, we're a little early, just wait a few years," Greeley said. "We're getting people ready."

Emma went back to her room and called Christopher to complain again about her surroundings.

"You might recall that the first move of dictators is always to control the media, even if it's a rag like the Arthritis Acres *Reporter*," she said.

"Get me out of here, or you will be hearing about me on the news. I will be leading a new revolution."

Her words were prophetic.

Sebastian's lantern flickered so many times that night that he suspected Arthritis Acres had been hit with a power surge.

FOURTEEN
Don't Get Me Started...

Harry, something's happening out there. I'm hearing from more people! Lots of people! People who think like I do and are afraid our country will be swirling the socialist drain soon unless somebody does something about it. Oh, there's a few nasty nuts and Ninnie-compoops mixed in too, but I just ignore them, and wish the rest of the country would, too.

Here's an example of what I'm getting, from Sarah in Savannah:

"Finally, somebody is saying what I have been thinking for a long time! The Ninnies are leading us down the road of ruin. Keep it up, Emma! The country needs you!"

Mildred in Minneapolis was enthusiastic, too:

"Finally, a voice speaking for all the rest of us, the real Americans, the traditional Americans, who subscribe to old-fashioned values and the American Way."

Lynette in Louisville:

"We are in perilous times. We are in a new civil war, when what we need instead is a new American Revolution!"

Fred in Phoenix:

"Being stuck in this restrictive Ninnie world is like being stuck behind the creep out in the freeway fast lane doing 40 mph. Get the hell out of the way!"

Mike in Michigan:

"You tell it like it is. It's hard to get real news anymore. You can't believe anything in the press, or anything the Ninnies say."

Remember Harry, when they called the press the Fourth Estate because it was supposed to be a check on nefarious activities and mischief that might be going on in the three branches of government? Well, instead, they have become the fourth branch of the Ninnie-Progressive-Socialist government. Now we need a Fifth Estate just to watch them, too, to keep the whole bunch clean. Today's partisan press is an embarrassment to the legitimate journalists of yesterday.

Sometimes I think they get their news tips from anonymous phone numbers scrawled on the walls of restroom stalls. "Brie at 555-5555" always promises a good time, maybe even a scoop.

Most of the stories in the resident newsletter here are made up, totally unbelievable. But I've learned it's best to just believe them. Even if they're not true, they might be soon.

The paper here is run by a guy, I hesitate to call him a journalist, who just yesterday told us scientists are working on a way to turn white people purple (they call it 'wisteria'), so that repentant racists can sign up to see what it's like to go through life a different color, thus escaping their dreadful, horrid whiteness and atoning not only for their past prejudice but for the sins of their ancestors as well.

A week ago we learned about hordes of happy young people applying to colleges under the Ninnies' new free-education-for-everybody program, and how colleges are wondering how to cope with what they think will be a sudden rush of sincere, earnest, ambitious degree-seekers headed their way.

Hah! What they're likely to get instead is a heap of loafers, druggies, high school dropouts and assorted other social misfits, seizing a golden invitation to party for four years or more at government/taxpayer expense.

Give me a break.

In one sense, that kind of Ninnie scheme would be good for the economy, because at some of the more notorious party schools, certain town merchants will be hiring more bartenders and bouncers and preordering more beverages, while others will be laying in new supplies of birth control items and nostrums claiming to be the new sure cure for hangovers.

Here's another example of what you're missing down here these days, Harry. According to our paper here, and it certainly appears this could be true, an illegal immigrant from Honduras sneaked into a movie theater in San Francisco, and when he was discovered by the Ninnie management, was ushered to the front row and showered with free popcorn, candy and soft drinks, given a season pass and told his kids' college educations would all be paid for.

"This is our way of apologizing for the years of depravation you have suffered," sobbed a sweet young ticket taker two months out of a top liberal university with a degree in multicultural studies. "Not only for the deplorable conditions in your own country, which the US could have helped solve with only a few billion more dollars in foreign aid, but for the uncomfortable, shameful, embarrassing way you were forced to sneak into this country illegally."

Harry, I am worried. The press has betrayed a once-noble and essential profession, and become opinionists and attitude shapers. Where are we supposed to get the straight story now? These people who are supposed to be impartial and just give us the facts have bought into an ideology. No wonder the rest of the world thinks poorly of us – all they know about us in some places is what they see and hear on leftist news networks and international editions of leftist US newspapers.

The Truth? They don't believe in the truth anymore. The truth is whatever coincides with their Ninnie personal biases and prejudices, a lot of it spoon-fed to them during their college years. Remember the line from that movie? "You can't handle the truth!" Well, today's press can't be trusted anymore with its original mission – finding and dispensing the truth. They are no longer interested in reporting the news, but in shaping public opinion, in telling us how and what to think, which is, of course, whatever the Ninnies think.

Their leftist opinions used to be confined to the editorial page. Now they are everywhere in the news columns, and headlines, too.

Their sins of omission are just as egregious as what they report and slant. They ignore major stories that don't advance their leftist agenda, betraying the public's constitutional right to know what's going on in their government and their politics. Big stories damaging to their agenda are ignored, or disappear, vanish. So there's no follow-up. How can they follow up on some Ninnie scandal they never reported in the first place?

Today's press has bought into the Ninnieness, selling their souls to a philosophy that wants to penalize and even prevent success and ambition, spread the wealth to slouches and incompetents. Well, they should look around at other corners of the world, where socialism has inflicted its own cruelty, suffering, unfairness and crime.

Just saying.

And the press loves to report on the people who make a living finding fault with America. Seems like there's a new apology coming from us every day now.

One of the first acts of the new Ninnie government was to apologize to the world for America being first to land a man on the moon, which had been so terribly hurtful and embarrassing to other nations.

The US apologized for letting Babe Ruth and Hank Aaron and Barry Bonds hit so many home runs while other nations were hitting few or none. No matter that they didn't even play baseball. We apologized to Britain and Germany and Vietnam, because so many GIs had come home with so many war brides.

Harry, we apologized for Henry Ford and the Model T, which had set off the mad race to destroy the planet. We apologized for digging the Panama Canal (who were we, anyway, to presume the world needed a shorter route between the Atlantic and Pacific, and besides, did anybody ask the Panamanians how they felt about this defilement and desecration of their country?)

We also apologized for inventing cell phones and texting, which set off that worldwide epidemic of pedestrians and cars crashing into each other. And we took full responsibility for all those people who were driven to suicide because they didn't collect enough "likes" or "nudges" on their social media page.

We were sorry that there was a backlash against Muslims just because "some people did something" on 9/11 and 3,000-plus people were murdered and millions of dollars in real estate obliterated in the process.

Well, as I recall, those "some people" were not Christians or Buddhists or Rosicrucians.

If they insist on apologizing for something, how about apologizing for California, or Minneapolis, or Portland?

Just saying.

Or we should apologize for allowing Al Gore to invent the internet, which led to that relentless flood of political e-mails, ads for erectile disfunction remedies, and social media pages where friends could tell other friends and even voyeuristic strangers how their latest bowel movement turned out.

Remember, Gore thus is responsible for giving us hackers, too.

Myself, I don't participate much in the artificial world of social media.

'Don't Get Me Started'

I read about a guy who had more than 4,000 friends on his page. Two people came to his funeral.

I can't keep up with it all. Facebook, Twitter, Snapchat, MySpace, Instagram, QQ, Zoom, WhatsApp, WeChat, Qzone, Tumblr, Skype, Pinterest, Linkedin, Reddit, Foursquare, Tagged, TikTok, Meetup, Buzznet, Nextdoor, CafeMom, Facetime... And there's more of them every day.

I'm sorry. I just don't want to share every detail of my personal life. I don't want to be in constant contact with everybody I know. For some of them, I don't *ever* want to be in contact. Leave me alone.

I've stopped watching the TV news. Lordy, some of them are even worse than the newspapers. They have 24 hours of "air" to fill, so they fill it with just that – air. We get overblown coverage of something, anything, to fill up that "air" – trivial crap that never would have been worth a mention in the newspapers of our era. Twelve TV trucks roll up to an intersection and film the remnants of a fender-bender, while a breathless bimbo interviews "eyewitness" neighbors and cops before a wondrous backdrop of whirling squad car lights.

They brag that an upcoming news event is going to be shown exclusively on "their air." And here I thought the air belonged to everybody.

Well, I warned you again not to get me started.

I fear very much that researchers and anthropologists of the future will get an absolutely skewed and false picture of what our era and society were like if the only source materials they can find are from leftist/liberal/progressive news networks and newspapers.

I can see it now: "Researchers digging into the ruins of a building that housed a major newspaper have discovered the remains of a room that apparently was called 'the Morgue'. In ancient times this referred to an area of the newsroom where old photos, news clippings and other reference materials were archived. In a later era it came to mean a room where facts, honesty and the truth were sent to die."

Well, that's enough crankiness for today.

For God's sake, Harry, when is somebody going to do something about all of this?

§§§

"Were it left to me to decide whether we should have government without newspapers or newspapers without government, I should not hesitate a moment to prefer the latter."

–Thomas Jefferson

FIFTEEN
The Celebrities

Emma steered clear of the two resident "celebrities" at Arthritis Acres, retired athlete Rocky Tosterone and his actress wife, Narcissa Nurottica, except when she saw an opportunity to insult them.

Rocky was just recently retired from his "career," and was resentful that Emma did not pay him the attention he felt he was due as a resident celebrity. He was insulted that she did not buy his book, *God of the Game*, or show up at his autograph-signing party, where he charged $100 for a signed photo, and fawn over him like some of the other residents.

"I wouldn't pay $100 for a signed photo of Adam and Eve," she told Sebastian.

Tosterone, short, stocky and swarthy, had been a star in the National Rock Skipping League, and the MVP for the Chadwick Valley Hoppers. Rock skipping now was a major sport, played in stadiums with flooded surfaces before thousands of people disaffected by the haughty and declining traditional pro sports leagues. Tosterone was one of its superstars, having developed a unique wrist-flip delivery that once let him bounce a rock 94 times on Lake Superior, a world record at the time. "Superskipper," they called him in the sports pages. Tosterone was forced to retire early, when an opponent's errant rock hit him in the elbow, altering his unique delivery.

He had been on the covers of sports and style magazines, and appeared regularly on TV talk shows dispensing his noxious brand of leftist talking points. Like many delusional celebrities, he had convinced himself that the world waited breathlessly for his every utterance, his every progressive, liberal Ninnie opinion, and was determined to use his wealth and celebrity status to save humanity from those evil, uncaring conservatives, no matter that most people valued his views about as much as they did those of your ordinary parking lot attendant.

Tosterone also had played professional cornhole at one time, and had even led a fruitless campaign to change the name of the game. Not only was he affronted by its alternate risque meaning, he believed the name was demeaning to farmers, especially in his home state of Nebraska, the Cornhusker state, and maybe even bordered on occupational and agronomical misappropriation.

"Corn is a vital commodity in our economy," he told a crowded press conference. "The name 'cornhole' implies it is a trivial crop. I think it should be called beanbag toss, or something less offensive. Nobody will be offended by beanbag toss. Nobody cares a hill of beans about beans."

That immediately roused the ire of harried bean farmers and bean aficionados, who were already under attack for contributing to the methane gas crisis, so when he was accused by the bean lobby of fostering hate speech he had to back away.

Fans of cornhole also were up in arms.

"Who's he to complain?" said one. "He's as dumb as one of his rocks."

Tons of advertising and TV money were now being thrown at rock skipping and cornhole. The traditional major sports had been in a slow decline for years, partly because they finally had priced themselves out of the market for many people. Athletes' salaries had driven up the price of a single National Football League end zone ticket to $2,700, and most families could not even consider it without taking a second mortgage or starting a GoFundMe page. Many fans also had turned away because so many crucial games were being decided by inept calls by referees.

"People got fed up," Emma told Sebastian. "They said enough, enough with the big prices, the big egos, the big salaries, the unwanted opinions, the wild off-the-field behavior, the disrespect to their country, enough with big muscle-bound college-graduate ignoramuses, some so dumb they couldn't even read the letter on their varsity sweater."

Women's sports had disappeared altogether, buried under an avalanche of biological boys claiming they were transgendered girls. The old women's achievement records were being broken at an astounding rate; a bearded sprinter now held the ladies' record in the 440, and a demure, hairy-legged, 260-pound figure skater with bulging calves permanently disabled his/her partner during a triple-throw Lutz when he/she threw him/her well beyond the judges' table and into the fourth row of seats.

Most sports now had two divisions – Men and "Other" – and negotiations were underway to just merge the two.

Sports fans also were angered when they continued to see the best seats at the World Series and Super Bowl occupied by grinning celebrities and politicians watching their first game of the season, maybe their first ever, while die-hard, dedicated fans who saved and scrimped all year to afford a single game were consigned to the nosebleed seats, if they were even that lucky.

Another major factor was the distaste and anger of many fans when rock-skipping athletes began kneeling during the playing of the National Anthem, originally to protest oppression of minorities, but later extended to all kinds of other social issues – white privilege, ageism, the death penalty, homophobia, sexism, agents who mismanaged their multi-millions, unfair labor practices, gender issues, inequality of health care, poor public schools, the disparity in quality of steroid brands, the lack of a cure for jock itch, the refusal of kids to pay $100 for an autograph, and the high price of their favorite athletic shoes, even though they got their promotional pairs free. One kneeling protester said he was protesting because there were too many protest issues.

And many fans had turned away from sports because it now took too long to play all of the anthems.

"It started with the blacks, who wanted a black national anthem to be played, too," Emma told Sebastian. "Then the Polish-Americans wanted theirs, and then the Greeks, then the Germans, the Latvians, the Irish and the Estonians, Hungarians, Mexicans and Rwandians and even the Northern Mariana Islands, who most people didn't even know had an anthem. Sometimes the afternoon games didn't start until dusk, and the TV networks were panicking because the games were eating into times for their popular reality shows, like *Naked Baking* and *Even Liberals Got Talent* and *The Real Leftists of Beverly Hills*.

"This is the melting pot idea boiling over into madness," Emma complained. "There's one anthem, one nation! This is diversity run amok!"

Emma had been a big baseball fan at one time, until she was priced out of the market.

"It's ridiculous," she complained to Sebastian, who also loved the game but had never been able to see one in person. "Utility infielders batting .165 hauling down $3 million a year. That's like a third assistant car wash attendant getting $200,000 plus a huge signing bonus."

So teams in major sports were playing before mostly empty stadiums, and the players and owners could not understand what was happening. Desperate promoters labored to create new popular sports out of pastimes that had once been considered simple parlor games.

Besides rock skipping and cornhole, there now were leagues for Tiddlywinks, Yahtzee, Monopoly, Scrabble, Risk and Clue. Moderate salaries were being paid to lure star players, who performed in cavernous arenas before huge crowds thankful again for a game they could watch for a reasonable fee.

A syndicate was formed to organize a professional Blind Man's Bluff league, but the new Ninnie government shot that one down.

"Hurtful and disrespectful to sight-challenged people," it declared. Promoters also feared it was too old-fashioned to ever appeal to a technologically-savvy younger generation.

A Chinese Checkers league enjoyed a short life until it was forced to dissolve before a flood of complaints from leftist culture warriors claiming that it was a gross example of cultural misappropriation, no matter that it had no connection with China whatever and probably was invented by Americans, based on earlier British and German games.

But salary demands were beginning again to push prices back into the stratosphere, and the cycle was starting all over. Promoters already were retrenching and turning to other activities to fill their stadiums – hopscotch, jump rope, jacks, distance spitting, guessing beans in a jar, breath holding, knuckle cracking, pie and hot dog eating contests, weight guessing, whistling, ear wriggling, apple bobbing and the like to fill their stadiums.

Severe, career-ending injuries such as Tiddly Twitch, Monopoly Elbow, Scrabble Finger, Cornhole Callus, Yahtzee Rot, Rock-Skipper's Rash and Clue Syndrome were becoming common. Some athletes, encouraged by the PC crowd to "get in touch with their feelings," did so, and quit lest they be involved in any incident where a competitor's feelings might be hurt, like in losing.

Sebastian was caught up himself in some of the new sports. He was in several Fantasy Tiddlywinks and Fantasy Cornhole leagues, knew all the player statistics, averages and league standings, and relayed to Emma every new scandal that cropped up.

"Toady Towson has been suspended from the Denver Twinks tiddly-winks team," he told her excitedly. "He was caught shaping the nail on one of his fingers, trying to get a competitive advantage. They also suspected he was on steroids, because the same finger seemed abnormally large.

"And Perry 'Park Avenue' Puddington has been released from the Minnesota Monopoly Club. Officials caught him with hundreds of Get Out of Jail Free cards hidden in his locker."

An adoring press continued to heap fawning attention on people who were playing games for a living, now child's games at that. The sports pages were filling up with accounts of hotly contested Clue championships, memorable Monopoly matches, challenging Cornhole competitions and savage Scrabble showdowns.

Every utterance of high-school dropouts was recorded and preserved for posterity. Some of them climbed up on the pedestals the press provided and began to speak out on issues of the day, running for political office, leading social causes.

Tosterone himself was the spokesman for a global environmental group vowing to save the Indonesian kumquat from extinction, lecturing the public in TV ads about their reckless attitude toward endangered species.

Emma lost whatever patience she had left when Rowdy Redbun of the Minnesota Monopoly Club announced he was running for governor on a Ninnie platform of redistributing all private box seats and season tickets to anyone who claimed they were indigent. The rolls of the indigent immediately began to swell.

"Who cares what some ignoramus playing Monopoly for a living thinks about anything?" Emma complained to Sebastian. "Out in the real world, some of these 'celebrities' would have a hard time finding a job shining shoes."

Tosterone's vanity and pretension also troubled Emma, especially when she learned that he had left instructions that after he died, admirers could take a copy of his obituary to any bookstore and redeem it for a 25% discount on his book.

Even though Emma tried to keep her distance from Tosterone, her resentment spilled over in the dining room one day. Tosterone, although retired, was in the news as a champion of the kneeling rock-skipping players. She confronted him as he was stirring his soup, and called him a traitor to his country.

"They are kneeling to call attention to America's continuing persecution of blacks, Latinos, women, gays, transgenders, bisexuals, conscientious objectors, vaccine-deniers, lesbians, meter-readers, baristas, vegetarians, left-handed people and all the other oppressed and persecuted minorities out there," he said defensively.

Other diners scattered for cover when Emma lit into him.

"You insufferable, insulting, ungrateful moron," she suggested gently. "Try playing your game for a living in, say, Somalia, or Haiti, or Liberia, and see how they treat you, what they pay you, *if* they pay you. If you're so concerned about improving the state of your fellow man, why not spread some of your concern and your multi-millions around in the ghetto, lifting kids out of crime and drugs and poverty, improving deplorable Inner City schools, or sending some deserving kids to college? Countless caskets have been carried to cemeteries with that flag draped over them, so you can be free to continue spouting your drivel. Put your money where it will do some good.

"Despite your excuses, as far as I am concerned, your kneeling for the National Anthem can only be interpreted one way: disrespect, contempt and disdain for the very country that has given you so much, enabled you to even be in this position. I take this personally. You are insulting not only me, but millions of others who love this country. You should be ashamed of yourself."

But Tosterone, blessed as he was with a generous dose of American good fortune, believed he was entitled to it, and that Americans would be so much better off if they would just listen to what he had to say.

"I think..." he sputtered before Emma cut him off.

"I don't give a damn about your opinions," Emma said, her voice rising. "I don't even care about your opinion of the toilet paper brand they choose to buy here or of the paint color they select for the walls. I put more stock in Punxsutawney Phil's groundhog weather forecasts than I do in the opinions of you and your celebrity friends. I don't give a rat's ass about the Ninnie causes you support or the products you endorse. The fact that you are endorsing them is enough for me not to buy them."

Tosterone again attempted a defense.

"Listen, there are so many oppressed, suffering unfortunates out there, people who have never known prosperity…" he started to say.

"Oppressed? Suffering? You don't know what hard times are!' Emma shouted, shaking her finger in his face.

Tosterone shrunk back, spilling his Italian wedding soup on his shirt. Other diners, who had already risen from their tables and fled, watched, alarmed, from the far corners of the room.

"The lowest income, worst-off people in this country live better than a lot of people in the socialist countries you admire so much. You take for granted all of the magnificence that you enjoy. Look around you – food, shelter, air conditioning, television, computers, luxury items, a comfortable retirement, an endless flow of consumer goods. This is called prosperity! Your problem is that you have no contrast, nothing to compare it to, because it's always been there.

"Well, I've seen hard times, and my parents lived hard times, and it ain't pretty. And you and your socialist ilk want to take us back there! And did you ever stop to think that in these prosperous times a lot of your 'unfortunates' brought their misfortune on themselves?"

To Emma, Tosterone was part of a sinister "entertainment" industry where Ninnie executives decreed that only their corrupting Ninnie views would be allowed on movie, TV and computer screens, while their Silicon Valley comrades manipulated social media to suppress conservative views and paint them as subversive, unbalanced, demented lunatics.

"For years you people have been inflicting on us an endless stream of movies, video games and music filled with blood, gore, vulgar language, immorality, violence, sadism, cruelty, disrespect for the law and our country and the very notion of decency, and all of it has been eating away at our culture," Emma said. "Listen to some of the lyrics in your rap music. They're not just vulgar, they're crude, coarse, revolting and repulsive to decent people. A lot of the other music we hear is just noise.

"With the help of lax parents, you are turning out a generation of desensitized adolescents – bad manners, bad grammar, bad language, lies, casual abortions, cheating, name-calling, finger-pointing. Everybody just shouts at each other."

Tosterone turned away angrily and went back to his lunch, although most of it now was on his shirt. How dare she speak to a God like that?

§§§

Rocky was insufferable enough, but his wife, Narcissa Nurottica, was another piece of work – the work of a long line of inept plastic surgeons. The two made a pathetic pair.

She billed herself as a former actress, and was not embarrassed when it was discovered that her acting credits consisted of one brief appearance in a horror film, as a corpse, and two seasons at the Nonesuch Summer Stock Theater in Michigan. The horror film, a huge hit, featured a band of zombies, Narcissa among them, who rose from their graves every election day and helped other rotting corpses cast their votes for Ninnies.

Narcissa was the victim of a succession of failed plastic surgeries, so many that her face now resembled a lump of Play-Dough after a two-year-old had finished with it. It was so hideously deformed that she carried a whistle with her to warn her family and especially others that she was approaching.

She also was from a long line, many generations, of rabid, toxic feminists. Born as Olga Brandt-Imhoff-Torgeson-Carlson-Hancock, she was totally unaware of the unfortunate last-name acronym her family's hyphenated marriages had created, until it became common for some people to address others simply by their last-name acronym shortcut. A good friend, Ima Sanford-Lewis-Underwood-Thomas, was known to slap people who dared address her in such a manner, but the issue became moot for Olga/Narcissa when she changed her last name for "professional purposes."

Emma thought Narcissa's doughy face and angry attitude made her a poster girl for toxic femininity. She was angry about male privilege, glass ceilings, unequal pay, gender stereotyping, tight bras, small purses, uncomfortable shoes, pedicures that did not last for more than a week, what she saw as the secondary role of women in society, and especially toxic masculinity.

"Funny, your kind didn't call it that when they were dying on beaches in the Pacific and in France, liberating concentration camps in Europe," Emma said. "My father was killed on Iwo Jima."

Narcissa had created a little theater group at Arthritis Acres, mostly so she could be the showpiece in her own Ninnie-leaning productions, which she wrote, directed and starred in. Her themes and plots usually involved beautiful, glamorous actresses or socialites who rescued single mothers from poverty, spousal abuse, workplace suppression, sexual harassment and other conservative and masculine depravities by day, and returned to their 30-room opulent mansions, staffed by cadres of servants, at night, where they worked on their lines of elegant designer clothes and purses and on their blogs, which typically were titled something like, "I'm So Wonderful I Can't Stand It."

Other productions also parroted the Ninnie line. One play, with Tosterone in the lead role as an evil, capitalistic factory owner, preached that the production of some commodities, such as mascara, lipstick, eyeliner and hair colorings, were vital "necessities" to national security and even civilization itself, and that as such their manufacture should not be taxed, much less entrusted to the control of greedy, private-enterprise profiteers. They should be awarded instead to the factory workers themselves, watched over by a benevolent government bureau.

Another Narcissa Nurottica play, with most Arthritis Acres residents participating, was a utopian, Brothers Grimm fantasy fairy tale depicting how control of a small-town bakery was wrested from the greedy, unfeeling owner and awarded to the workers. Production immediately increased, workers were deliriously content with the new sharing system, and everyone lived happily ever after.

This one was a musical, called *Flour Children,* set in snowy Buffalo, with catchy numbers like "Whistleblow While You Work" and "Take This Job and Shovel It." Workers were delighted with a new product introduced by the new management – doughnut holes selling for $12 each.

"If they can do it with cupcakes, why not doughnut holes?" said a happy technician at a frosting machine.

Emma got wind of it and offered an alternative version of *Flour Children*, which Narcissa immediately rejected. Emma's version showed the whole thing collapsing when the conscientious bakery workers began to resent the lazy workers who still got the same pay, and when starving workers began to eat the products coming off the assembly line because they were paid so poorly they could not afford groceries.

"I can't imagine why she turned it down," Emma huffed in mock indignation. "It's such a wonderful 'miserable-ever-after' socialist ending."

Emma was offered a role in one of Narcissa's productions, playing a Ninnie schoolteacher taking her students on a class trip – pilgrimage, really – to the Socialist Hall of Fame. This one was a musical comedy, featuring a chorus-line finale of tap-dancing peasant girls in babushkas strutting their stuff to the rousing socialist anthem, *The Internationale*.

"No, thank you. I would rather lick a gas station toilet seat," Emma said diplomatically.

Then, fearful that she had not made her point clear enough, she added: "Or must I spell it out for you in crayon?

Emma did not waste any time wondering or worrying why she continued to dine alone.

Sebastian was doing his homework that night when his light came on.

SIXTEEN

Don't Get Me Started

Harry, I seem to have started something here. I'm getting more and more comments on my posts, thousands of them now, most of them agreeing with my rants. Apparently there are a lot of people out there who are absolutely fed up with the way things are going these days.

"Somebody's got to do something about this before it's too late," Mary from Maine pleaded. "We can't let this go on or the country we knew and loved will disappear. It's being eaten away from the inside."

Harry, it's a different world down here since the Ninnies took over. For one thing, phony, cardboard 'celebrities" are everywhere now, trumpeting the Ninnie line of political correctness and socialism, their every utterance reported and venerated. To me, their bloviations are as memorable and lasting as a block of ice in the Sahara.

I don't get it. Our society seems to be fixated with empty-minded, breathless attention on trivia, on so-called celebrities, following their every move, their lifestyles, their opinions, even their employees, as if their views and wealth carried any more weight than the janitor down at the high school or the power company guy climbing a utility pole.

Who cares what celebrities think about anything, or what they do? There's a couple of them at the retirement home here, left-wing Ninnie nuts, and they are living proof why the gene pool needs a lifeguard. They are so caught up in their supposed self-importance that they've forgotten they are just playing a game, or an adult version of make-believe.

I envision seeing some day soon a TV bulletin interrupting an episode of *The Young and the Clueless*, where a Walter Cronkite-type dramatically removes his glasses, sighs, looks up wearily at the clock, and tells us solemnly that just a moment ago, in Hollywood, the fairy-tale union of Brick Brockton and the lovely Patty Pulchritude, the fifth marriage for both, had been dissolved in a divorce proceeding, after three weeks of wedded bliss. Both claimed extreme mental cruelty.

Give me a break. Who cares? Where are our priorities these days? Some people spend more time following the lives of hollow celebrities than they do in weighing seriously who should be leading the government. I wish the PC police would do something useful, like protect us from these celebrity idiots.

The most famous Americans these days are not the achievers, the doers, the innovators, the people who are actually accomplishing something, contributing to the common good, setting an example for others. No, no, it's those so-called celebrities leading tinsel lives or being hauled off to jail for trying to cheat their kids' way into prestigious colleges, or illegally doping their way into athletic halls of fame. Wherever the Ninnies go, they seem to attract and foment crime and absurdity.

Harry, the Ninnie PC people are running amok, forbidding this, prohibiting that, issuing new decrees every day, protecting us from hurtful words and hateful speech. Well, the Ninnies are the experts at it, aren't they? They indulge in more hateful speech than anybody else. They like to shout down and insult anybody who dares voice a contrary opinion. They call their opponents Nazis, when it's really them who are goose-stepping America toward extinction.

But still, they want to protect the rest of us from hurtful thoughts. For example, they now have a whole list of song titles they find objectionable. Why don't they clean up movies and video games and rap music instead?

Many of our favorite old numbers are now banned from the airwaves. It started with what they say is the pro-rape anthem *Baby It's Cold Outside*. After all, she said, "I Really Can't Stay..." didn't she, so I guess that means she was being held against her will, chained up in a basement and subjected to unspeakable depravities.

Give me a break.

Now they are moving on to a bunch of other old songs that they consider repulsive and revolting. We have to watch out now that we are not caught humming disgusting tunes like *Thank Heaven for Little Girls* ("Who grow up in the most delightful way....")

Pedophile perverts!

Check out these other banned old favorites on the new list just released:

Beat Me Daddy, Eight to the Bar (Horrors! what were they thinking?)

Come On-a My House ("I give you candy...") – Another glorification of enticement and rape.

Standing on the Corner ("Watching all the girls go by...") – sexist pigs!

Mule Train (cruelty to animals; hear that whip?)

My Prayer (no religion, please)

March from The River Kwai (offensive to Japanese)

Brother, Can You Spare a Dime (disparages the homeless – there is no homelessness in the perfect Ninnie society)

In a Shanty in Old Shantytown (same reason)

Indian Love Call and *Poor Old Kaw-Liga* (cultural appropriation and belittlement)

Too Fat Polka (body shaming)

Rudolph the Red-Nosed Reindeer (cruelty to animals, bullying, shaming, violates wage and hour laws)

Even some later songs aren't safe from the PC police:

Do That to Me One More Time (OMG! More submission, domination)

Shop Around (demeaning to women)

Get a Job (mocks the disadvantaged, unemployable, disabled, motivationally deficient)

Short People (self-explanatory)

Walk Like an Egyptian (demeaning, cultural disrespect)

Maybe I Mean Yes (OMG again! Seriously, how did that ever get through?)

There's a whole bunch of songs in the male domination and male toxicity category: *You Belong to Me, Let Me Go, Lover, Will You Love Me Tomorrow, I Will Follow Him, Don't Sit Under the Apple Tree*" ("...with anyone else but me...")

Give me a break.

Harry, remember when a love song was just a love song, with no suggestion or hint of sexual aggression or domination?

Yeah, me, too.

And here's the last straw: They are proposing a ban on one of my all-time holiday favorites. It now appears that *White Christmas* is offensive to some people. Implies white superiority and white privilege and all that, you know, plus it discriminates against people who live in southern climates and never see snow, and is offensive to non-Christians besides.

Well, you can see where this is going, Harry. Bing Crosby, come back and save us from this insanity.

And there are lots of other PC lists.

One of them deals with cultural appropriation violations. For starters, they want to rename all the states with Indian names. You know – Iowa, Oklahoma, the Dakotas, Utah, Massachusetts, Michigan, Wisconsin – there are a lot of them, and they never asked permission of the Indians. Minnesota, too, which in the Ojibway language means, "Place that elects wrestlers, comedians and AINOs to high office." I heard the Ninnies in Minnesota are going to put up a dandelion for governor next year and a free-range chicken for attorney general.

Just saying. Where is this all going to end?

I can see it now. Wisconsin becomes Cheeseria. Iowa is Cornucopia. Ohio likes Buckeye better anyway. Idaho shifts to Spudland, even though it turns out the name Idaho is not Indian after all but might have been invented by a white man... All the more reason to change it, say the PC police.

I fear that one of these days Christmas and Easter will be banned because they offend a powerful, combined lobby of atheists, Buddhists, Muslims, Rosicrucians, agnostics and Scientologists. Already, Christmas carols like *Silent Night* are vanishing from the airwaves and malls and being replaced with safe, secular vanilla froth like *Frosty the Snowman*, *Jingle Bells* and *Winter Wonderland*.

Happy Holidays, Harry!

If the Ninnies get their way, we should probably look for new, equal-time songs soon. How about *I'll Be Home for Ramadan, It's Beginning to Look a Lot Like Scientology, Oh Come All Ye Infidels, We Three Buddhists, All I Want for Christmas is Shariah Law, The 12 Days of Kwanzaa,* and *It Came Upon a Winter Solstice.*

I fear they might also toy with another one close to my heart. Look for *Grandma Got Run Over by a Bedouin Camel.* Well, no, that probably won't happen. Offensive to Muslims, you know.

Don't get me started, I said, but you wouldn't listen...

I lay some of this absurdity at the feet of the entertainment industry. Harry, remember all those great patriotic World War II films of our childhood, films that swelled our chests with pride and made you so proud of your country? Films like *So Proudly We Hail, The Purple Heart, Thirty Seconds Over Tokyo, A Wing and a Prayer,* and *God Is My Co-Pilot.* And later, movies like *Apollo 13* and *Miracle.*

Harry, what's happened? There was a movie made a while ago showing the first two American astronauts landing on the moon. The producers wouldn't show our guys planting the American flag on the moon because they said it was a "human achievement," not just an American one.

"Human achievement" my ass. Yeah, like Jonas Salk's polio vaccine was a "human achievement," or Thomas Edison's inventions were a "human achievement," or the development of the internet was a "human achievement." That brilliant visionary inventor Al Gore was an American, wasn't he?

Then there was that movie about Wonder Woman, an American creation if there ever was one. But no, Hollywood removed her red, white and blue, star-spangled uniform because they were aiming for a "universal" audience. Give me a damn break. What's next? Superman in orange and black, or United Nations colors? *Captain America* becomes *Captain Global*?

I'm afraid the Ninnies will try to revise the voting system next, letting Americans vote from home permanently, by mail or from their TV easy chairs, just like on the TV talent shows, some of them responding to whatever Ninnie candidate is promising the most free stuff at the moment. Isn't this a recipe for disaster, opening up the election process to tampering and fraud?

Just saying.

There is no end to the Ninnie nonsense, Harry. Listen to this: There was a prestigious Ninnie art show somewhere featuring pretentious feminist "conceptual art." A woman was shot in one of the galleries, and she died there because nobody came to her aid – they thought it was "art," part of the show.

Give me a friggin break.

Oh, don't get me started on feminism, Harry. You know I'm all for equal rights for women. My problem is with the ones who exude toxic femininity, want to play professional football, prefer a world with no men at all. I have a cure for them – a quart or two of laxative.

Some of them resent the so-called "secondary" role of women as nurturers, wives, mothers. They want to defy biology. Haven't they noticed

125

that they are *different* — in size, voice, shape, strength, temperament? Well, most of them, anyway. They are the only sex equipped to bear children, at least so far. They can deny it all they want, but it's evident to almost everyone that from an early age, boys and girls are wired differently. Don't they mind if their daughters have to use the same restrooms as questionable trans-genders?

Give me a break.

Some of these people would follow their feminism out the window. They wouldn't care if the candidate was a mass murderer, a child abuser, a crackpot who was convinced that dandelions talked to her — if she's a woman, vote for her! Be careful of what you wish for.

These are the people who will crucify a political candidate at the slightest rumor of sexist behavior — unless it's one of their Ninnie candidates, of course.

They are now campaigning against fairy tales, if you can believe it. Damaging to women and children, you know. *Snow White* and *Sleeping Beauty* — both had to be saved by a man, of course, but who really needs men anymore? *Little Red Riding Hood* — another helpless female, and those predatory wolves are all alike. *The Ugly Duckling* and *Cinderella* — bullying, and besides, Cinderella needs that unnecessary man again. Same with *Beauty and the Beast*, although you could make the argument that's he's not really a man, unless you subscribe to their belief that there's really no difference — beast/man. As for *Hansel and Gretel* — a blatant case of child abuse. And by the way, the Ugly Duckling is now to be referred to as the Pulchritudinally Disadvantaged Duckling, please.

Oh, give me a break.

Because of these people, marriage — the foundation of a functioning, cohesive, upright society — has been debased. There's less real commitment to marriage, to children, and to country, and the country suffers because of it.

If you ask me, it doesn't take a village to raise a child; two loving parents works a lot better.

It's getting so bad down here, Harry, that now the feminists want gender-neutral language. They don't like words like "him" and "her" anymore. Today, in their double-talk, you would be described as a "male-presenting person." Even the word "mother" is objectionable to some of them, who now prefer "birthing people." And gender-neutral pronouns now, please. They prefer gibberish like ze and xe and hir and xis. To all this I say: #@#$%&*%#!

A big thing down here now Harry are women who were assigned the term female at birth, but now identify themselves as a man. Maybe they are on to something here. I was born poor, but can I now identify myself as wealthy? Will that make it so?

Just saying.

And these same people demanding a gender-neutral society are the ones also demanding a female president. Go figure.

No more policemen or firemen, either, or freshmen or manholes (personholes?) or sportsmanship or penmanship.

I expect they will be boycotting Mensa next, and issuing a sheifesto declaring that several pages of dictionary words like mandate, mandatory, manipulate and manager should be avoided or altered. Oh, and also menstruation. Especially menstruation.

Well, that's my rant for today. Where is this all going, Harry? Somebody should DO something.

A-*men*!

§§§

"America is another name for opportunity. Our whole history appears like a last effort of divine providence on behalf of the human race."

–Ralph Waldo Emerson

SEVENTEEN
The Politician

Park Barile had spent his life awaiting a magnificent political destiny that he was sure would arrive some day, but never did. He did, however, climb as high once as Tweedle County Mosquito Control District Commissioner.

Now he had retired to a place, Arthritis Acres, where he could safely practice the timeless arts of political corruption and meddlesome bureaucracy. In the tradition of politicians past, he had weaseled his way into the inner sanctum of Arthritis Acres administration, and become Josef Stallingski's left-hand-man. Stallingski, always an admirer of people skilled at intruding needlessly into other people's lives, had appointed him the home's chief bureaucrat.

So he was at home now, interested only in the perks of office and clinging to power. But he did miss his old world, where Ninnies threw $20,000-a-plate fund-raising dinners where they could denounce the greed and selfishness of the wealthy, and bash capitalism.

Emma discovered to her dismay that she had to go through Barile to accomplish even the most mundane of tasks, such as procuring a simple picture hook to hang a family photo on her wall.

First, she had to prepare an elaborate sketch showing exactly where the photo would go, including the number of inches from floors, corners and ceilings. Then the photo itself, including dimensions, underwent intense scrutiny and approval. She had to provide a list of the subjects for vetting.

"Who are these people?" Barile demanded to know. "Will they be visiting? Will they be bringing guests? Have they ever voted Republican? They will need electronic passes and be recorded for our face-recognition entry system. We need their complete histories to do routine security checks."

So Emma dutifully complied. Besides one of her family, she applied for permission to hang a gallery of portraits, including William F. Buckley Jr., Barry Goldwater and Ronald Reagan.

"I also would like to hang a photo of my favorite horse," she told Barile with a straight face. "I think you'll like the name."

"A horse? Quite unusual. What is it?"

"Proletariat, a triple-crown winner."

The refusal of her request was immediate, except for her family and Proletariat/Secretariat. She was not particularly attached to Secretariat, but was learning to take her little victories wherever she could.

Emma tried again with some favorite works of art she brought from home.

Napoleon Crossing the Alps was rejected because it was "too militaristic, symbolic of empire-building." *Liberty Leading the People,* well, the female figure of "liberty" leading a revolution for freedom just would not do because she wasn't black. *The Scream*, by Edvard Munch, passed easily.

"It could have been painted here," Emma muttered under her breath.

So in the end, Emma had to be satisfied with *The Scream,* Secretariat/Proletariat, and photos of Harry, Christopher and Sebastian, although she did sneak in Sean Hannity at the last minute, telling Barile that he was a nephew, confident that Barile was not familiar with many conservative media figures, since he watched only the far-left liberal networks.

Barile was a comical figure, extremely corpulent, not only from all those years slurping at the public trough but also the thousands of free meals devoured on the campaign rubber-chicken circuit. He was too vain to wear glasses, even though it was obvious to everyone that his ill-fitting toupee was one color and what was left of his own hair quite another.

Barile spent hours each day at Stallingski's bidding, handing down rules and regulations for the other residents to follow, just for the sheer pleasure of snooping, interfering and meddling in the lives of others. Often his dictums and edicts were at odds with each other.

"Yesterday he sent around a notice warning that there was trouble with the phone service," Emma complained to Christopher. "Then he sent another one saying, 'Call the office if you are having phone troubles.' Today, he sends out an e-mail blast telling people not to send e-mail blasts because they are overloading the system.

"Next, he'll be advising illiterates to write for free help."

Like all toadies, Barile had created an exalted title for himself. He was First Assistant Chief Executive Officer, arranged a cushy office, secretary and built-in raises for himself, and in the best traditions of politicians everywhere, had exempted himself from all the mundane rules he made up for other residents to follow.

This was all with the approval of Stallingski, who enjoyed the same perks. Emma discovered that both were ensconced in their positions in perpetuity, thanks to a decree they had imposed guaranteeing that they would never be bothered with anything so pesky as re-appointment or term limits.

This was fine with the absentee owners of Arthritis Acres, a conglomerate that dutifully handed down every day from Ninnie headquarters the latest updates to the already oppressive rules and regulations for retirement homes, which now numbered 22,456 pages.

"You can even find in here the prescribed sizes and colors for doorknobs, pillows, window shades, wastebaskets, doorbells, light switches, toilet lids and drawer pulls," Barile gloated. "I love it!" He would have waved the rulebook in triumph, but it was too heavy.

Besides his Mosquito Control District pension, Barile had hoodwinked lax oversight boards into seven other pensions and stipends from previous "offices" he had held in government, including a Sewerage Control District, a Standing Commission on Gender Discrimination Case Resolution, and a Rickets Suppression Committee, even though there had not been a case of rickets in the area in 137 years.

Life at Arthritis Acres was tightly regulated, thanks largely to Barile. Emma's dining hours were restricted to a precise 29 minutes for breakfast, 37 minutes for lunch and 52 minutes for dinner, with resulting demerits if you dared overstay on your bowl of granola or grilled cheese sandwich. A huge spreadsheet tacked to his office wall detailed the allocated times for each resident, and tracked their progress or lack of same in adhering to the schedule. Emma did not have many gold stars.

His allotments were based on elaborate calculations of how long it should take a relatively healthy 80-year-old to consume a breakfast consisting of a bowl of oatmeal, a cup of yogurt or a helping of scrambled eggs, bacon and multi-grain toast. The calculations for dinner were more generous, given that most of the residents did not have all of their own teeth anymore and it would take them longer to dispose of, say, a steak.

Barile had no patience for residents who complained about his heavy-handed approach to leisurely dining.

"Seniors as a group tend to overeat," he said, "mostly out of boredom. So we need to get them out of here and into the exercise room and the activities room. And we also must avoid overloading our kitchen and staff, many of whom, shall we say, are ambitionally-disadvantaged."

Barile was oblivious to the irony of the situation – a portly, rotund bureaucrat issuing decrees on health and diet to people in much better shape than he was. As it was, he could not maneuver his substantial bulk through Arthritis Acres doorways without taking a deep breath and slipping through sideways.

Emma had noted with alarm that Barile, in adhering to Ninnie policy, had recently decreed a minimum wage of $37 an hour, even for dining room busboys, which meant her residential fees were going to go up correspondingly. But she needn't have worried, because Stallingski intervened when it became apparent that management could not continue to operate if they paid the help that generously.

"The concept is called minimum wage because these are minimum jobs!" Emma protested successfully. "You people obviously have never run anything more complicated than a rummage sale."

Residents also were given guidelines on appropriate clothing, which led Emma to fear that uniforms for everyone might be coming next.

"Mao jackets, maybe?" she protested to Barile. "Oh, yes, dress all the little proletarians in identical gear. Don't let anybody express any individuality. We will all look so smart marching in lockstep in the May Day parade!"

Barile bristled. He was not used to people challenging his edicts. He wished fervently that this irritating woman would find another place to reside. Perhaps they could just reassign her to one of the Ninnies' maximum deprivation and discomfort facilities, the former penitentiaries now emptied of maniacal murderers, serial rapists, anarchists and arsonists.

They were now being used instead to punish criminals of a far worse sort.

Among those serving attitude adjustment sentences there was Tad from the Teterboro *Times*, who had the audacity to accurately report what a conservative candidate actually had said at a debate. History teacher Beulah Bagglethrop from Bemidji had discussed Hiroshima with her students without heaping adequate censure and condemnation on the US. Pippi Porter from Pittsfield was turned down by the A-Line Fashion Design School because her admissions essay did not properly acknowledge the contributions of plus-sized people to the industry.

Author Algernon Auberge did not have a single minority character in his new novel, and Hector Hogarty was sentenced and his name removed from the dormitory he paid for at Kissimmee A&M when he was over-heard saying he believed that all lives matter. Samuel "Suds" Sliperthy of the Acme Soap Co. got five years and lost the contract to supply a very woke hotel chain when he insisted his firm could not economically produce black soap flakes. The Equal Opportunity Employment Commission caught up with Hiram Hastermint after it was told by an informer that his sole proprietorship did not have any women in executive positions.

The whole thing came to a head when Ninnie authorities investigated a complaint of flagrant violations in the local public-school system. They had to back away when they discovered that the culprit was little Lexi Lufferton, 5, who had inadvertently spelled out GOP with her kindergarten alphabet blocks, and then compounded the violation with OAN.

Barile thought a week or two in the social deprivation slammer would be good for Emma, and give him some respite from her constant criticism. "Oh, yes," he said to himself. "I must speak to Stallingski about that."

Emma learned that haircuts and styles were regulated at Arthritis Acres, too. No Mohawks allowed. No nose or lip rings, either.

"Are you kidding me?" Emma sputtered. "Most of these guys don't have enough hair for any kind of haircut, let alone a Mohawk. Nose rings? Lip rings? The last one who tried that caught his lip on a fork and needed twelve stitches."

However, she did agree with some of the restrictions, such as no tank tops or bikinis allowed in the public areas. Although most of the residents were quite fit, some were not.

"I have absolutely no desire to see some of these behemoths in tank tops or bikinis," she told Barile. "A bikini on some of these people would be like two Band-aids on the Washington Monument. If they all got into the pool at the same time, people in neighborhoods for blocks around would swear global warming and rising sea levels had indeed arrived. Tank tops? Some of them sport tank tops that would fit around a Panzer."

Barile's minions, like politicians and bureaucrats everywhere, were obsessed with regulating every facet of life at Arthritis Acres.

Emma seethed over an encounter with the inspector from the home's Knitting Needle Inspection Team (KNIT), making her regular snooping round of the ladies at Arthritis Acres. The inspector found Emma to be in serious violation of one of the house rules.

"Your knitting needles are too long."

"What do you mean, too long?"

"The new national standard is 12 inches maximum. They could poke your eye out, or somebody else's. And besides, they appear to be from a country not on the approved knitting needle trade and tariff list."

"My grandmother brought them here from Ireland in 1892."

"Oh. Well, then you'll have to apply for an exemption."

"You mean like, so I can have them grandmothered in?"

"Yes. She'll have to attest to where and when they came from."

"She's been dead since 1972."

"Oh. Well, then you'll have to fill out this 22-page form…"

Sometimes the regulations and inspections handed down from above were so ridiculous that even some of the Ninnie-leaning residents found them amusing.

Stallingski was quite upset when a Ninnie inspector from the National Bureau on Toilet Seats arrived at the home, unannounced.

He was following up on a complaint by a gentleman who lived a few doors down from Emma. The inspector discovered that the descendance rate of the gentleman's self-lowering toilet seat was excessive, could be accelerated accidentally, and had caused serious injury.

"You might be wondering how this could happen," Emma told Sebastian, laughing so hard she could hardly get her story out. "It seems that the gentleman's little grandson was visiting, and while he was standing at the toilet attending to a bodily function, the seat slammed down, and, well..."

Sebastian winced. He didn't think that was so funny.

Emma complained that most of the employees at the home were hopelessly incompetent, ranging from the wait staff ("We wait, and wait, and wait, and then wait some more") to the housekeepers, who did not keep the house in the best condition.

Then she discovered that employers no longer were allowed to ask of potential hires such inflammatory and patently discriminatory questions as, "Do you have any skills or experience or training for this job?"

Emma wondered if these same new Ninnie rules applied now to doctors interviewing at hospitals, or architects designing high-rises.

She began to spend more and more time on her blog, where she was finding the company much more to her liking.

Sebastian's magic lantern was getting a workout.

EIGHTEEN
Don't Get Me Started...

Harry, I am getting to know some really nice people on this blog. I think there might be hope for our country after all. I am hearing from a lot of folks who are fearful of this drift toward socialism, of what's happening to a generation of youngsters who don't know any better and have been filled with drivel and twaddle by leftist Ninnie schools and colleges.

I saw a shocking poll that said half of young people today embrace socialism. God help us. Let's hope they grow up soon.

But I'm also hearing from a lot of other people in the alphabet generations – Gen X, Gen Y, even Gen Z (What does that make us? Gen G, for Geezer?) – who aren't buying the Ninnie nonsense. Maybe they will turn out to be Generation R, for Rescue/Relief, and save us from this current generation of politicians, Generation Zero.

Don't get me started on bureaucrats and politicians! There's a former professional politician here at Arthritis Acres, a leftist who spent his life working for the government, so naturally he thinks government is the cure for everything. I shouldn't really call him a former politician, because with that breed they are never really retired, spend even their declining years lusting for power, even if it's over a gaggle of senior citizens, drawing up rules here, posting them there, never really retiring because it's in their blood, like a deadly virus eating away not only at their own self-respect but infecting everything they touch.

When there's a national emergency, like a natural disaster or a pandemic, these Big Brother leftists see it as an opportunity to wrest more power for government and away from the people, who are not likely to ever get it back. If they can get citizens accustomed to the idea that the government is the fount of all wisdom and efficiency, the Great Problem Solver, then the easier it will be when the emergency is over to make the crisis rules permanent and continue whittling away at more of our liberties and independence.

Before you know it, they are decreeing which car you are allowed to drive, stipulating the size of your soft drink, looking over your shoulder menacingly awhile you dare to read such publications as the *Epoch Times*, telling you where you can live and what kind of mustard you can buy.

Politicians! They never seem to get anything done. Too many of them spend more time squabbling, accusing each other, investigating each other, than they do on the nation's business. There are people in high office who care more about their party politics, about getting re-elected and hanging on to their precious perks, in enriching themselves, than they do about running and preserving a great country. Their whole focus is on obtaining power and holding on to it forever, or prying it loose by whatever means necessary from those who do have it.

Why don't they DO something? Where is the leadership? It seems all they ever do is react to things that have already happened, instead of heading them off.

Just saying.

We have allowed the rise of a professional class of politicians and bureaucrats, a closed system where the pros circle the wagons to repel any outsiders, any non-professionals, who dare to challenge their autocracy.

It's no better at the international level. The United Nations spends a lot of its time passing useless resolutions, most of them against the US. Some of the stuff they do is laughable. Its Human Rights Council is stacked with members like Cuba, China and other nations who have wretched histories of persecuting, mistreating and even executing their own citizens.

What's next? Let's put Iran in charge of Israeli security, China will keep the world safe from deadly viruses, and Russia will secure the safety of dissidents everywhere.

Oh, don't get me started again.

Instead of squabbling like children, here's a few things the politicians could tackle to make themselves useful for a change – affordable health care, immigration, poverty, broken families, abysmal schools, crime, cybersecurity, a strong military. Some of them want to decimate defense spending. Don't they get it, that without a strong military there won't be anything left to defend?

But no. Instead, they are introducing crucial laws to stipulate the number of kernels allowed to be left in a popcorn bag after the popping is finished, or designating the exact ratios for peanut butter and jelly in PBJ sandwiches, or specifying how many jerks have to actually live there before a town can be officially classified as a jerkwater.

OK, so I exaggerate. But give me a break.

Or they could do something to protect the integrity of the voting process, one of our most sacred rituals. There are suspicions about crooked elections, ballots disappearing or tampered with, noncitizens voting, outcomes manipulated invisibly by political parties, social media and even other countries. There are stories about truckloads of preprinted ballots arriving mysteriously, the checkboxes next to a preferred candidate already conveniently filled in.

Harry, this is a threat to our very existence as a free nation, to our civilization. The people in our own country who would violate our tradition of transparent and honest elections, manipulate them for their own devious ends, nullify the sacrosanct decisions of voters, should have their citizenship revoked and spend the rest of their lives in jail. Too harsh? Not for a crime that is this malicious, as destructive to our country, as actual treason. Again, a lot of us would look forward to seeing them paraded through the streets with shaved heads.

If you ask me, Harry, why don't you need an ID to vote? You need one to drive, to buy liquor, to license a pet, to get a bank account, a job, medicine, food stamps, welfare, a hotel room, cigarettes, buy or rent a house or car. You need one to gamble, board a plane, marry, buy a gun, get employment. And unemployment, for that matter.

So what's the problem with making someone prove their identity, and citizenship, at the polls, especially in a time of proven instances of voting fraud? And don't sing me that tired old racism song again. How tough can it be these days to prove who you are? If you care about yourself and want to survive in an ID society, get an ID. Something so essential to a democracy should not be that hard to get.

If it is, make it easier! There's something useful that legislators could do. But it seems, Harry, as if the politicians have abandoned any pretense of ever making it an honest profession. Everywhere you look there is corruption, graft, favoritism, influence peddling and waste. It's a dangerous thing when it appears that the government is for sale.

All of this, whether real or suspected, makes people distrustful and suspicious of both government and big corporations, some of which pay no federal taxes, if you can believe it. Some of the biggest firms, just saying, seem to be more concerned with their worldwide sales, sales even to our enemies, than they are with the security of their own country.

And the legal system, too. There is a feeling out there that if you have enough money you can buy your way out of anything with a team of high-priced lawyers. Judges soft on criminals and with little regard for victims don't help, either. The government spends millions to rehabilitate criminals but nothing for their victims.

The Ninnies used to be known as Progressives, but now they are socialists or even communists. They are obsessed with victimhood, multiculturalism, hate speech, identity politics, political correctness. What's "progressive" about an ideology that would reverse hundreds of years of a supremely successfully experiment in self-government?

Hate speech? What is that? Well, the Ninnies and the universities also call it "dangerous speech." There would be no America if some very smart people long ago hadn't engaged in some very "dangerous speech" against the Crown, as in the Declaration of Independence.

George III probably was offended, hurt even, at being called an oppressive tyrant, but the world is much the better for it. Wonder if Old George retreated to his Safe Space with his comfort porcupine. And across the channel, I'm sure Robespierre was offended when his own head rolled off the guillotine. Talk about hurtful.

"Dangerous speech" to the Ninnies means shutting down and shouting down the opposition. Oh, no, they say, this is not about censorship. It's about "communication and starting a conversation, and creating awareness," whatever that friggin double-talk claptrap means. Hate speech to them is any speech they disagree with. Hate speech is OK if it's *their* hate speech.

It really means that you are not entitled to an opinion that differs from theirs or they will try to harass and intimidate you into silence, just as Hitler did. They also would remove your ability to defend yourself, especially against them.

They demonize anyone who dares oppose them or has a contrary opinion. "Dangerous" conservative speakers at colleges struggle to be heard over the juvenile din of demonstrators.

Remember when it was common to shrug off opposing or disagreeable opinions by saying, "Well, it's a free country..."? No more.

Harry, free speech is the only defense and antidote to idiotic, sinister, dangerous, twisted opinions.

The 'hate police' try to shut down any talk and debate that is anti-global-society, or anti-diversity, and brand it as racist or xenophobic. The Ninnies like the idea of globalism; then they could turn the entire world into one socialist global disaster.

They like to twist the language into ridiculous PC contortions to avoid 'offending' anybody, and manipulate it to promote and protect their own causes. The old "global warming," for example, has become "climate change," which lets them blame the evil polluting Americans for any manner of global climate event – record cold or heat, record droughts or floods, tornados, hurricanes, sudden clouds of gnats that disturb the Ninnies' annual picnic.

How can "global warming" be blamed simultaneously for today's droughts, hot weather and fires, and also for harsh winters, record snow and cold? Well, even the Ninnies could see the problem there, and switched to "climate change." Maybe they believe that our era is an exception, that eons ago, droughts and extreme temperatures did not alternate with ages when your oxcart wheels were frozen to the ground... Ask Noah about rising sea levels. Even the Sahara Desert, scientists say, has experienced alternating periods of wetness and dryness.

America is always the bad guy to a lot of global environmentalists. China and India are never held to account for their pollution-belching smokestacks. Maybe because nobody can see them through the smog.

Just saying.

And speaking of science and thoughtful inquiry, whatever happened to our universities, those bastions of free speech and the free exchange of ideas, where neither of these are now permitted? To the Ninnies, freedom of speech is acceptable only if it's in line with their own views and doesn't offend some snowflake.

Before you know it, Harry, there's likely to be a new Ninnie department governing hurtful speech, where you'll need to apply for a permit before you can call your degenerate, deviant, lying, cheating, dirtball scumbag neighbor a degenerate, deviant, lying, cheating, dirtball scumbag.

Oh, don't get me started on the bureaucracies, Harry. There's one now for nearly everything. The Ninnies love bureaucracies. What is it that makes them think they have to control everything, even down to the mundane minutia of everyday life? There are so many bureaus now regulating our behavior and consumption habits that there is a new bureau that regulates all the other bureaus. We might as well be living in China.

Speaking of, some of the dreamland progressives seem oblivious to the threat posed to America by the Chinese, the Russians and others. "Let's just all be friends, let's teach the world to sing, and we'll all live happily ever after."

Give me a break. The Chinese communists don't want to teach the world to sing. They want to teach the world to grovel before them.

We're dreaming if we think China just wants to coexist peacefully with us. They are overrunning the world like a flood, financing nations that probably can't pay it back except by capitulating to them. Look no further than Hong Kong for a lesson in what happens after they take over – digital surveillance of the population, re-education camps, restrictions on religion and freedom of thought and movement. Some of us will forever suspect that they loosed a plague on the world while experimenting with germ warfare.

Because of our internal divisions, our decline in national unity and patriotism, they see us as a soft pushover. They plan to take over the world while we worry about wrong pronouns and rules for bathrooms and getting in touch with our feelings. I can see it now – in the next war, we will shout abusive, politically incorrect pronouns at opposing troops, and then watch gleefully as they shrink away in abject, crushing defeat...

Give me a break.

If the Chinese and Russians are so creative, how come they survive and prosper by infiltrating our universities and institutions and industries, hacking and stealing our military and trade secrets, our patents, literary works and films, buying up American companies so they can tap into their technology?

If they're so clever, let's see them invent a leaf blower that doesn't make so damn much noise. Nobody else seems to be able to do it.

'Don't Get Me Started'

Maybe they don't have what it takes to invent their own stuff? More likely, they're just too lazy. It's easier to just steal it. Why expect a government with no morals, no scruples, no ethics, to honor or respect what belongs to others?

Just saying.

What happens when the flow of stolen American ideas, technology and art is finally cut off, disappears? You're on your own, Russia and China. Will they then collapse from inertia because they don't have the motivation and savvy to create the new technology needed to survive?

Remember, they have no culture of rewarded innovation and ambition – that's one of the terrible evils of capitalism, right?

What's the chance of some proletariat drudge toiling away in some windowless concrete Soviet-style bunker building ever inventing something really exciting? Even if he does, all the credit and reward is going to go to somebody else, or to everybody. So why bother, the drudge is thinking.

Aren't Russia and China supposed to be socialist paradises where the wealth is shared and everybody has everything they need and the masses live in total bliss? Then how come they have their own oligarchs, their own billionaires, who live lifestyles the "masses" could never dream of?

Just saying.

Well, I apologize for rambling on like this. Sometimes I get carried away in my rants.

But why doesn't somebody do something about all of this?

§§§

"If ever a time should come, when vain and aspiring men shall possess the highest seats in Government, our country will stand in need of its experienced patriots to prevent its ruin."

–Founding Father Sam Adams

NINETEEN
The Moocher

Few of her new 'companions' offended Emma as much as Lazuli Leech, a shiftless slouch with a name to match.

Emma had stopped by to say hello shortly after Lazuli's arrival, hoping as always that fate might deliver a new resident who might actually be proud of her country, hold reasonable political beliefs, somebody she could talk to, someone sane.

No such luck.

Lazuli arrived in a chauffeured limousine. Her possessions, in 12 large crates, were brought to her apartment by two attendants.

"Things must be tough in Europe," Emma said. "Now they're sending their retired and deposed royalty over here."

Emma never liked to make snap judgments about people or say unkind things about their appearance – well, hardly ever – so this time she confined herself to observing, "My, she certainly does cast a formidable shadow. She's very easy to see."

Lazuli was tall, wide and wobbly, and supported herself on two canes as she lurched up the walk toward the front entrance, canes that always became unnecessary as soon as she was out of sight of observers. Her full name was Lapis Lazuli Leech; her father had been a vagabond mineral prospector with a fondness for precious stones who named his other children Hematite, Agate, Quartz, Jasper and Obsidian. After he died in a mine cave-in, her mother took permanent advantage of government programs designed to help her get through an emergency.

Lazuli was 65 and somehow had managed to live her entire life free of any of the responsibilities and burdens that most people have to shoulder. That was not surprising, since she had grown up in a family of six children who all had lived off of the government for 60 years.

"Work is for idiots," her mother had told her. "If you do it right you can assemble a pretty decent life from all the programs that are out there for you."

Lazuli was an excellent student. She had surveyed the opportunities and survived for years on a combination of government benefits.

Food stamps provided her basic needs there, and even allowed her to buy ice cream, soft drinks, junk food, bakery – lots of bakery – and even an occasional fast food burger and fries.

As a mother of four, all by different fathers, she had collected on, or made good use of, Aid to Families with Dependent Children, day care, Head Start, rent and utility subsidies, nutrition and other child care assistance, and if it got tough to make ends meet, which sometimes happened, she just had another baby and collected additional sums.

"You know, I'm one of those who's paying so you can live like this," Emma said, always diplomatic and gentle in her opinions, regretting she had ever stopped by. "Have you no shame?"

Lazuli was unfazed. She had heard this before.

"Well, I thank you," she said. "Thank you very much for your kindness and generosity. I am indeed grateful. What a wonderful country.

"But I'm entitled to this, and I deserve it, because of my disability."

Lazuli was on Social Security Disability, having successfully conned a lax and pushover hearing judge into believing that her obesity, from a lifetime of overeating and indolence, interfered with her ability to get in and out of cars, let alone public transportation and elevators in office buildings, or to go up and down stairs.

The judge nodded sympathetically and blinked back tears as Lazuli fabricated for him a lifetime struggle with a limited range of motion and an inability to sit or stand for longer than five minutes, all of which precluded any chance for employment. She had discovered to her delight that not many employers were looking for people with her particular set of attributes.

"But I saw you sprinting toward the dining room the other day," Emma said. "You lifted two tables and cleared a bunch of chairs to make room for yourself."

"I was feeling a little stronger that day," Lazuli conceded. "And I was in a hurry to get there before anyone else, because I need my space. I also have Multiple Chemical Sensitivity, which means allergies to perfumes, candles, flowers and deodorants, among a lot of other disagreeable things that you find out in public spaces."

"That includes work, too, I'm sure." Emma sniffed. "And explains why you smell like that."

Lazuli, too, was immune to sarcasm and insults, so proud of her membership and expertise in the parasite class, so unaware of the revulsion it stirred in others, that she eagerly shared an anecdote about one of her fellow "sufferers" who was eager to claim a disability check.

"He shot himself in the foot," she giggled, blissfully oblivious to the delicious irony of this particular phrase in this particular situation. "And when that didn't work he had to shoot himself again. Last I heard, he only had two toes left."

Lazuli had never held down a job, unless you count the time when she was between welfare applications and momentarily impoverished, and reluctantly signed on with a company that consulted with real estate firms in exorcising ghosts from haunted houses.

She was not very successful, but when it ended she was able to collect unemployment for 26 weeks, and then another 26, and she would have had 26 more if the lavish Ninnie state program had not run out of money. She also was able to collect workman's compensation benefits when a ladder fell on her – pushed, she successfully claimed, by one of the hostile ghosts she was seeking to evict. She developed a great fondness for this ghost, which she came to call Clyde.

The whole experience instilled in her a great incentive – not to work or look for another job, certainly, but to research other lucrative government programs for the shiftless and "motivationally deficient."

"Mother was right," she concluded. "Why work?"

Lazuli did not know many employed people, but even those she did know did not inspire her to join the workforce.

"My cousin, he had to turn down raises because it would push him into an income category that would jeopardize his freebies. It's just so unfair."

Emma discovered that Lazuli had lived in a 3,000 square foot house on a lake, with a huge garden and sculptured hedges, swimming pool, a boat dock and a gatehouse. All of this was possible because of disability payments, unemployment, housing assistance, low-income energy vouchers and weatherization subsidies, plus a multitude of other government programs intended to help the truly needy.

She was at Arthritis Acres because it had all become too much for her.

"I just couldn't keep up with it anymore at my age and with my disabilities," Lazuli said. "My gardener had retired and I couldn't find a new one. It's so hard to find good help these days. The cabin cruiser needed to be replaced, the Olympic-size swimming pool had a leak and my pool attendant was so unreliable that the pool was covered with algae and I was getting an allergic reaction to it. Plus, the golf course dues kept going up. It was just too much of a strain."

"You poor soul."

Lazuli plunged ahead.

"And that's not the worst of it. Because of my size, the airlines were now charging me for two seats and I had to give up my annual trips to Spain and Bali. By the way, do you know if the rooms here have 65-inch TVs and therapeutic pop-up chairs, and if there's a stairlift elevator? I hope so. I'm going to miss mine."

Emma could not suppress her coughing fit.

Lazuli also enjoyed a free cell phone and minutes, subsidized Internet access and free legal assistance. The kids had received free breakfasts and lunches. She needed her late-model car to shop and get around, so the gasoline assistance program helped her there. And she needn't bother about taxes, either; indeed, she received tax credits.

"What about car insurance?"

"Oh, I just take my chances."

Emma was speechless at her irresponsibility. Lazuli barged ahead.

"They make it all so convenient, especially for somebody with my disabilities. For food shopping, I just use my electronic benefit transfer card. What a country."

"What do you do about health care?" Emma asked, knowing full well the answer.

"We just go to the emergency room," Lazuli said. "They have to take you. And now I'm on Medicaid besides."

She relished telling Emma a story about the 84-year-old man she knew who applied, unsuccessfully, for Medicare coverage of his penis pump.

"Penis pump? What's that?"

"You know, if you're having difficulty, um, um, you know... I can't imagine why he needed it. He can't even get to the bathroom by himself."

Lazuli collapsed into laughter.

"I get the idea," Emma said, her anger rising. "What about educating those children?"

"Educational grants, free tutors, that kind of stuff. Can't wait for the Ninnies' free college program to start. I even home-schooled them for a while. But I wasn't very good at it."

"No kidding," Emma seethed.

She was becoming more appalled by the minute. Emma did a quick calculation in her head and concluded that Lazuli's many welfare equivalents were worth considerably more than a lot of hard-working people pulled down after a 40-hour week of intense, difficult, stressful labor.

"You know, you'd better enjoy all of this while you can," Emma said finally, heading for the door. "If this keeps up, this whole system, this taxpayer gravy train, this moochers' paradise, is going to collapse."

Lazuli, oblivious as always to criticism, smiled sweetly.

"Well, I hope it lasts at least until I'm gone."

"How selfless, how thoughtful of you."

Lazuli ignored her. She was busy checking her food stamp balance on her cell phone.

Emma backed toward the door. She sensed that she and Lazuli would not become good friends.

"I've got to get out of here," she told herself again.

Sebastian was busy with homework that night when the lamp lit up.

TWENTY
Don't Get Me Started...

Harry, it's getting worse down here every day. The Ninnies are bound and determined to protect everybody from everything, do everything for everybody. How in the world is that ever going to end successfully? They are big on showing kindness, sensitivity, charity and understanding to the "less fortunate" – which includes homeless drunks, welfare cheats, druggies, loafers, disability phonies, criminals, dropouts.

Interesting way of putting it – "less fortunate." Does that mean that the "fortunate" only got there because of good luck, and not hard work and ambition? Of course! So that lets the Ninnies take over and make sure that the 'luck' is spread around evenly to everyone, even to some who have done nothing to deserve it. They are even talking now about mandatory house loans to indigents. Seems like a good way to wind up with lots of trashed housing.

Oh, how the Ninnies love to talk about 'spreading the wealth.' Remember free-market capitalism? The harder and smarter you worked, the more your self-respect and wealth increased. But that results in income disparity, so the Ninnies want to carve it up and share it with the slugs, slackers, slouches, shirkers and sloths. Why do they deserve a share of someone else's achievements? Go out and earn your own.

Seniors control a lot of the country's wealth, after working for 50-60 years to amass it, so that's our wealth the Ninnies are talking about spreading around. We pay a hefty share of the taxes, yet we are accused by the slackers and slouches, those who pay little or no tax at all, of not paying our fair share.

Huh?

Some of the ever-so-compassionate, gentle, and touchy-feely Ninnies are even saying seniors eat up too much of the nation's health care, that we should just live with our maladies instead of treating them.

I guess what they're really saying is, "Why don't you just get out of the way, suffer in pain and then die, you old buzzard?"

I'd like to transfer some of my arthritis and bladder problems onto them. Especially my bladder problems.

What's next, Harry? Go to the back of the line in the emergency room? ("Oh, excuse me, Mr. Illegal Alien. Did I cut in front of you?") The new triage policy is going to be by age. If you're over 80, forget it, see your funeral director instead.

So that's going to create a run on plastic surgery. Back in the day, we used to lie about our age to get a drink; now it's to get an operation so we can look younger and delay mandatory death a little longer. What's the next big breakthrough for treating ailing seniors going to be? Gas chambers?

Just saying.

I see a day coming when there will be "Coot Patrols" – Ninnies in hazmat suits and with big nets, out trolling the streets for stray seniors in wheelchairs, with limps, canes or other obvious infirmities, and hauling them off to the Geezer Disposal Grounds.

Which reminds me. I am quite disturbed that the same people who are in favor of unrestricted abortions want to be in total charge of our health care.

Don't get me started...

Harry, it is so bad down here that if you are good at gaming the system through various forms of government assistance – food stamps, child care, unemployment, housing, disability, Medicaid – you can wind up in better shape than people who actually work. In some states, half of the people are supporting another half made up in some degree of people wallowing in inertia, drug dependency, questionable disabilities, ignorance, and just plain laziness. You can see where this is going.

We have one of those professional moochers here at Arthritis Acres. I like to address her as "Your Indolency." She loves it. She's so ignorant she thinks it's a compliment.

This is what happens when government is controlled by people with absolutely no real-world business experience – the Ninnies from academia, nonprofits, the bureaucracy, community organizers. They have no concept of how to pay for all of this, except to raise taxes, and then raise them again, and then...

Don't get me started.

The Ninnies know full well it is human nature to take handouts, to want something for nothing. So they are encouraging and creating a permanent underclass of professional welfare loafers who are perfectly content to let the support system carry them forever. They are being robbed of ambition, of their right to seek a rewarding life beyond subsistence.

The Ninnies like to take money from those who work hard for it and give it to those who refuse to work, who like to be spoon-fed and safe on the government plantation. These people should not be allowed to vote It's a conflict of interest.

Harry, I can't figure out some of these Ninnies, people who shouldn't be Ninnies at all, like big bankers and celebrities and financiers. Now that they have their pile, all provided by the free market system, they want to lift the 'oppressive yoke of capitalism' from everybody else by redistributing the wealth – everyone else's wealth, that is, but not theirs – to lazy louts and welfare cheats. Are they so dumb they don't realize that a lot of the wealth that is going to be redistributed is going to be theirs?

They wouldn't have any wealth if they lived anywhere else but America. They need to be careful. Where do they think the Ninnies will be constantly looking to finance their free-everything-for-everybody scheme?

I suppose they should be admired for their concern for the "unfortunates." It will be interesting to see what happens when their do-gooder instincts collide with the reality of their vanishing fortunes. At what point does your own welfare trump your idealism?

The Ninnies treat people like squirrels. Just keep handing out free nuts, like welfare, supplemental income, child and health care, all designed to make them forget how to fend for themselves, and pretty soon they have a docile, obedient class dependent on the government.

Cockroaches and mice die in traps because they haven't figured out why the bait is free. And just to stretch this a little further, chickens and cattle are blissfully unaware that the guy feeding them is the same guy who will slaughter them. Just like socialism.

The 'safety net' has become a hammock for too many indolent, lazy and shiftless freeloaders. War on Poverty? Well, poverty is winning, if you let the Ninnies have their way.

Just saying.

Don't get me wrong. There are people out there who are truly needy, because of medical conditions, job losses, tragedies or misfortunes over which they have no control. I'm talking here about the able-bodied people who consciously choose to be wards of the government. We need to be able to tell them apart.

How come we are constantly told that Social Security and veterans programs are running out of money, but we never seem to run out of money for food stamps and welfare and illegal alien benefits, and raises for politicians?

And please don't call food stamps, welfare and the like "entitlements." They are entitled to nothing, except in the eyes of Ninnies who would reward people for doing nothing to help themselves. They are entitled in this great country only to go out and make a living, to earn their own way, to seek their destiny.

The politicians have been tinkering with Social Security for years, redirecting the money elsewhere. This is a real "entitlement" – we paid in for 40-50-60 years and now they want to make it harder to collect, like upping the Social Security age while the pols vote themselves another plush benefit.

We all might be able to have free health care if the politicians would get serious about eliminating the fraud in Medicare/Medicaid and the Social Security disability system. Most of us know of perfectly healthy loafers who go on disability and then they're seen out shoveling snow, mowing the lawn, lifting children, running marathons, swimming the English Channel, climbing Mt. Everest... Well, so I exaggerate. But not by much.

I don't know about you, but nothing irks me more than seeing a guy with a handicapped sticker on his car sprinting into a supermarket, while a little old lady with a cane has to hobble in from nine lanes away because he's got her disabled parking spot. And there never seem to be any consequences for these jerks – they get away with it.

§§§

'Don't Get Me Started'

To all of you wonderful people out there who are following this blog, and commenting on it, I sincerely appreciate and cherish all of your observations. It is so heartening to know that there are so many other people out there who feel as I do, that the promised land we live in is under threat these days from every quarter.

So I want to get you involved here in something. I want you to tell me what America means to you, what comes to your mind when you think of our great country, its history, its promise.

For myself, one of my favorite images of America always has been that of a football team. Just look at a typical lineup, whether high school or college or professional. The roster is made up of guys with names like O'Brien, Robinson, Mendelsohn, Archambeau, Yamamoto, Lopez, Bloomquist, Bartolutti, Singh, Abboud, Kowalski.

The roster of a typical football team in Poland might be one guy named Kowalski plus ten more whose names all end in -ski or -czyk.

Isn't that amazing? We are the melting pot, indeed.

What about you? What is your favorite image of America?

§§§

"When half of the people get the idea that they do not have to work because the other half is going to take care of them, and when the other half gets the idea that it does no good to work because somebody else is going to get what they work for, that my dear friend, is the beginning of the end of any nation."

–Adrian Rogers

TWENTY-ONE
The Veteran

Except for Deuteronomy Diaz, the caretaker and building engineer, and Sebastian, who came and went, Emma had few allies at Arthritis Acres, which catered to a Ninnie-leaning clientele. She fretted constantly how she had ever wound up in this Ninniebin, how long she would have to stay, and was perpetually angry at Christopher for sentencing her to this den of leftists.

"Didn't you research this place? When it's your turn, I hope Sebastian returns the favor," she scolded. "Maybe he can find a nice uncomfortable gulag for you, too."

Christopher didn't need any reminders that he had betrayed his mother.

"I'm sorry," he said. "It sounded so good in the brochure. I didn't realize what this place was like. I'm looking for something else for you."

"Well, hurry. They can make socialism and communism sound good in the brochures, too. Same for colonoscopies and root canals and amputations. I don't want to spend my last days in a godless socialist utopia. I hear they won't let you through the Pearly Gates if this was your last earthly address."

So she was happy to make friends with Col. George Patton Collins, 85, a black retired West Point grad and Vietnam veteran who was from a long line of military men. His father was a Congressional Medal of Honor winner from World War Eleven, er, II, and had been a great admirer of Patton, thus the distinctive name bestowed on his son.

Although disabled from an encounter with a Vietcong land mine, Collins was still trim and fit with ramrod-straight military posture, limped into the fitness room every day to work out, and called everybody Sir or Ma'am. He and Emma would become fast friends and allies.

Collins had a chestful of medals, including a Purple Heart and several Bronze Stars, but seldom displayed them, saving his uniform for special occasions like Ronald Reagan's birthday and the solemn annual observance of Rush Limbaugh's demise, which he knew would infuriate most of the other residents and staff.

"I thought most blacks were liberals," Emma told him shortly after they met, in what Collins liked to call the Arthritis Acres Mess Hall.

"Not on your life," he said, taking off his glasses and running a hand through his gray crewcut. "Not many I know of who served in the military, anyway. The military kind of gives you a different perspective on life and duty and patriotism, on your obligation to serve and honor your country, on the crucial importance of a powerful defense.

"A lot of ambitious, talented blacks today realize there is no place for them in a leftist ideology that suppresses personal achievement and individual accomplishments. There still are some delusionals who think Lyndon Johnson is some kind of a saint. Myself, I'm with the people who think LBJ and his Great Society of expanded welfare programs helped to destroy the black family."

Emma raised her eyebrows.

"Think about it. Single mothers, of whatever race, really, were eligible for welfare as long as there was no man in the house. So they married the government. All those programs just deepened dependency on the government, reduced personal initiative. It made the black husband, the black father, dispensable. Broken families breed instability, dropouts, drugs, crime. Look at the legacy of all those burned out, crime-ridden, crumbling neighborhoods."

"So how did you wind up in a place like this?" Emma wanted to know. "You are too sharp to have been so easily lured into the Arthritis Acres Ninnie Trap."

"Oh, they made it sound so good," Collins said. "I had to do it by mail. I didn't know what I was doing. I didn't research it very well. By the time I got here and saw it for myself it was too late."

"You have to meet my son," Emma said ruefully.

Collins winked at her. "But I don't intend to stay."

"Me neither."

It was the beginning of a cabal.

§§§

Emma discovered that Collins led a secret life away from Arthritis Acres. He disappeared for several hours every day, which intrigued Emma no end. Most of the residents stayed put, except for occasional outings sponsored by the home, such as the trip to the annual Ninnie picnic downtown marking the 1917 Russian Revolution, or to watch the yearly parade celebrating the anniversary of China's suppression of Hong Kong.

So she asked him what he was up to.

"Come along and find out," he said.

They climbed into his immaculately maintained 1977 butterscotch-colored Buick station wagon, which he called Agent Orange, and set off. A half-hour later they were at a Veterans Administration hospital.

"I like to visit my boys, especially the ones with no family nearby. It means a lot to them to have visitors. Some of them are confined here for long periods and nobody ever comes to visit."

Emma accompanied Collins as he strode through the wards and poked his head into rooms here and there. She was impressed by the respectful reception he received, from the patients, the nurses, the doctors. She could tell they were in awe by the way they looked at him.

"Hello, colonel," said an ex-soldier doing rehab exercises for a knee replacement. "I hope you don't want me to do any deep knee bends today."

"Not a chance, Hank. But we do want you to be in shape to genuflect again."

He knew most everyone by their first names, and if he didn't, he introduced himself. But even the new patients already knew about Col. Collins.

"He even knows my wife's name, my kids," one GI told Emma. "He knows where I'm from, where I served. He's amazing. He even bought me a subscription to my little hometown weekly newspaper. Last month he reminded me about our wedding anniversary coming up."

"Believe me," Collins told Emma. "I get just as much out of this as they do."

A widower now, Collins had been married to his childhood sweetheart, who had accompanied him to posts all over the world.

"She died from breast cancer quite awhile ago," a nurse told Emma. "And do you know what he did later? He married a woman whose husband died in Iraq and who was left with six children to care for. I don't know if he actually loved her, at the time anyway, but he told me, 'She can't raise those kids all by herself.' Their mother's gone now, but all of those kids still are in contact with him."

Collins and Emma made one more stop before returning to Arthritis Acres. He pulled up in front of the bus station and parked.

"The bus comes in once a day. I wait for a couple of minutes and sometimes there's a soldier or two getting off, on leave, or discharged, or whatever. So I see if he needs a ride to wherever he's going next."

While they were waiting, a sailor carrying a duffle bag emerged from the station and stopped at the curb, looking anxiously up and down the street. Collins made a move to get out of the car and approach him, but stopped short when a middle-aged couple and a pretty young woman ran toward him, arms outstretched.

"He's in good hands." Collins said, smiling, and got back into the car.

Back at the retirement home, Deuter Diaz filled Emma in on more Collins stories.

He told her about one soldier Collins met at the bus station who was on leave and on his way home to attend his father's funeral.

"His connections were tight," Diaz said. "He probably wasn't going to make it. So Collins drives the kid to the airport and pays for him to fly home.

"Same thing with a Marine who was on her way home for her sister's wedding. She wasn't going to make it either because of a bus breakdown, so Collins puts her in a taxi and prepays for the 100-mile trip.

"Another time he picked up a GI hitchhiker and asked him where he was going. It was to a town 150 miles away. So he drove him there, 150 miles! When he got there he was invited to have dinner with the family and stay overnight, and then he drove back. Amazing!"

There were more classic Collins "interventions."

"He was watching a marathon race that passed by Arthritis Acres one day, and spotted a scrawny kid who was struggling to keep up with the group," Diaz said. "So he fell in beside him and ran the rest of the way with him, pumping him up, encouraging him, like a gentle boot camp. The kid finished third!

"I told him one day that my neighbor's shy, introverted granddaughter was dejected because it was prom time and she knew what was going to happen, again. So what does he do? He tells me to tell her to get ready for something special and apparently he fixes it up with the principal, then shows up at her door with a corsage, and takes her to the prom!

"'Grampa, you should have seen it!' she told her grandfather later. 'We come through the door and then everybody stops and stares at this handsome, buff officer in all of his ribbons and medals, twirling your wallflower granddaughter around the floor!'

"And that wasn't the end of it," Diaz said. "After they saw what she looked like all spruced up, she had to beat the boys off with a stick."

Emma smiled wistfully, thinking back to a time when she had been a prom queen. Now she admired Collins even more.

"And I was with him downtown one day," Diaz added, "when we saw a young guy standing out in front of an office building. He was pacing nervously back and forth, looking at an image of himself in a store window, adjusting his tie, his clothing.

"The kid obviously was prepping for a job interview, maybe his first, so Collins, well, you know Collins, he takes him aside, re-ties his tie for him, spiffs up his suit, then gives him a pep talk on how to go into an interview with a confident air that says, 'You're a fool if you don't hire me. Don't let me get away.'"

"So what happened?" Emma said.

"Well, two weeks later the kid shows up at Arthritis Acres and wants to take Collins out for lunch with his first paycheck. Collins goes, but won't let the kid pay and picks up the tab himself, of course.

"Another time I watched him out back, you know, where that pasture is, behind Arthritis Acres, where that nice young couple keeps a bunch of horses. One of the horses was mired up to his belly in a mud pit. The other horses were very nervous as they watched a veterinarian and his crew trying to get a sling under their pal, to get him out, pacing back and forth, stomping around. So Collins sees this and he goes out and calms them down and coaxes them over to the fence so they can watch the rescue operation. He has a great touch with animals, too."

"Maybe he was with the cavalry," Emma said, grinning.

Even the elderly widows at Arthritis Acres, with whom he flirted constantly, had Collins stories. His courtly manners and gentlemanly ways had set many an aging heart aflutter.

"He just makes us feel so special, so attractive, so desirable," one of them told Emma. "We know he's lying, but they're such delicious lies."

Emma learned that Collins was a remarkable man in many other ways, too. He held some very definite views about society, which Emma found interesting, to say the least.

"I don't get it," he told her one day after a late lunch. "Some blacks complain about their surroundings, then go out and loot and burn and make them even worse. They blame whites and the system and white privilege and anyone else for their situation, accept no responsibility for themselves.

"They're always victims, when they could be trying to help pull themselves out of poverty and crime. The police are accused of 'excessive violence.' Well, how about 'excessive crime'?

"If you are born white, why does that automatically make you a racist? Most whites I know want to help this situation, not make it worse, to live in peace and harmony. If you ask me, racists are a dwindling minority. My own mother used to say, 'Why should all of today's whites be responsible for what happened years ago? They weren't there, they had nothing to do with it. How you gonna' change what happened?"

Collins shook his head.

"We've all come a long way. Our job now is to stamp out the rabble rousers and prejudice that remain. Let's move on, let's move up."

"Amen," Emma said.

Sebastian's lamp glowed again that night.

TWENTY-TWO
Don't Get Me Started...

Harry, I have a friend here, a military guy, a patriot, and he is a daily living reminder of what a great country we live in. A country whose foundations are now being threatened by ignorant people who don't realize how good they've got it here, in this remarkable mixture of cultures and customs and legacies.

We all came from somewhere else, but once here we built a marvelous system that is distinctly American – a receptive incubator for new and free ideas. We created a world where you are free to do anything, become anything, say anything, worship as you want, start a business, become a millionaire, all without government approval or management, without burdensome rules and ridiculous regulations.

You can even try to sell Korans in a Jewish neighborhood if you want, and then learn firsthand about some other great American freedoms, like the freedom to try, the freedom to fail, the freedom to then try something different, having learned something in the process.

Well, this works most of the time, except when you let the Ninnies have a say, when you let them get their nose in your tent with their rules and regulations. I know of one city where they make you purchase an expensive license if you intend to go *out* of business. And in one state there is a law against sleeping on trains. Another state exempts igloos from minimum ceiling requirements. Really. They love procedures and directives and laws, the more intrusive and ludicrous, the better.

There's a story about a West Virginia guy who had a small one-man coal mine in his back yard. They threatened to shut him down unless he equipped it with a stretcher.

'Don't Get Me Started'

Harry, our glorious American system is under attack. There are people among us plotting to turn whites against blacks, women against men, young vs. old, "fortunates" against "unfortunates," citizens against cops, gays vs. straights, polka people against hip-hoppers, rum-raisin ice cream fans against the pistachio people... Well, you get the idea. They want to fragmentize us – what's the old saying – divide and conquer?

It's plain common sense that we are stronger together than we are divided. Together, we should be enjoying all the fruits of this blessed land.

But some days it seems like their plan is working, that all we do is argue and bicker and call each other names. Call me old-fashioned and naive, but I think we need to go back to a kinder, gentler, patriotic time, the one represented by my military friend.

Harry, on this blog I'm hearing from so many wonderful people who think like we do about this glorious country, and resent what is happening to it. I certainly started something when I asked them in my last blog to send me their own images of America.

This is from a lady in Topeka:

"My America is written in its songs: *Oklahoma*! and *Show Boat* and *The Music Man*. Loretta Lynn's *Coal Miner's Daughter* and Dolly Parton's *Coat of Many Colors*. John Denver's *Take Me Home Country Roads*, George M. Cohan's *You're a Grand Old Flag*. I think of the *Battle Hymn of the Republic*, songs like *Shenandoah* and *Home on the Range* and *City of New Orleans,* and Eddie Arnold and LeeAnn Rhimes singing *Cattle Call* together. Neil Diamond, Johnny Cash, Leonard Bernstein, Irving Berlin... We are so blessed to live here amid such creative genius..."

A guy from Albuquerque wrote me:

"My America is the Grand Canyon and Yosemite and Yellowstone, the mighty Mississippi, the Great Lakes, the Rocky Mountains, the great prairies and waves of grain stretching to the horizon. Never has God blessed a country with such natural beauty, bounty and splendor.... This is the Promised Land."

Some of the responses were quite poetic, like this one from New Hampshire:

"It is the natural human condition to be free, to be unencumbered, to be able to soar, to run, to reach and to strive, to test the limits of your ambition. I picture a child, sun in her face and wind in her hair, racing across a field of green, toward a horizon of unlimited promise. Anyone or thing that opposes, restricts, belittles this image of my America, stands in the way, is the enemy..."

This is from a man in Tucson:

"I believe in an America of Fourth of July parades and kids running through water sprinklers, of the Budweiser Clydesdales, of families on picnics, of lemonade stands and baseball games, of church suppers and swimming holes, of street parties and neighbors talking to each other across back yard fences..."

A woman from Iowa wrote: "My America is BIG – a big country with big vistas, bighearted people, big dreamers with big ideals, big ideas and big achievements – people like Clara Barton, Henry Ford, Frederick Douglass, Thomas Edison, Martin Luther King, Babe Ruth, Amelia Earhart, Henry Aaron... But my Big America does not extend to big government, to Big Brother."

And here's another one, from a guy in Idaho:

"When did it become corny, or passe', to thrill to the sight of your high-school band leading the Fourth of July parade, or to sing *The Star Spangled Banner* with thousands of others at a ball game, or to shed tears at your first glimpse of the massive, stunning Statue of Liberty? She is still a beacon of hope, just like she was for those millions from abroad escaping oppression and poverty and political suffocation, and who knew on sighting her that their lives were about to start over."

Another, from an ex-Marine in Florida:

"America gave us Elvis, John Wayne, baseball, postage stamps, radio stations, skyscrapers, the Wright Brothers, Jackie Robinson, peanut butter, lasers, GPS, country music, potato chips, cotton candy, the light bulb, frozen food, doo-wop, chocolate chip cookies, a man on the moon, Bob Hope and Bing Crosby, Eddie Murphy and Phyllis Diller, disposable diapers, credit cards, cell phones, cowboy movies, Gene Autry and Roy Rogers... The list goes on, and on... And don't forget all those eccentric creative tinkerers, like the guy who invented a meter to tell if tomatoes experience pain when they are sliced (He says yes, they do)."

Harry, I didn't know we invented the potato chip. And I apologize now to all those tomatoes I sliced and tortured.

From Alabama:

"My America is *Superman* and *Batman*; *Wonder Woman* and *Catwoman*; *Captain America* and *Captain Marvel*; *Spiderman* and *Plastic*

Man; *Mickey Mouse* and *Donald Duck*; *Dick Tracy* and *Brenda Starr*; *Hagar the Horrible* and *Herman* and *The Far Side*; and all of the other unforgettable characters and creative artists that roamed across our newspaper pages and comic books."

Disney World and Disneyland were mentioned often, Harry, but I was surprised to learn that *It's A Small World After All* is not a universal favorite.

"'It's been 20 years since I was at Disney World, and I still can't get that dang tune out of my head," said Barry from Birmingham.

Another recurring theme, from a lot of people, was country music.

"How wonderfully, typically American," a man from Georgia wrote. "Country music is a marvelous blend of Scottish and Irish and African music and instruments, with a generous dose of American originality thrown in."

Over and over again, Harry, my new friends mentioned banjos and guitars, fiddles, square dances, Bluegrass, and patriotic songs like Lee Greenwood's *God Bless the USA* and Brooks and Dunn's *Only in America*. There were a lot of mentions of country classics – Patsy Clines' *Crazy*, Hank Williams' *Your Cheatin' Heart* and *I'm So Lonesome I Could Cry*, Marty Robbins' *El Paso*, Bob Wills' *San Antonio Rose,* and Carrie Underwood's *All-American Girl*. And what's more American than country churches, gospel music and African-American spirituals?

Our delightful American sense of humor came through again and again in allusions to other songs. A guy in Buffalo claimed that the world would have been better off without *You're the Reason Our Kids Are So Ugly* by Loretta Lynn and Conway Twitty. Sam in Sioux City liked the Statler Brothers' *You Can't Have Your Kate and Edith Too.* And Theresa in Tacoma was a fan of *If My Nose Was Running Money (I'd Blow It All on You).*

Harry, if we ever lose that irrepressible sense of humor, we are done for. We will be as sober and dour as the Germans and the North Koreans.

Another guy told me he found his America, and its lasting influence, on a trip overseas, to France.

"Go out into the countryside, and you are reminded that they have not forgotten World War II," he said. "In a remote little town in Normandy, the elderly proprietor of a restaurant recognized us as Americans and came up to us with tears in his eyes. He just shook our hands over and over again, and showed us an old photo of four smiling GIs standing in front of the very same restaurant, alongside a guy who obviously was this man's father."

Well Harry, that little anecdote was only one of several similar stories.

"We were tourists in a little town in southern France and stumbled across a street fair," a man from Wisconsin wrote. "They were cooking sardines and sausages right out on the street. After I bought a plate, this young guy who was operating the booth extended his hand and said earnestly in hesitant English, 'Thank you for Normandy.'

"I was blown away. He couldn't have been more than 25 years old!

"There was an accordionist there, and as this wonderful evening wore on I asked him to play *La Marseillaise*. They were so honored to hear a request like that from a visitor that they toasted us at every opportunity, and some of them even made a stab at *The Star-Spangled Banner*. What an evening. We did not feel so good the next morning."

Harry, America's influence is still felt in Europe in lots of other ways. A lady from Fargo wrote about an experience she had in Germany, when her group came upon a big street party in the huge central plaza of a big city. "As we sat down at a picnic table, the band struck up a familiar tune, John Denver's *Country Roads*. The entire crowd, and there were thousands of people there, spontaneously began to sing along, some in perfect English, some giving the lyrics a bit of a Teutonic twinge!"

A man in Florida told me about a place he rented in a little town in Italy. A prominent feature was a group of three big cypress trees in the town square. He asked why they were there, if they symbolized something.

"They were planted as saplings in memory of three American soldiers who died here during a skirmish toward the end of the war," the mayor told him.

Yes, Harry, America has left an indelible mark on the world.

A man in Michigan told me a World War II story about his uncle, who was in a troop transport heading toward the front, which turned out to be the Battle of the Bulge. As they bounced along he saw a road sign with the name of a little town on it: It was his own name! This was the ancestral town in Belgium that his grandparents had emigrated from in the last century.

I remember, Harry, and you do too, when the whole world watched, mesmerized, as Apollo 11 landed on the moon and two Americans walked on its surface, and then returned. Nobody else could do that. That's MY America.

But perhaps my favorite story of all tells you something about the America I know and love. It's about Col. Gail Halvorsen, an Air Force pilot who took it upon himself in 1948, during the Berlin Airlift, to drop packages of candy to destitute German children trapped by a Soviet blockade of the city. He would wiggle his wings on approach to signal to the children he was coming. What began as one American's effort to bring some joy into the lives of people ravaged by a long war turned into a nationwide cause when American candy companies and citizens learned of Halvorsen's campaign and joined the effort to help keep the "Uncle Wiggly Wings" crusade going.

Maybe my view is romanticized and sentimentalized, but what's wrong with that? It also seems to be the view of thousands of patriotic Americans I have been hearing from on this blog. We have been blessed, and we should all thank our God every day that we were born here, into this particular place, instead of some backward, corrupt, diseased pocket of the world.

And yet, Harry, there are those people in our own country who do not appreciate what we have, who would change it, modify it, corrupt it, to fit some misguided complaint that our system, our way of life, is not perfect, that some people still suffer, that we have made mistakes.

Of course it's not perfect! Is anything? People suffer all over the world. But it's certainly way ahead of whatever is in second place. And socialism isn't even in the top twenty!

We live in a world marred by greed and violence, and unless someone figures out how to change human nature, it's likely to stay that way. A strong democracy like America, with noble principles and aims, is a brake on the chaos and cruelty of brutal dictators, tyrants and socialist dreamers all over the world. A PC culture is not going to be useful in a world where we have to be tough and fight our enemies with everything we have.

America is a living, breathing, beautiful, wondrous thing. And there are those who are hunting it, who want to kill it. If it goes extinct, the world will slip into another Dark Ages from which it might never emerge.

Harry, I'm afraid we are on the brink of a new civil war down here. The sides have been forming for quite some time. Free and honest elections, the two-party system, are in danger. When the Ninnies are out of power, they don't want the country's problems to be solved, because somebody else would get the credit, because then they wouldn't have anything to complain about, to use as leverage to get back into power. This amounts to putting their own interests ahead of the country's. They apparently don't believe in one of the bedrocks of any successful society or culture – cooperation and compromise.

They have rejected our system of government. The opponent who wins must be removed from office or at least obstructed every step of the way. Individuals who threaten their path to power must be destroyed.

They want to suppress any media that supports an opposite point of view, which is not much of a problem, because most of the media is in their pocket anyway. You have to look hard these days to find any news media that are fair and impartial chroniclers of events.

Harry, somebody has to do something. I can't take much more of this. If it comes to civil war, though, I guess I should not be overly concerned, because our side has guns and the other side has Safe Rooms and Comfort Chickens and Trigger Warnings and a choice of pronouns.

Well, our generation has saved the world from Nazism, from socialism, from dictators and tyrants before. We put those fires out. Do we have to do it again?

§§§

"Over the years, the United States has sent many of its fine young men and women into great peril to fight for freedom beyond our borders. The only amount of land we have ever asked for in return is enough to bury those that did not return."

–Gen. Colin Powell

TWENTY-THREE
Horace Aappel

Perhaps the most sinister person at Arthritis Acres, and that's saying something, considering the conglomeration of clueless idealists and misguided zealots who walked the halls there, was Horace Aappel, the information technology person.

Aappel had worked for Silicon Valley's biggest social media platform, a behemoth called Barney that was created in a burst of tech mergers and acquisitions. It had absorbed all of the major newspapers and radio and TV networks, phone and tech companies, and social interaction platforms until it was the sole means of communication, information and social contact in the country, a perfect complement to a Ninnie dictatorship and thus also its biggest financial supporter by far. It was hard to tell the two apart.

There even were calls to rename the country, to United States of Barney, but there was too much opposition from supporters of alternative names, especially those who fancied United Socialist States of America. Another Ninnie faction favored "Fagam," created from the first initials of the corporate tech titans that dominated American life and were the core pieces of Barney.

That one lost a lot of support, especially among mapmakers, when it became obvious that North Fagam and South Fagam would be incongruous oddities on a new map of the world, to say nothing of the turmoil it would create at the United Nations and with songs such as *Fagam Pie* and movies like *Fagam Graffiti*. Several major corporations also stepped in to protest, concerned at having to change their logos and stationery to Fagam Airlines and Fagam Express. Traditionalists, of course, were aghast at the prospect of having to sing "God Bless Fagam" and "Fagam the Beautiful."

Barney knew everything about everybody, and rented its vast library of information to a captive crowd that had nowhere else to go anymore. Advertisers could buy priceless inside information on shopper preferences. Pollsters knew your political and social views, and thus so did the Ninnies, so you had to be careful in your e-mails and in what you read or said online and which sites you visited.

Medical researchers got extremely personal health data about citizens, sometimes disturbing information about illnesses the citizens themselves did not yet know they even had.

"Why am I getting all these e-mails advertising Gleevec and oncology clinics?" Alex in Annapolis wondered innocently, then ominously.

Frank in Fergus Falls panicked when he was solicited by VD clinics offering their help for his "problem," and had to watch anxiously every day to beat Sarah to the mail.

And you had to be sure there was nothing on your computer that might arouse Barney's suspicion.

"Hmmm," said the bishop, after Barney alerted him that something might be amiss at St. Oswald's. When he tapped into the parish's web page, besides Father Brennan's report on last Sunday's receipts, he also found a spreadsheet record of the pastor's success, or sometimes lack of same, in playing the horses, hidden in a file labeled "Indulgences."

"No wonder there's no money to fix the roof," said the bishop. He made a note that in his upcoming annual financial address to the priests of the diocese, which he called "The Sermon on the Amount," he would have to warn them against such sinful practices.

Barney knew what kind of toilet paper you bought, so you were likely to be bombarded with solicitations not only from a variety of toilet tissue purveyors but also from your favorite brand, imploring you to remain loyal or they would be wiped out, so to speak.

For a fee, Barney also allowed you to become privy to some quite intimate details in the lives of others.

"I didn't know you were so unhappy," Betty in Baltimore said tearfully when she learned her husband was renting a motel room three times a week in another part of town.

"Well, I didn't know your 'bridge club' sessions were in the bedroom of our neighbor, George, either," her husband said.

'Don't Get Me Started'

Some people were extremely happy with the new behemoth called Barney.

"I love it," enthused Olivia, 78, of Oshkosh. "Barney knows so much about us, makes life so easy, offers solutions to crucial lifestyle decisions. It knows I bought an electric toothbrush and then thoughtfully suggested other personal items, such as my new vibrator.

"It knows we went to San Francisco last year and now it's offering deals on syringes and inflatable homeless shelters and poop scoopers. And how does it know I'm almost out of hemorrhoid ointment? Maybe it's because my personal assistant device overheard me complaining about that pain in the ass next door...?"

But Barney had some weak spots, too. It was not good at screening junk phone calls, so you still might be pestered 15 or 20 times a day by people trying to scam you out of your Social Security number or imploring you to buy their extended warranty on your toaster.

"If you ask me, companies that are so concerned about an extended warranty don't have much faith themselves in their own product," Emma grumped,

And Barney had a tin ear, which often led to misunderstandings. After Olivia bought a six-pack of Budweiser, funeral homes began flooding her with discount offers on biers. When she bought a breakfast cereal two-pack, she was besieged by a video-streaming website touting their new serial on serial killers. And the shopping trip with her granddaughter to look at wedding gowns brought a solicitation from *Horse and Bridle* magazine and a special discount on riding boots.

Olivia suspected that Barney also knew she was a closet drinker, and about those secret vodka bottles stashed all over the house. Her suspicions were confirmed when her supply ran out and Barney automatically sent her a new batch, based on her past purchasing habits, plus a pamphlet on Alcoholics Anonymous.

Barney also noticed she had not voted in the last presidential election, so it took the liberty of voting for her this time. She wondered who she had voted for.

In their delusional delirium, cities were naming streets after Barney, there was a new electric auto called the Barneymobile and an ice cream confection called the Barneysickle, and Barneyburgers were a staple in restaurants. The rock-skipping championship game was renamed the Barney Bowl.

"How about Barney?" Ludmilla from Laramie suggested excitedly to her husband from her maternity bed. Another little Barney thus joined thousands of other little Barneys in the next census.

Mysterious, unknown, anonymous Barney 'managers' in dark rooms decided, based on the vast volumes of 'evidence' now available to them, if you were a danger to their Ninnie society and should be marked for 'surveillance,' although they called it 'attentive awareness.' Barney would not disseminate over its vast information network any opinions it deemed detrimental to society, meaning the Ninnie philosophy.

Corporate and big tech titans now had access to your most personal information. People were being fired, or not hired at all, because they knew you watched Fox or Newsmax, or got a sandwich from that place that made no secret of its Christian values, or sent $10 to that foolish candidate who declared you should have to prove you were an American citizen before you could vote.

Your social media page was apt to disappear mysteriously if you didn't think the US should be appeasing China, or if you backed the "wrong" team in athletic contests, meaning the one that didn't have a transgender head coach.

If Barney learned your company had donated to a political candidate or cause that was out of favor, it would soon be losing its government contracts, and some of your employees might be transferred to a firm that was more woke, even if it was in another state. If you fancied enrolling in a right-leaning college, your grades transcript might be doctored and you'd be lucky to find a horseshoeing or mortuary school that would take you.

"I wanted to go to Hillsdale College and they're making me go instead to LGBTQ State Polytechnic," protested Shawn from Saginaw.

In the new, official cancel culture, you could be publicly ridiculed and humiliated because of your opinions, blackballed because of your choice of companions or activities.

"My date and I wanted to watch an inspiring old patriotic movie," muttered Craig from Coeur d'Alene. "But instead of *Miracle*, they made us watch documentaries on the scandalous US repression of obese, ugly fashion models and its brutal discrimination against blind air traffic controllers."

'Don't Get Me Started'

There was no end to big tech/government snooping and interference. Hiram Higginhelter's season tickets to football games at his alma mater, Acme A&M, were revoked when the college learned he had once donated $4 to a conservative candidate for Crabgrass Control District Commissioner. Arthur and Alma from Abilene were turned down by an adoption agency because they had once signed a petition against same-sex marriages. Tad Tumulty of Trenton complained that his auto insurance policy was cancelled because he drove a gasoline-powered pickup, and then the company doubled down and voided his homeowners' coverage too when they learned his hedge trimmer, lawn edger and lawnmower were not electric, either.

"They warned me not to be seen praying anywhere but in church," grumbled Esther from Elmhurst. "Then they also wanted a list of the people I intended to pray for.

"I told them to go to hell."

Farmer Phineas Finsterminster lost his milk contract with the co-op when it was discovered he had a firearm. He argued that it was common practice on farms to keep a gun, to protect chickens from foxes and other farmyard varmints, but his plea was ignored by a city-slicker bureaucrat who thought eggs came from an egg-making machine in a special back room in the supermarket and who told him to reason with the intruders instead.

Pete the Plumber refused to respond to an emergency call when authorities warned him that the homeowner displayed a yard sign for a conservative candidate. And Mayor Rex Rifflesworth of Raleigh was not only recalled but held up to social media humiliation when he advocated that America return to observing a Thanksgiving Day, long since abolished by the Ninnies. They were advocating instead for a national Apology, Shame and Reparations Day.

The few opposing news networks that remained were constantly harassed. Fox, Newsmax and One America News Network broadcasts were repeatedly interrupted by the obnoxiously loud tests of the Emergency Warning System, sometimes 10 or 12 every hour. Whenever an opposition political figure appeared on a show, the screen was likely to dissolve into a jittery confusion of random pixels and shimmering images, and the dialog disintegrate into indecipherable fragments. Sometimes the sound went dead altogether and the substituted subtitles expressed the opposite of what the person had actually said.

Even abbreviations and internet shorthand shortcuts were being policed. LOL now was outlawed because too many people were Laughing Out Loud at preposterous Ninnie edicts, and citizens were being told that if they intended to use OMG, it now stood for Oh My Government. As for WTF, even though they didn't touch that one, it's what a lot of people were wondering.

§§§

"Why did you leave Barney?" Emma asked one day, hoping fervently that perhaps Aappel might be recalled to duty and thus removed from her life.

"Had to retire early," Aappel replied. "Eyesight was failing, plus rheumatism. Doctors said it was from too many years staring at secret cameras monitoring private homes, analyzing algorithm patterns, installing hidden microphones in dark, dank places. I don't see how the KGB and the SS did it. Maybe that's why so many of those Storm Troopers were all hunched over and wore thick glasses."

"That's too bad," Emma snorted. Silently, she mused that Aappel couldn't see much else, either, especially the evil menace of his own "profession."

So now there was a Barney2, installed and monitored at Arthritis Acres by Aappel, who even though a retired resident himself, was also Stallingski's chief intelligence officer. From a bank of computers in a back room he could monitor every resident's comings and goings, their personal information, their bank accounts, and even tap into their laptops, tablets and cell phones.

He was watching everyone at Arthritis Acres through cameras, sensors and microphones concealed in everyday devices like televisions, telephones, doorbells, personal assistants, light fixtures – even toasters, air conditioning vents, seat cushions, candles, and, for a time, toilet paper holders. He abandoned that when he couldn't decipher the sounds he was picking up.

Aappel's miniature Barney system knew where you were, what you were doing, who you were with, what you were buying, what you were saying and to whom, whether you had regular bowel movements or were constipated, just like the bona fide Barney of the outside world.

Emma suspected from the start that there was something very rotten about Aappel. Her misgivings about his intentions and capabilities were confirmed when he sent her a message recommending a certain sleep aid.

"It worked wonders for me," he said.

"How the hell does he know I'm having trouble sleeping?" Emma seethed, livid at the implications.

Other residents soon were on to him also, and some tailored their behavior accordingly. Everyone had heard about the incident with Priscilla Plowski, who couldn't find her false teeth one morning and was pacing about her apartment talking to herself when an ominous voice came from her bedroom chandelier saying, "They're on the stand next to the toilet."

"Did I tell you about the birthday cake fiasco?" Emma said to Sebastian. "Sunflower Squance had a birthday party for Simper, and Horace planted a tiny microphone in the cake to monitor the conversations of any subversives who might be there, such as me."

Emma began to giggle uncontrollably.

"So then he couldn't retrieve it before they cut the cake, and Simper ate it."

She had to wipe her eyes with a tissue.

"Now all Horace can hear are bubbly burps and growling gurgles and restive rumblings. It must sound like he tapped into a volcano."

She collapsed on a couch in laughter, holding her sides.

Aappel, as Stallingski's chief tech person and spy, had compiled extensive dossiers on every resident and visitor, and knew, for example, where Simper hid a pot stash in Sunflower's room, that Professor Salters trolled online dating services catering to sex-starved seniors, and even that Stallingski himself kept his porno magazines in a file marked "Recreational Outlets" in a back room of his office.

He knew that Park Barile slipped into Hepzibah Sigalthaler's room some evenings and did not emerge until early morning, that Rocky Tosterone kept his copies of *Gay Pride* magazine in the ah, closet, and that Slant Greeley had a contraband miniature TV set in his bathroom where he could secretly watch Fox News, OAN and Newsmax, although he called it "monitoring."

Aappel made it difficult for residents to access information through anything other than Ninnie-approved, leftist communication outlets. He set up an Arthritis Acres "intelligence" system that mirrored the larger one the Ninnies managed in the outside world.

For starters, he "managed" the occasional so-called elections that Stallingski set up as a feeble, bogus show of fairness.

"I need to get rid of Colonel Collins as a board member," Stallingski told him in advance of a resident board election. "He's honest and straightforward. Quite deluded. Thinks this is some kind of democracy. Can't have that here. He's a bad influence on the rest of the advisory board."

The board, with Slant Greeley's help, immediately began a disinformation campaign against Collins. Stories in Greeley's paper questioned his character, his background, his taxes and his ethics, belittled his hairstyle, claimed he really was a spy for a rival retirement home, Multiple Maladies Manor, and even quoted a document purporting to show that Collins had promised some residents he could erase their demerits in a *quid pro quo* deal for their vote.

When Collins fought back, Greeley produced "evidence" that a right-wing pro-military group had tried to influence the election on his behalf by tampering with the voting machines, and was not embarrassed when Collins pointed out that Arthritis Acres did not use and had no need for voting machines.

"Maybe it was the Russians again," Emma offered helpfully.

Aappel pulled the levers of his communications apparatus and Sunflower Squance won in a landslide, which surprised her somewhat, inasmuch as she didn't even know she was running. A close inspection of ballots would have revealed that 27 residents of the home who had died in the 1990s had been happy to support her campaign, and even Pucci, Narcissa Nurottica's little pooch, had barked her approval.

Emma's festering dissatisfaction grew even more with this affront to her patriotic military friend.

"This place is like a prison," Emma told Christopher. "Maybe worse. I hear even San Quentin serves better meals."

Christopher, whose guilt mounted every day his mother spent at Arthritis Acres, had been looking desperately for an alternative, but so far could find nothing suitable. The Ninnies had packed the retirement home regulatory boards with so many fellow-travelers that it was difficult to find one anymore that had even a chapel or library.

Emma had been accepted in the first place only because Christopher had lied on the application papers, attesting that she was a member of the League of Leftists (LOL) and contributed significant sums regularly to the SS (Society of Socialists) and Anarchist Nation United States (ANUS).

Fearful that her real political leanings might be discovered, she had been keeping a fairly low profile at the home, but no more. Instead of surrendering, Emma decided to fight back.

With the help of Deuter Diaz and Sebastian, technological titans in their own right, she did a sweep of her living quarters. What they found made Emma very angry.

The ceiling fan contained a hidden radio transmitter that sent her every conversation to an unknown destination, but Emma was pretty sure she knew where that might be. In the light tower of her favorite painting, a lonely, wintry, windswept lighthouse, they found a miniature camera that sent images of her room back to HQ, which Emma again figured was Aappel's office.

Her "personal assistant" was the mandatory little box on her counter that could keep track of her appointments, play her favorite music, program her computer and doorbell and even her refrigerator, change TV channels, remind her to take her pills, convert meters to inches and grams to ounces, and in an electronic, feminine voice, provide instant, accurate answers to such crucial trivia questions as, "Can you get butterflies in your stomach from eating caterpillars?"

It could even intrude on your conversations.

"I don't like the color of the device," Emma told Deuter. "It's such an ugly green."

"I only come in green," said the device. "You have a dress in your closet that's the same color, so what's the problem?"

"Well, aren't you a snippy little bitch," Emma said.

"That's hate speech and I must report you."

So most of Emma's conversations descended into whispers.

"It's like Siri and Alexa had a baby," she told Deuter. "I'm going to call it Mata Hari."

Emma also discovered that her computer had been tampered with. By some unknown and sinister means her every keyboard keystroke could be monitored and deciphered. Deuter eventually traced the problem to the electrical receptacles, which were not standard issue.

"Look," he told Emma. "There's a hidden wi-fi device in here that probably alerts Aappel whenever you work on your computer."

"You'll have to be careful now with the blog," Sebastian whispered. "We need to set up a workaround."

"This means war," Emma vowed.

The workaround he came up with was ingenious but laborious. Sebastian created a code template that converted her computer's top row keyboard numbers and special characters to letters of the alphabet, so messages that might read, "Help! I am a prisoner in Arthritis Acres Retirement Home!" would appear to any spy as "1@3$5 ^7**9 0_=+-)9(8 &6^ %443#2@^. When Sebastian applied his template to the gibberish on his end, the text would be converted back into sense.

That sufficed for a while, but Emma had to use a tedious hunt-and-peck system to make it work for her blog. After Deuter discovered how Aappel's keystroke detector worked, he was able to disconnect and reconnect it whenever necessary. While he was at it, he disarmed the system's forbidden-word censor as well.

As a test, he had Emma send him a message. It said, "Now is the time for all freedom-loving libertarians to come to the aid of conservative radio talk show programs." When there were no repercussions, they knew they were home free.

Once her computer was cleared of Aappel's bugs and perpetual surveillance, Emma spent a lot more time on her blog, sending it on to Sebastian via their secret signal system. She also amused herself for hours on end by composing fictitious messages that she knew would torment Aappel.

"Your order for an anatomically correct female inflatable 'companion' has been shipped," said the order confirmation Aappel received from an online adult toy store. "Remember to remove the safety tape from all orifices." Somehow the message also got sent to all Arthritis Acres residents.

Aappel was intrigued when he received a lucrative, hard-to-believe job offer from another retirement home, and was disappointed when he investigated and discovered exactly why it was so hard to believe.

174

It took him weeks to unsubscribe from *The Epoch Times*. He could have done it earlier, but became so fascinated by the contents that Stallingski feared he was about to go over to the other side.

And Aappel's e-mail to Stallingski apologizing for the stench in his office and outlining his search for a cure to his uncontrollable flatulence also somehow was disseminated throughout the building.

Emma was having so much fun that she decided to distribute the abuse evenly.

Sunflower Squance received an alarming call from the relative of a former resident.

"You might want to consider asking for a different room," the voice on the phone whispered ominously. "My hateful socialist aunt died in that room and I know her spirit is still there. Haven't you heard the muffled voices in the night crying for more taxes on the wealthy and free funerals for everyone? You probably have noticed strange noises and sudden drafts of cold air."

Sunflower hadn't. Until then.

Stallingski himself was not immune. With the aid of a secret Emma ally in the kitchen, his Cokes sometimes tasted more like soy sauce, his creme donuts were filled with mayonnaise, and that ice cream sundae he ordered looked instead like mashed potatoes with gravy topping and a cherry tomato.

"Wheee!!!" Emma exulted. "This is like being back in middle school again!"

She extracted what satisfaction she could from wherever she could.

She taped a photo of Ronald Reagan over the lighthouse painting tower light, and changed it out every couple of days with portraits of Eisenhower, Nixon, Ford, the two Bushes and Trump, and once even with a drawing of an extended middle finger.

Stallingski suspected she was the instigator of all this mischief and retaliated by suspending her access to the fitness room, which was fine with her because she didn't put much stock in excessive exercise anyway.

"Have you ever seen a smiling jogger?" she asked Sebastian.

But she was very upset when he restricted her access to art classes.

Emma had discovered that there was something about painting that soothed her soul. She found relief from the Ninnie demons around her by indulging her latent talent.

Portraiture had become her favorite recreational outlet. She was quite good at it, and loved creating hideous caricatures of Adolf Hitler, Pol Pot, Josef Stalin, Idi Amin and Chairman Mao, as well as Stallingski himself and the other tyrants at Arthritis Acres, which she then smuggled back to her room and used as dartboard targets in games with Sebastian, Deuter and Collins.

"Bullseye!" Collins shouted when his dart neatly cleaved Hitler's sinister mustache.

When the portraits were in tatters from too many holes, Emma worked them into the rotation on the lighthouse tower light.

Emma also had a special affinity for landscapes. Her favorite watercolor was the one she did of San Francisco, the one in various shades of gray that she painted using a photograph of Hiroshima-after-the-bomb as her model.

She called it "Legacy of the Left" and it hung in the front lobby. Briefly.

Stallingski took it down and said henceforth she was allowed in the art room only on every fifth Thursday in months ending in 'q'.

Emma was at the end of her rope.

Sebastian's lantern lit up again.

There would not be many more such times.

TWENTY-FOUR
Don't Get Me Started...

Well, Harry, Big Brother is here. Except now it's called Big Barney. These days we are no safer than the Russians or the Chinese or the North Koreans from government snooping.

The social media monsters have become so powerful that they now can influence elections with hidden, innocuous tweaks. Who needs the Russians or Chinese anymore to interfere with our elections? We can do it ourselves, thank you.

Even Arthritis Acres now has its own version of Big Barney. This one we call Barney2. And it is frightening, terrifying, alarming what they can do. This has got to stop, Harry. This is America!

There is a new retired guy here who in his spare time is the Resident Attitude Tracker (RAT), which really means chief spy. He knows where you are, what you are doing, who you are with, what book you are reading, how many cholesterol pills you have left, your blood sugar level, and often will scold you from a hidden camera-speaker if he thinks that blue scarf you just put on doesn't go with the rest of your outfit.

Give me a break. This is going too far.

Barney2, like its father, also polices our language. They're good at that, the Ninnies. Besides erasing 'hurtful' references from speech and print, they also like to disguise words and meanings, and change perfectly adequate terms into something that won't offend people like those pitiful little cupcake failures who get trophies for finishing last and hide in their Safe Rooms during thunderstorms.

But don't call them failures, please. They are just "achievement deprived," as if it's somebody else's fault that they are such zeroes.

And yet these Ninnies are the same "sensitive" people who abuse police, riot in the streets, burn down businesses and mobilize to shout down and threaten speakers who dare say anything they don't agree with. They obviously are not averse to hurting somebody's feelings there.

Hypocrites.

Even crossword puzzles have become endangered. The people who create them can't use common terms like queer or dwarf or midget or moron or spinster anymore because they are so offensive to somebody or other. What queer, dwarf-brained morons.

What's next? Rid the language of all disagreeable words? Let's start with Ninnie.

Just saying.

I guess this all began innocently enough when used cars suddenly became "pre-owned" or even way back when the newspapers shied away from the simple, direct word "died" and came up with more pleasant alternatives, such as "gone to his reward" and "went to meet his maker" and "gave up the ghost" and even "passed." How do you make "death" more pleasant?

Harry, the Ninnies have created a new agency called Security from Hurtful and Unwelcome Speech Habits (SHUSH), where busy little bureaucrats are thinking up new names for what used to be straightforward, common sense terms.

Illegal aliens now are undocumented, or transient, or foreign nationals, or some other euphemism for "illegal" and "alien". Young criminal hoodlums now are "justice-involved youth." Terrorism is "legitimate protest" or "man-caused disaster," or "justifiable forceful disagreement," and our effort to combat all of this supposed non-threat to our country is a "hysterical overreaction."

What's next? How about doing away with disagreeable words like "disease" and "murder," which conjure unpleasant images. In place of murder, somebody has suggested we just say "unauthorized elimination of a human presence." And instead of body odor and bad breath, how about "abnormal and atypical anatomical aromas"? When it comes to this whole PC crowd, don't forget that very useful phrase of mine, posterior body cavities.

Just saying. Is this really where we are going?

Anyway, now the perpetually aggrieved Ninnies even want "cultural competency" tests to make sure we are properly indoctrinated into their leftist bilge and will toe the line. Social sites even now are correcting our internet language into politically correct terminology, and the new guy here is doing the same thing at Arthritis Acres.

When I railed once in an e-mail against "liberal, leftist, progressive, delusional, socialist-communist sleazebags" he changed it to "broad-minded, one-world, gifted collectivist realistic thinkers."

You get the idea.

It's dangerous these days to use the word "right" in any manner or context whatsoever, because it drives the Ninnies nuts and triggers their offensive-word alarms. They are paranoid about the word. You might even say they are righteous in their paranoia. If you have been using "righty-tighty" when you're grappling with a wrench, for example, better find some other way to remember it or risk being officially reprimanded.

Right also means "correct," of course. "Left," on the other hand, is associated with apathetic terms like "leftovers" and also has a litany of other negative meanings, such as abandoned, deserted, discarded, dumped, forsaken, neglected and rejected. Sounds about right to me.

Try looking up "conservative" or "libertarian" these days on search engines and social media: They will take you to sites dealing with mass murderers, pedophiles, sex traffickers, child abusers, wife beaters, gang rapists and other despicable characters, like those people who put gravy on their breakfast cereal, wear blinking plaid bowties, add ketchup to peanut butter and jelly sandwiches or wear knee-high black socks with shorts.

Persons suspected of harboring conservative views are routinely re-fused admittance to theaters and restaurants now, forced to ride at the back of buses, and use separate bathrooms and their own water foun-tains. There is a bill in the Ninnie Congress that would require conserva-tives to submit to a forehead tattoo ID. Jim Crow for conservatives.

Is this what "Progressive" means – marching us backwards into histo-ry? Socialist are good at that kind of thing. Shall we look next for signs saying, "No Conservatives, Dogs or Sailors Allowed," or "Catholics, Jews and Conservatives Keep Out," or "Conservatives Seated in Rear"?

Just saying.

It is not even safe anymore for conservatives to go to restaurants. There are gangs of roving thugs out there who will hunt down and follow them, even into restrooms, or maybe even douse their entree with chili pepper or nuclear hot sauce.

My God, what's next? Little red tags for our lapels? Obscenities scrawled on our windows? Isn't the next step a Night of Broken Glass?

Well, if they want to play that way, I say it's time for a food fight. Most Ninnies would look quite fetching with a coconut cream pie smashed into their face, don't you think, Harry?

Just saying.

Well, anyway Harry, it turns out my "private life" here is not so private. The powers that be suspect that I am up to something, so I am under constant surveillance as a subversive. With Sebastian's help I smuggle this "inflammatory" blog out into the world. He found a rogue website somewhere that helps you sneak seditious material, such as truth and facts, onto the internet. It seems there are a lot of these sites springing up these days in response to Big Barney's heavy-handed Fascism. How encouraging! The spirit of liberty and freedom still exists out there!

But I suppose they will figure out soon how we do it, and we will be shut down. It's just as well. I think this whole thing is coming to a head soon anyway.

I told Sebastian that the Stasi in East Germany probably didn't have a spy network as efficient as the one the Ninnies have created, or even like the one at this place. He didn't know what the Stasi was.

So I told him about that official state security service, the oppressive, brutal and quite effective intelligence and secret police agency. People lived in terror of it. Pure socialism at its best. Or worst.

In fact, the new national Ninnie bureau charged with monitoring and snooping on citizens was at first named the Special Tracking Agency for Sensitive Intelligence, until someone called attention to the acronym it created.

Harry, this place is so oppressive now that we are getting demerits for unacceptable behavior. They know what we eat, where we shop, what we read and watch.

Oh, some of the demerits are benign enough. If you don't walk enough for exercise during the day, you get a demerit. If you have a donut for breakfast instead of yogurt, you get a demerit. But some of them are Ninnie-level sinister. If you dare sneak something like *The Epoch Times* or *National Review* or the Washington *Times* into Arthritis Acres, you get double demerits.

There are demerits for patronizing places that have declared a conservative point of view, for mentioning Fox News, for associating with anyone that Barney2 deems conservative, i.e. subversive. I guess that's why nobody talks to me anymore.

There are demerits for contacting suspicious organizations like the Heritage Foundation, Turning Point USA, Judicial Watch, and the Burlington Meadows Crocheting Club, which never registered with the front office.

I complained mightily once when I got a demerit for turning up my thermostat two degrees. Wasting energy, you know.

"It's winter, you idiots. This place is not exactly Palm Springs."

Double demerits are levied for especially egregious transgressions. If you are thought to be indifferent about the concepts of white privilege or toxic masculinity, or to societal repression of blacks, Latinos, gays, lesbians, transgenders, one-armed tree pruners, red-haired parking attendants or any other kind of minority or disadvantaged person, they will see to it that you become quite disadvantaged yourself.

And if you are caught defiling the planet by not re-using your toilet paper until it is in shreds, or by sitting under anything brighter than a five-watt light bulb to read the paper, there will be consequences.

So as you can imagine, Harry, your naughty Emma's demerits are starting to add up.

I have to go to the back of the line to get cosmetics, food and snacks, medications, toothpaste, deodorant and gas-relief tablets; I'm last in line for outings and trips and movies, not that I wanted to see anything by that cadre of Hollywood leftists anyway.

My dining hall portions have been reduced. Worst of all, by the time I get to order, all of the liver and onions Saturday Special is gone.

Demerits reduce allowable visits by family and friends. As my demerits rise, so do my monthly fees. At this rate, I might never have visitors again, and I'm going to have a tab here bigger than a sewer worker's laundry bill.

And just like outside, my neighbors here can reduce their own demerits by snitching on others. Slant Greeley is especially good at this. He turned me in one morning after breakfast when he saw me help myself to an extra pat of butter. I was sure he would complain when I called him a latter-day Joseph Goebbels, but he took it as a great compliment.

Funny how we start life in a kindergarten, watched over because we're not good yet at taking care of ourselves, and wind up in an eldergarten, watched over because we're not good anymore at taking care of our-selves. We go from one set of diapers to another.

Harry, I think they are on to me, and I don't know how long I can keep this blog under their radar. They know I'm up to something, haven't quite figured it out yet, but I suspect I am the primary target of Aappel's spying apparatus, and am being punished accordingly.

My mail and packages often are delayed or even show signs of having been opened. The box of chocolates from Amazon was missing a Cash-ew Cluster, and there was a bite out of the Cherry Cordial.

My laxative bottle from a mail-order pharmacy was half-full when I opened it. At first I was angry; what kind of thief does that?

Now I admire their intestinal fortitude, so to speak. They must have had a desperate need. I wonder if everything came out all right...

Sometimes I'm not even told of upcoming events. Damn! I missed the lecture on "Art and Socialism" and the seminar on "Ten Ways to Ap-pease Your White Guilt."

And I am subject to frequent "inspections" where Aappel scans my computer or stops by to look for dangerous, subversive publications. So far all he's found are *Reader's Digest* and *Croquet Gazette*, and computer bookmarks for *Arthritis Monthly* and the National Cremation Society.

They are doing their best to make life miserable, as if it could get any worse here. Their latest tactic is to keep changing the security codes to the computer system. In the name of security, and fear of hackers, they have created a system of passwords and double passwords and secret codes and verifications made up of letters, characters, symbols, numbers, upper/lower case, all of which needs to be changed once a week.

I tried to use IamaRobot as a password but it was rejected – no num-bers or special characters.

So here's my new one: $crewUba$tards2!

Harry, I know they are listening to my conversations, either through that lighthouse painting or that lip balm in my purse.

They're probably thinking these are just the rantings of a hysterical old woman slipping into senility. Well, they ain't seen nothin' yet.

Harry, I'm done. I can't take this anymore.

§§§

'Don't Get Me Started'

"Why stand we here idle?... Is life so dear, or peace so sweet, as to be purchased at the price of chains and slavery?"

–Patrick Henry

TWENTY-FIVE
Don't Get Me Started...
Blog 11: September 5, in a year not too far away

This is it, Harry, I've had it. I keep saying somebody's got to do something about what's going on down here, but nobody ever does. Why aren't the red-white-and-blue-blooded Americans, the die-hard patriots, the moderates, the rest of us, rising up in outrage about what is happening to our country?

When did we become a nation of sheep? How long are we just going to sit here? Are we going to twiddle our thumbs while China and Russia take over the world, while home-grown terrorists burn down our cities, taunt and goad our police? Are we going to just sit here while our schools turn out a generation of socialists and communists, while the cancel culturists cancel our culture, our history, our American Dream, while the media takes sides – always the same leftist side – while we drown in political correctness, while Big Tech tries to influence what we believe and how we vote?

How long must we put up with a partisan press, with illegal aliens flooding across our borders, with misguided "entitled" people who do not appreciate what we have here? When do we say enough with the constant cries of racism, white privilege and reparations, with social media censors who would rob us of our right to speak freely?

Well, I'm saying "enough." I guess it's up to me. I'm going to do something.

I've been hearing from a lot of people, Harry. And I mean a LOT of people. I find it heart-warming and gratifying that so many wonderful folks out there have found my blog and feel like I do about this magnificent country. They are as alarmed as I am about what's happening to it.

'Don't Get Me Started'

It's getting worse every day.

You can't advertise for an employee who is "hard-working and reliable" anymore, because that offends people who are lazy and unreliable.

Department store Santas are being told to stop with the ho-ho-ho because it scares children, and besides, "ho" has that other meaning and PC parents don't want to have to explain that to their kids.

College students can't be vetted to see if they are likely to pay back their loans, because that's so obviously discriminatory, so insensitive, so politically incorrect. So nobody is turned down anymore for loans, or for admission either, because it's so unfair to pick winners and losers, you know. You can see where this is going.

Give me a friggin break.

Believe it or not, math is now racist. It's too "white," according to some people, the whole discipline pervaded by white values and expectations, and too much credit given to Europeans like the Greeks for its development. And besides, too many math teachers are white.

How far are we going with this? Teaching English and history is racist? All those white Europeans again, you know. Chemistry? Too many white chemicals and powders. Physics? Better make sure you have equal numbers of black and white atoms. Where does this crap stop?

Math is under attack from another direction, too. It's too hard for some of the snowflakes.

Well, I agree. I think they could make math a lot simpler. Take seven times nine, for example. The answer is an odd number, hard to remember. Let's make it some even number instead, like 86. That's easier, because it's my age, too. Then next year we can change it to 87. How simple.

The Ninnies might buy that. They're already trying to change and smear and put a new spin on our history, so why not take on math next.

We are now being told that Easter eggs are to be called "spring spheres" because, well, that's a Christian holiday. We are not to condemn ISIS for terrorist acts or observe a moment of silence for the victims of 9/11 because that might offend the terrorists and their religion of "peace" and encourage Islamophobia. Well, this is MY country, too, and memories of the people behind 9/11 offend ME mightily, and nobody seems to give a damn about ME and people like me.

Don't get me started.

Here's the final straw: Now the Ninnies want to codify all of their PC rantings, diversity derangements, environmental mania, social snooping, free speech suppression and big-government socialist slime into law. There is an omnibus bill before Congress, a socialist dream, that would do all this, that would change America forever. We cannot sit still for this. No more.

Oh, Harry! I have my own dream. And all of you good folks out there who follow my blog are going to help me make it come true. I am asking you, and I am told there are millions of you now, to jump in and help me launch a crusade to save our country.

This is what I am going to do: I am going to do what neglected and dissatisfied and angry Americans have always done, from the very beginning. I am going to rebel, I am going to launch a revolution. You, me, we, are going to peaceably assemble and redress our grievances. Remember the Minutemen? You might call us the Freedomfolks.

I am going to organize a march on Washington, to the Capitol, where we will present our gripes and our demands to the Ninnie Congress, insisting that they drop this latest package of socialist and PC drivel that they want to force down our throats. They will get something done for once or we will answer them at the ballot box.

Some of the radicals in this new generation are very big on marches, Harry. They march against poverty, against oppression, against the police. They march against offensive brand names, Civil War generals, hurricane names that are not ethnically inclusive, Supreme Court nominees who do not exactly fit their rigid socialist mold. Next, they will be rioting over watermelons with too many seeds and pizzas with not enough cheese, burning down roadside watermelon stands and attacking cheesehead Packers fans in the streets.

They always seem to be against something. Aren't they ever *for* anything?

Well, we can march, too. We are *for* something. We are *for* the grand idea called America, for American values and a noble vision of a world living in peace. We will march peaceably, without violence, without malice, to make our point.

We're a little older now, and have lost a step or two, so let's call it something else, something gentler and more dignified, befitting our status as the elders of our nation.

186

Let's call it the *Ramble* on Washington. We will ramble in as if we own the place, which we do, and present our list of grievances. And if the Ninnies want to turn our Ramble into a rumble, so be it.

So all of you people out there who have responded to my blog, who think America is in dire danger, who think what's happening in America today is a threat not only to ourselves but to future generations and the world itself (picture what the world would be like without an America!), who want to do something about this downhill slide toward socialism before it's too late, please say you'll join me, not just in the Ramble itself, but with all the details of putting it together. Now is our hour! We can be the silent majority, the silent generation, no more. But I need your help.

Please respond, if only with your encouragement. If everyone would send me just one dollar, we can pull this off. Please also volunteer your many varied talents to help me get this crusade off the ground! Besides financial support, we need people with expertise in logistics, organizing and coordination, transportation, housing, food, communications, health, legal, and all the rest.

Enough! This is our time. Unless we do something, our kind is on the way to becoming a minority, or even extinct, replaced by a culture that takes our prosperity and liberty for granted, does not appreciate or subscribe to our belief or value system, does not have the same patriotic fervor and love for this country and its history. We will not let all of this slip away.

We care only about preserving this country and its ideals, and we don't care who gets in the way. We are coming for you, we are coming to take our country back. You have abused our trust. What kind of political party is based on hate, greed, victimology, anger and economic envy, which loves and craves power more than they love their country?

There are indeed two Americas – the one that subscribes to the template that has brought us so far, and the one that sees only our faults and wants to stop us dead in our tracks. One America wants to work and succeed and move on, and one wants to mire us down in guilt and mediocrity and sameness. One wants its citizens to be strong, independent and self-sufficient. The other wants government to provide a cradle-to-grave insulated bubble for everybody.

In the Ninnies' America, they would take from those who have achieved and succeeded, and give it to those who don't, or won't. They call this socialism; I call it just plain old-fashioned robbery. Does not one of the Ten Commandments clearly state, Thou Shall Not Steal?

They want to deny the successful the fruit of their labors and intellect, and reward the unsuccessful for their failures. Shouldn't you be rewarded, or not rewarded, depending on your choices, your effort in life? In America, you are given a head start on the pursuit of happiness just for having been born here, or for being accepted for citizenship. Happiness and socialism are two words that do not fit well together.

To the Ninnies, everybody is the same, to be treated the same, regardless of effort or ambition, and lest anybody be offended or hurt. How does this square with their almighty holy grail of diversity, their obsession with the many variations among us?

The hordes of dreamers who left stagnant, warring, constrictive societies behind and explored, pioneered and developed this greatest free nation the world has ever known are now being betrayed and sabotaged by menacing misfits who want to turn the American Dream into an American Nightmare.

§§§

Call us what you will – senior citizens, golden agers, fogeys, geezers, dinosaurs, codgers, coots, the Over the Hill Gang, whatever. We prefer "We, the People." And We, the People, are coming for you.

We are leading the charge back up that hill, so get out of the way. We have at least one good fight left in us, the most important fight of all, the fight to save our nation and our way of life before our fading voices are stilled forever. We might be the last line of defense, the last barricade in front of a vanishing America.

Some say we are old and tired. Yes, we might be a little lame and slower of step now, harder of hearing and more uncertain of eyesight. But we have lived full, rewarding lives and want our children and grandchildren to continue to enjoy the blessings this land has bestowed on us.

Old and tired? Maybe. But we are not tired in spirit.

Let me tell you what we ARE tired of:

♦We are tired of hearing that someone else is always to blame for crime, violence, poverty and discrimination; of endless complaints, excuses and grievances, of blind racial and cultural allegiance. People are responsible for themselves, but we all want to help them escape miserable conditions, create opportunities to succeed, improve their neighborhoods.

♦ We are tired of political correctness. We are going to PC ourselves into another kind of PC – a Paralyzed Culture. We don't care if we offend somebody, especially those who deserve it. It is our right to speak freely, to object to what we believe are offensive ideas. We do not buy into the game of language camouflage. We will not call a terrorist a "freedom fighter." We will not call a true patriot an "agitator" or an illegal alien "documentally disadvantaged."

♦ We are tired of those who shout "racism" as the reason behind every conceivable situation they don't like. We believe outright racists and hatemongers are on their way out these days, and we're working on getting rid of the rest. Most folks just want to live in peace, take people for what they are, and get on with their lives. The early execution of America's promise was not perfect, to be sure, but in the years since, the responsible people among us have been striving to improve and perfect the great idea that is America – the idea that all men are created equal. We have come a long way. Let us complete the journey, ignore the people who want to mire us in constant guilt and turmoil over our "great national sin" because it is the last tool they have left to bludgeon America and democracy.

♦ We are tired of being lectured about white privilege and oppression. All people must be treated the same, but all races and cultures should be recognized for their unique accomplishments. Oppression? You know what my grandfather, an immigrant, would say about white privilege and oppression? He would say, 'Well, we are the freedom-loving people who fled oppression, founded and developed the greatest open government and civilization the world has ever known, and then we invited everyone else to come and join us – legally, and live and work in universal 'American Privilege.' We don't like to think about the kind of country that Ninnies and snowflakes would have, or even could have, built.

♦ We are tired of talk of "reparations." We shall not pay for the sins of our fathers. We acknowledge that some of yesterday's common practices were abhorrent and repulsive by any standards of decency and fairness. We were not there, we were not part of it. So let's move on.

♦We are tired of socialists, Fascists, deluded young people and the press all defining riots and anarchy as acceptable, justifiable "demonstrations."

♦We are tired of judges legislating from the bench – stay in your own branch of government! – and we are tired of light sentences for brutal crimes.

♦We are tired of politicians apologizing for us. Apologize for what? Without America, half of the world would be speaking German and the other half Japanese, and maybe Arabic and Russian and Chinese are next. If you are resentful and afraid of us because we are big and wealthy and powerful, good. Be resentful and afraid. We might be all that stands between you and enslavement.

♦We are tired of a national debt that can hardly be measured. We have to live within our means. Why doesn't Congress? And by the way, why do we get a 1% return on our savings but credit card companies can charge us 29% interest?

♦We are tired of corporate irresponsibility and dishonesty, of obscene salaries, perks and pensions, of huge bonuses awarded just before bankruptcy. Corporations, especially, should be models of the American Way. We are tired of corporations cozying up to China despite their obvious intention to displace us, by whatever means necessary, as the globe's most influential superpower. And we want to know why no one is ever held individually responsible for corporate crimes, corruption and behavior that lead to national economic disasters.

♦We are tired of sending federal aid to countries that sabotage and hate us. Spend it here, on veterans, health care, education, on making college affordable.

♦We are tired of an entertainment industry and Big Tech conglomerates that often erode and belittle our uplifting and inspiring American culture. Times have changed since the Constitution was adopted, but the bedrock principles of a free and unfettered democracy have not. Some things are basic, universal and essential, like decency, honesty, fairness, civility, patriotism, compassion for your fellow man. Aberrations like violence, gutter language, corruption and cruelty are not, despite Hollywood's emphasis on them.

♦We are tired of holding our tongues, of watching and waiting for someone to speak. We have been quiet long enough. This is our time. We want to keep the best of the Old America we grew up in and love, while welcoming and adapting so much of what is new and good. But we reject much of what is being called the New Normal. In many ways, we prefer the Old Normal.

"Enough!" That is the credo of our crusade.

We are too old to live under the Ninnies' new socialist pyramid scheme.

We have become fond of toilet paper, electricity, airplanes, cars, cows, shoes, clean water and food.

We like the idea of store shelves brimming with merchandise.

We do not want to stand in line for hours to get a potato.

We do not want to participate in meatless Wednesdays, bread-free Saturdays, fasting Fridays and long lines for water, or sign up to get a gallon of gasoline a week from Monday.

Socialists specialize in that kind of stuff, so let them have it.

Every generation is required to leave something of beauty, of lasting value behind, for the next. To this generation we leave the precious idea called America that we ourselves inherited. We have tried mightily to polish it, to improve on it, sometimes with success, sometimes with disappointment. So we say, pick up the torch, and lead the way forward, until at long last we are indeed a land where all men are created, and treated, equal.

So with that, onward!

Enough! Let's Ramble!

§§§

"America will never be destroyed from the outside. If we falter and lose our freedoms, it will be because we destroyed ourselves."

—Abraham Lincoln

TWENTY-SIX

Getting Ready
September 20, in a year not too far away

Harry would have been astounded. Emma's blog, which had been growing steadily in readership and popularity, now went viral. She was hearing from more and more people, of every age, from all walks of life and political stripe, from every state, even from foreign countries.

Generous Americans had responded with more than just dollar bills to help finance the march – the 5's and 10's and 20's, checks and money orders, and even 50's and 100's, kept coming and coming. The company that was hired to manage credit card contributions had to take on extra help. Emma added a payment button to her blog. Her tech team also helped create a podcast, which enabled her to spread her message to even more people.

She opened a bank account and called in Sebastian and Christopher to help handle all of the emails and correspondence. By their count, her followers now numbered in the multi-millions. Her one-woman shop was being overwhelmed. The post office box Christopher set up had to be emptied three times a day.

Emma was dumbfounded. Never in her wildest dreams had she imagined that her little blog, which started as an outlet for her patriotic idealism, would take on a life of its own and become a national phenomenon.

All of the local news channels wanted to talk to her. Fox News came to Arthritis Acres to do an interview, which had to be conducted surreptitiously at a coffee shop downtown. Retirement magazines planned cover stories. Conservative talk show hosts vied to be the first to get her on their shows.

She told producers from several leftist liberal channels to "stick it where the sun don't shine."

Christopher took time off to help organize the march, and allowed Sebastian to join the effort, too. Deuter Diaz and Col. Collins became indispensable allies and coordinators.

"Sebastian will get a better education in participatory democracy, civics and patriotism than he ever would in school," Emma said.

Her enemies tried all of their familiar tricks to try to stop Emma's bandwagon. The BSN network – Broadcast Socialist News – searched desperately for something in her past that would embarrass her and derail the entire movement.

And sure enough, they found something. It wasn't long before detrimental stories began to appear.

"We have discovered that Emma O'Doud still has an unpaid parking ticket from 1969 on her record," a solemn anchor intoned one night as the network's main story. It also produced a retired 99-year-old librarian who thought she remembered that Emma had not paid an overdue 50-cent book fine back in 1951. But she wasn't all that sure.

"It might have been 1851."

The BSN talking heads all clucked and flapped their elbows and shook their heads in disgust over this alarming abdication of personal responsibility. The network redoubled its efforts to show Emma up for the sickening, revolting, irresponsible criminal grandmother that she surely must be.

So one night the network broke into its proudest jewel, a prime-time, behind-the-headlines news exposé show called "Slime Time," with the sensational report that in the 1960s Emma had been a member of some kind of sinister, subversive group that held mysterious meetings at her house. Its crack investigative team was about to "blow the lid off of this town" with its report when Emma, feeling it was best to come clean, to get out in front of this looming scandal, headed them off with a press conference.

"I must confess that long ago I was indeed involved with an exclusive organization," she said before a bank of cameras and an audience of millions. "I was a Cub Scout den mother and held frequent den meetings at my house. Even worse, we all recited a subversive oath."

She put her hand over her heart and provided it: "On my honor I will do my best to do my duty to God and my country, and to obey the Scout Law, to help other people at all times, to keep myself physically strong, mentally awake and morally straight."

That should have been enough to send her enemies slinking back to their holes, but then they tried to make an issue of the Scout law that urged members to be thrifty, that they should "work to pay their own way," which was heresy to the Ninnies, and they also sniffed suspiciously at the rule that said Scouts should be reverent toward God.

The public was not buying it, because the added publicity only intensified interest in Emma's march and boosted contributions, but still, the effort to subvert and sabotage her campaign continued.

"I have here Emma O'Doud's report card from the fifth grade," smirked an anchor one night on the leftist evening news. "It is quite interesting to note that she received a "C" in Deportment. Ms. O'Doud could not be reached for comment."

If she had been reached, and it wasn't difficult to do, she would have told them that Billy Sinclair had yanked on her pigtails and that she turned around and smacked him in the nose, but that the teacher saw only the reaction to the action.

A capitol newspaper was set to go to press with a four-part series on how Emma had once lobbied a school principal to get Christopher moved to the class of another teacher with a sterling reputation, but shelved it when the only sane editor in the newsroom said, "Wait a minute. Haven't we all done that?"

Thirty-three vice presidents of Big Barney, the high tech communications conglomerate, met in emergency secret session at the direction of the Ninnie-controlled Congress, and were ordered to thwart this rapidly developing threat to national security. But the rogue, underground internet apparatus that was disseminating Emma's blog from an abandoned mine in a remote mountain range in Michigan's Upper Peninsula, confounded and circumvented their efforts. Emma was able to maintain instant contact with other Ramble organizers and followers.

But there was no letup in the harassment of Emma's group, even up to the eve of departure.

"The leader of this so-called 'march' actually plans to ride at least part of the way in a bus," sneered a bright young thing on BSN, blissfully unaware that most people did not intend to actually march or walk the entire distance, especially if they lived in, say, California or Oregon or Washington, not that there would be that many people from California or Oregon or Washington joining the march anyway.

"They'll never make it," hooted an insulting editorial in the student newspaper at a big California university. "The geezers will need car carriers for their wheelchairs, tank trucks for their oxygen supplies, maps to help them get out of their houses, nurses to tell them where they are going and to remind them of their names and to take their medications. And even if they get there, they won't remember why they came."

The New York *Clarion/Ledger,* in a frenzy of cultural misappropriation fury, editorialized that the organizers obviously were unaware that "*ramble*" in the ancient Numukokuko Indian language was an insulting, derogatory term for shiftless, indolent tribesmen who declined to join in the hunt but were quite eager nonetheless to share in the food that the real hunters provided.

Percy Soaring Eagle, a Numukokuko elder, protested.

"There is no such word in the Numukokuko language," he wrote in a letter to the editor. "Perhaps they are thinking of the ancient fable about a conscientious, industrious, ambitious ant named Rhambul, who stored up food for the winter, only to have his hoard redistributed to lazy loafers like the grasshopper. Today, we would call them socialists, or maybe even Progressives."

The press finally gave up after a leftist radio station claimed that before she moved to Arthritis Acres, Emma's car had been seen parked in front of a tavern, night after night. That scandal dissolved when her yoga instructor indignantly replied that a room above the bar was the only decent place she could find to conduct her classes.

Emma ignored all of the flak from the press and plunged ahead. She eagerly accepted offers of help and expertise from corporate executives, managers and all manner of other experts – lawyers, accountants, ministers, transportation executives, community organizers; from restaurants, caterers and other food prep experts; from housewives and factory workers and students; from nurses and doctors and hoteliers and pharmacists; from computer and insurance experts and countless other folks familiar with handling large numbers of people.

"Look at this list, Christopher," Emma marveled, showing him the support network that was building. "A lot of these people are not even old, much less retired."

"You are doing God's work," wrote a mechanic from Ohio who sent along $10. "He's looking over your shoulder."

Emma used Christopher's house to finalize many of the arrangements for the march, because it was becoming too dangerous to work from her bugged apartment at Arthritis Acres. She held multiple teleconferences with colleagues to go over preparations and fine-tune the logistics.

Regional rendezvous points were set up at four locations around the country, to accommodate the flood of supporters expected to pour in from all corners of the nation. All four streams would then converge outside Washington before descending as one on the capital.

Now there was only one matter left to attend to at Arthritis Acres.

§§§

"These are the times that try men's souls. The summer soldier and the sunshine patriot will, in this crisis, shrink from the service of their country; but he that stands by it now, deserves the love and thanks of man and woman. ...The harder the conflict, the more glorious the triumph."

–Thomas Paine

TWENTY-SEVEN

The Breakout

September 22, in a year not too far away

Stallingski and the rest of the Ninnie cabal at Arthritis Acres – Aappel, Barile and Greeley – were quite aware by now of Emma's crusade, and threw up every roadblock to thwart it. They had been severely criticized by national Ninnie figures for letting the situation get this far, and were under enormous pressure to nip the protest before it received any more traction and publicity.

While Big Barney mounted a search for the rogue website that was enabling Emma's blog, Aappel continued to search her computer every day for clues and for subversive material, but it was clean, thanks to Deuter Diaz and Sebastian.

"I can't find anything there except recipes and an ancestry site showing she has 0.00025% Norwegian blood," Aappel reported. "She claims she's Irish; maybe that's how we can stop her, bring her down, expose her as a fraud. Let's see if she's writing to Norwegian agencies asking if she is entitled to any special benefits, like a lifetime income or free college education, or at least if she's allowed to join the Sons and Daughters of Norway."

They suspected that Sebastian might be the carrier of contraband material, so he was searched after every visit. It did not occur to anyone to inspect his hollowed-out eighth-grade required-reading Ninnie-approved history book, *Lincoln Exposed: Pedophile and Porn Addict.*

Stallingski ordered Aappel to institute 24-hour surveillance on Emma.

"If we can shut off her blog, this whole bizarre campaign will fizzle," Stallingski said. "We must cut off the head of the snake, find out how she's managing to publish this thing."

But Emma was just as determined to survive.

The next time Aappel looked in on her through the hidden camera in the lighthouse painting, he saw Vladimir Putin's face beaming back at him.

"There's one sure way to shut her down," an exasperated Stallingski said. "If we lock her in, she won't be able to lead that march."

So he put Deuter Diaz, the building engineer, in charge of securing all the exits.

"Nobody goes in and out of here without my say-so," he said. "That goes especially for Emma O'Doud. She's been nothing but trouble since the day she got here."

Diaz nodded sympathetically. "You bet, boss. "I'll take care of it."

§§§

Emma, Diaz and George Patton Collins met secretly several times in Collins' apartment to plot their escape. Diaz would arrange for an unlocked exit, Collins would provide transportation so Emma could lead her regional contingent of the Ramble toward Washington, and Sebastian and Christopher would meet them outside Arthritis Acres with some of the logistics and strategy team.

But first, they wanted to leave behind for their Ninnie handlers and neighbors some souvenirs, reminders of all the good times they hadn't shared together. None of the three Arthritis Acres musketeers intended to return to their prison.

"A roomy cardboard box down on Skid Row is more appetizing than this place," Emma said. "If the Ninnies stay in power for long, we're all going to be living there."

Late that last night, they tiptoed up and down the corridors, replacing all of the Marxist slogans on the walls with quotations from Ronald Reagan, Candace Owens, Victor Davis Hanson, Thomas Sowell and Rush Limbaugh. The intercom system was rigged to play *God Bless the USA*, *Stars and Stripes Forever* and *You're a Grand Old Flag* in a constant, unstoppable loop.

The dining room menus were reprinted to feature only hot dogs and apple pie, superimposed over the grill of a 1953 Chevrolet with a baseball hood ornament.

'Don't Get Me Started'

The water in the three outside hot tubs suddenly turned red, white and blue.

Every computer in the building sported a new screensaver image: the famous Revolutionary War painting "Spirit of 76," depicting a flag-bearer, a drummer and a fifer.

In the morning, Stallingski would find on his desk an official-looking letter.

"Mr. Stallingski," it said, "we regret to inform you that your services are no longer needed because Arthritis Acres has been purchased by a new chain dedicated to making life comfortable for aging conservatives. You are welcome to stay, of course, but the only opening at the moment is Third Latrine Officer."

Helicopter parent Sunshine Squance and her snowflake son Simper found that they could only get Fox News and *Three Stooges* reruns on their TV set. Simper received an early trigger warning that the draft had been reinstituted, with newly liberal age limits, and advising that he should prepare himself for boot camp and some quite hateful speech and hurtful situations.

Professor Budleigh Salters was tormented with a steady TV diet of old cowboy and Indian movies and documentaries about Columbus. When he turned in desperation to the radio for relief, he would find only conservative talk show hosts. Salters also was informed by letter that his progressive Ninnie university had been absorbed by conservative Hillsdale College, and he was offered a chance to come back and teach a course there on the History of Conservative Thinking.

The trio got physical with Park Barile, the politician-bureaucrat who loved making up ridiculous rules for residents to follow. When he did not show up for breakfast in the morning, Stallingski went to investigate, and found him tied to his bed, wrapped in 100 yards of red tape.

The front page of Slant Greeley's latest newsletter sported a startling headline: "Greeley Accused of Molesting 15 Arthritis Acres Widows." The story described in some detail how he crept into their rooms at night naked and attempted to slip into their beds.

And as for Rocky Tosterone, he was notified by the new conservative owners of Arthritis Acres that since he liked to kneel so much, he had been assigned to permanent altar boy duty in the new chapel.

And there was something else for Tosterone.

"We thought you would enjoy knowing that in the best spirit of Ninnie philosophy, your lavish retirement pension is being redistributed among drug pushers and welfare cheats," said a letter from his old National Rock-Skipping League.

Toxic feminist Narcissa Nurottica was informed that her letter of application to become a server at a popular "breastaurant" had been received, and she was to immediately provide a portfolio of steamy photos showing her in various stages of undress. She also was sent an initial screening form, consisting of a bra and directions to "fill this out."

Lazuli Leech was notified that her government ID cards had been revoked because of abuse. With the notice was an interest-bearing bill for all of the fraudulent government benefits she had received over the years, now totaling $873,000, due in 30 days.

When Horace Aappel attempted to sign on to his computer in the morning, he found he now needed to change his password to a combination of 22 letters, six numbers and five special characters, in a specific order, not to be repeated, and that it must be revised twice daily.

Mischief Mistress Emma was quite pleased with the night's pranks.

"What a way to go," she reflected as the departure hour approached.

"Our work here is done."

§§§

Emma and Collins moved silently to a side door, where Diaz waited. Beyond, in the dark, she could see a plush tour bus idling at the curb.

"A bus?" she said to Collins, eyebrows raised. "I thought we were using school busses and vans."

"It's more than just a bus," Collins replied. "It's a coach bus, like the ones entertainers use, with a bathroom and kitchen and office, the whole works. We can't have our leader arriving at the Ramble in a plain old school bus. This is the Ramble's rolling headquarters."

The coach had been donated to the campaign by country music star Crash Cooley, who was between road tours at the moment. He'd even written a patriotic song for the occasion – *Rambling to the Rumble.*

Collins and Deuter escorted Emma to the vehicle. As she climbed aboard, she could see Christopher and Sebastian waiting in the first seats. Behind them were some of the logistics people, planners and organizers charged with making the Ramble run smoothly. More would join along the way.

When they saw her, a chant began and then swept through the coach: "Em-ma! Em-ma! Em-ma!"

She blushed, and then grinned and waved.

"Welcome to the Ramble!" she shouted, and turned toward the driver.

She stopped dead in her tracks.

"Simper? Is that you?" Emma could not believe her eyes.

"Yes it is," said Simper Squance, professional student, basement dweller, snowflake, Ninnie disciple and apologist. "I used to drive a bus, you know."

"What are you doing here? Are you sick?"

"Yes, I am. I am sick of the shallow, empty life I have been leading. I have listened to you all this time, at first with animosity, and gradually with respect as I realized you are right about a lot of things.

"This is my chance to do something worthwhile, to leave a mark, to make a difference, to help save my country from fools."

He grinned at Collins, who had come up alongside them.

"Simper and I have had a lot of long, rewarding talks," Collins said.

Simper grinned sheepishly.

"Listen," Emma said. "Forget that draft notice that you'll find in your mail. You are now honorably discharged.

"By the way, what happened to your comfort chicken?"

"I ate it. Fricasseed. Delicious."

Simper grinned again. The coach lurched ahead, on its way.

§§§

"I have sworn upon the altar of God eternal hostility against every form of tyranny over the mind of man."

–Thomas Jefferson

TWENTY-EIGHT
The Ramble
October 1, in a year not too far away

W hen Emma's signal came, caravans of her supporters began to roll toward Washington from all regions of the country.

They poured out of subdivisions, apartment blocks, condos and trailer parks, out of bingo halls and retirement communities from Florida to Idaho, from Arizona to the Carolinas.

They came out of nursing homes, assisted living centers, even hospitals and Alzheimer's homes, accompanied by family members or attendants.

"This is important," Ophelia from Omaha told her petulant husband, Oscar, as they boarded their bus. "You can finish that crossword puzzle when we get back."

"What's a six-letter word for annoyed?" Oscar said.

A very determined cohort boarded their special buses with wheelchairs, canes and walkers, and even crutches, some of them carrying their own oxygen supply.

Some even came by Shank's Mare, and had to explain what that meant to mystified young reporters who asked.

"No, it is not a bus company or a horse," Pete from Poughkeepsie said patiently. "It means walking."

They came from veterans' posts and organizations for disabled veterans. There were people from families who had lost a son or daughter, a husband or father, while serving in the military.

They came from churches, synagogues and mosques. They came from civic clubs and fraternal lodges and ethnic organizations.

"This is not just a march, it's a stampede," commented an awestruck TV reporter in Youngstown, Ohio as bus after bus emblazoned "Ramble on Washington" rolled by. "This is not just a march, it's a revolution."

Golf courses emptied. Shuffleboard, badminton and croquet courts were abandoned in mid-game, bingo cards were left half-marked in church basements from North Dakota to Texas.

"Damn, and all I needed was B-13," lamented Larry from Laredo, looking back sadly from the steps of his bus.

They came in automobiles, in pickup trucks, in buses, in vans, by train. A huge caravan of sprightly, fun-loving seniors arrived from Wisconsin on riding lawnmowers, sometimes stopping along the way to mow an unsightly lawn here and there. Thousands of RVs bearing anti-socialism patriots rolled along highways from Florida, Texas and Arizona. Curiously, or maybe not so curiously, there were only three RVs from California, and even then they had to sneak around their border checkpoints in the dead of night.

The RVs and other caravans picked up escorts along the way – throngs of veterans and other patriots on motorcycles, American flags flying from the handlebars.

"This is more fun than the rallies at the Harley mother church in Milwaukee," said one grizzled Vietnam veteran.

Emma's call was answered by countless other patriots who viewed the march as their chance to help save their country from socialists, thugs and communists. And although the heads in the crowds shaded heavily toward gray, there also were many young marchers from entities like Hillsdale College, Prager University, Turning Point USA, Young America's Foundation and other hubs of young American conservatism.

"I have heard inspiring stories all my life about The Greatest Generation," said Tim from Tallahassee. "My grandparents were part of it. Now it's my turn. I am not going to stand by while their America, their values, what they fought so hard to protect, slip away. We are going to be the Payback Generation."

Leftist reporters roamed among the marchers, struggling to understand why otherwise respectable citizens would stoop to demonstrate in support of a corrupt, antiquated, unfair, outdated concept like democracy, and the despicable country that enabled it.

"I'll tell you why, dear," said Clara from Kansas City. "It's so unappreciative, empty-headed twits like you can continue to live in freedom and ask stupid questions that have obvious answers!"

And among the hordes were fathers whose daughters had been assaulted or killed by illegal aliens in sanctuary cities and whose attackers were let off with light sentences; mothers fearful for daughters who had to use public restrooms alongside self-described transgenders; men and women with relatives who died on 9/11 because "some people did something;" a Boston man whose son was killed by "protesters" during a marathon race.

Milton from Minneapolis, whose business was torched by militant "peaceful protesters," marched alongside Pauline from Portland, whose policeman husband was hospitalized when he was hit by a "protester's" brick.

There was a woman whose toddler son was rescued from a burning building by a fireman exercising some toxic masculinity; a Chicago minister whose son was radicalized by a college that was supposed to educate him; a man whose daughter was delivered in the back seat of a squad car by a "heartless, abusive" policeman when they couldn't make it to a hospital in time; a promising young black student whose path to college had been cleared for him through the support of a "privileged" white teacher.

Emily from Albuquerque was marching because she disagreed so strongly with the concept of affirmative action. "I am here because my gifted child's place in the college of her choice was awarded instead to somebody far less qualified," she said.

There were many other parents whose children had no hope of college at all because of miserable public schools that had failed to prepare them, and who had nowhere else to turn because of ingrained Ninnie and union opposition to charter schools. Many parents, and students, too, were marching because of the obscenely high costs of higher education.

"I have an idea," said Schuyler from Schenectady, a sophomore at Woonsocket State who was already struggling with a student loan of $147,000. "Let's have the colleges co-sign all those student loans they are forcing us to take."

And then there were the many thousands of protesting Americans with "ethnic" names like O'Brien, Horowitz, Chan, Boudreau and Villanueva, resentful and angry because of America's immigration policy, or rather the lack of it.

"My great-grandparents came here legally, stood in long lines at Ellis Island, studied to become citizens, worked their way into the American Dream," said Eugenia from Elmira. "Nobody gave them free health care, free educations, driver licenses, the right to vote after sneaking into the country, like today."

There were no flags of Ireland, Poland, Israel, India, Mexico or any other country among the marchers. They all carried the flag of their America.

And every marcher had his or her own fond memories of a vanishing America they knew and loved, memories of small-town parades, swimming holes, patriotic songs, two-parent families, 1950s baseball, Walter Cronkite, *Leave it to Beaver*, the Beatles, Art Linkletter, Elvis, Apollo moon missions, and a national mood of optimism, that anything was possible...

§§§

When Pemberson Prittchard, congressional leader of the Ninnies, got wind of the angry hordes headed his way, he at first dismissed it as just another futile attempt by conservative radicals to disrupt the well-oiled levers of power that the Ninnies had labored so hard to capture and control.

"Watch," he told an underling. "This will fizzle out just like that bunch of protesters last year who tried to take away our inalienable congressional rights to free food in the cafeteria, free limousines, free health care, free trips home, free housing, free junkets to Tahiti to study the effects of coconut leaf blight, and our free passes to Patty's Pole Dancing Parlor."

So he was not at all pleased when an aide interrupted his poker game with lobbyist cronies to tell him that they had vastly underestimated the number of people who had answered Emma's call.

"Boss, we are getting ominous reports from our people in the field that they are creating traffic problems all the way from here to California. It's not so much that they are disrupting and slowing traffic. It's that so many people are abandoning their cars by the side of the road and climbing aboard the buses!"

Prittchard still refused to take the march seriously.

"Most of these people are old and tired and crippled. What kind of threat can they pose? Half of them will probably die on the way here!"

Prittchard laughed loudly at his own crude slur. His aide perceptively turned his face away before a wave of whiskey-and-peanut-flavored bad breath could engulf him. He had been Pritchard's aide for quite some time.

"That's not what we're hearing," replied the aide, a seasoned Washington veteran who was himself warming up to the idea behind this march. "Most of these people are very fit. These are not your parents' grandparents. They work out, they walk, they run in marathons, they play golf and tennis and pickleball, they swim, they're mentally active, they play bridge.

"Most of them are quite agile. Just watch them jockey for position when the Early Bird Special line opens, or the senior citizen discount sign lights up. If you're in their way you could get trampled.

"Some of them, I'm told, can do a difficult Sudoku or crossword puzzle in minutes – most of them even know that the plural form of isthmus is isthmi."

"I didn't even know that," Prittchard grumbled.

"I heard that a lot of them can play six or seven Bingo cards at the same time," the aide continued. "And you don't want to challenge some of them in video games, either. They can shoot down alien spacecraft, save imaginary kingdoms from monsters, and race their friends on kart tracks with the best of them."

Prittchard did not notice the aide's smirk.

He scoffed.

"I just hope they can remember how to get home!"

He laughed so hard at his own bad joke that he spilled his drink over the poker chips of the lobbyist for the Amalgamated Association of Lint Trap Manufacturers.

But Prittchard sobered quickly when he saw helicopter news footage of the enormous crowds gathering at the marshaling yards outside Washington, in Pennsylvania, Virginia and Maryland. He turned the color of a bedsheet when he heard one of the chants coming from the crowd, a chant that struck terror into the hearts of politicians everywhere:

"Go green! Recycle Congress!"

That stirred him into action.

First, he tried to get Emma's permit for a parade and protest rally revoked. That proved to be impossible because the office responsible for issuing such permits was closed, this also being the new Ninnie holiday called Diversity and Understanding Day (DUD). And besides, the veteran bureaucrats in charge of the office had joined the march.

Next, he tried to have the police department step in to protect the city against the anarchy and depredations of an unruly mob. The police looked into it and could find no unruliness and not a single depredation. The marchers were turning out to be a very orderly, law-abiding bunch.

"And besides," pointed out Capt. Homer Renningen, "most of my senior officers have taken a leave day to volunteer as security for the march, concerned about the safety and welfare of our own parents and grandparents."

As for the younger officers, they were looking forward eagerly to the overtime pay they would be racking up as a result.

Prittchard had to give up when his last, desperate attempt to stop the march also fizzled. It was his own fault, really. In his attempt to get the Supreme Court to step in with an injunction at the last hour, on grounds of national security, he petitioned Justice Mordecai Bumbleton, unaware that Bumbleton, 94, had volunteered to be the Grand Marshal for the big parade.

§§§

Emma's group gathered that last night in a huge meadow near Gettysburg, Pa., offered by a thoughtful farmer who had been following Emma's blog from the very beginning.

"Pickett's charge?" the farmer said. "Hell, this is Emma's Charge!"

Emma had her own name for it.

"We are gathered on the eve of a momentous undertaking," she told Collins, with a nod to the Constitution and the Declaration of Independence. "This is the PreRamble!"

Enterprising entrepreneurs circulated in the huge crowd offering souvenirs. T-shirts emblazoned with slogans like, "I Survived the Ramble on Washington," and "Geezer Power" and "Sorry If My Patriotism Offends You" were hot sellers. There even was a shirt bearing a cartoon likeness of Emma above the legend, "Go Granny, Go!" But the most popular item by far was a shirt trumpeting the message, "Gray Lives Matter."

Emma had to fight against being overwhelmed by the immensity of what she had started with her little blog. She tried hard to concentrate on the details, to make the Ramble effective and memorable, but it was difficult to get her head around the size of the response she had created.

"I have obviously tapped into something huge," she told Christopher and Sebastian. "There is a powerful current out there that the politicians have been ignoring. Maybe this is going to work."

That night before the Ramble, the four huge regional caravans, only miles apart now, set up roaring bonfires, toasted marshmallows, made S'mores, imbibed a pick-me-up or two, and sang old campfire favorites. It is not likely that neighbors will forget the chorus of thousands of seniors serenading them with old standards like *Show Me the Way to Go Home* and *On Top of Old Smokey* and *You Are My Sunshine* and *Good Night Irene.*

One former schoolteacher from Wisconsin tried to start up *99 Bottles of Beer on the Wall,* but had to flee the encampment under threat of a dousing with many more than 99 bottles of beer. Notably absent was any attempt to sing *Kumbaya,* or *I Want to Teach the World to Sing.*

In the morning, at the appointed hour, the word finally came from Emma's blog:

"On to the Capitol! Let's Ramble!"

§§§

And so Grandma Emma O'Doud, 86, unlikely hero or anarchist, depending on Prittchard's view or that of her legions of followers, marched into town on a bright, clear autumn day at the head of a column of millions. They streamed across the Arlington Memorial Bridge from Virginia, in rows 32 abreast, spread across all six lanes and two sidewalks, toward the Lincoln Memorial. They had come from everywhere, from bucolic small towns, farms and hamlets, to sophisticated, complex metro areas.

But they were of one mind. To send a message to the people they had entrusted to run their country.

'Don't Get Me Started'

As Emma mounted the steps at the Lincoln Memorial, she overlooked a scene right out of Forrest Gump. Her supporters lined the National Mall and the reflecting pool all the way to the Washington Monument and beyond. Many carried signs: "I Miss the Country I Grew Up In," and "Gray Lives Matter," and "Take Back Our Country." Many seniors brandished signs with that catchline from a memorable movie: "I'm as mad as hell and I'm not going to take this anymore!"

While they waited for the main event, the marchers splashed their legs in the reflecting pool and sat in the grass with their picnic lunches, books, laptops and reading devices, their knitting projects and decks of cards, or relaxed in the pup tents that suddenly appeared everywhere.

"They all seem to be having the time of their declining lives," the leftist Washington *Courier Transcript* noted snarkily. Except for the average age, it could have been Woodstock; the *Courier Transcript*, a bastion of Ninnie thought and dogma, even gave it a name: Graystock.

Many of the old bands and groups from the '50s, '60s, '70s and '80s, sensing a good thing, had reunited for this special occasion. Throughout the day they entertained the sprightly and spry crowd, many of whom got to their feet frequently to dance and sing to old chestnuts – *Good Golly Miss Molly, Lipstick on Your Collar, Runaround Sue, One Way or Another,* and *Do You Wanna Dance.* They certainly did.

"This was our song when we were going steady," Charlene from Cheyenne told a reporter as she and Ralph swayed together to *Earth Angel.*

"We did this at our wedding reception," said Gloria from Greenville while she and Gary showed off their moves doing *The Twist.*

And even though everybody had heard about the licentious behavior supposedly going on at some senior retirement havens in Florida, there didn't seem to be a lot of uninhibited sex happening, although there was that one elderly couple who were spied behind the huge seated Lincoln figure *in flagrante delicto.*

"I didn't know you could even do that in a wheelchair," observed a very interested bystander, Hugo from Hoboken.

"You should see what's going on back there in some of the tents," responded Priscilla from Pittsburgh, with a wicked grin. "It really is intense."

There weren't many drugs, either, unless you counted assorted nostrums for blood pressure, arthritis, cholesterol and muscular aches and pains. One sprightly lady, Laura from Little Rock, told a young reporter who had never heard it before that she was accompanied on the Ramble by several trusted gentleman friends – Ben Gay, Arthur Itis, Will Power, Charlie Horse and John.

A few seniors were seen smoking "medicinal" pot, but most were tending to their aches and pains at booths dispensing liniment, ice packs, aspirin and anti-acids, or sometimes even at the Mobile Assistance for Senior Hurts (M*A*S*H*) shelter, or the emergency dentistry tent, which was handing out free samples of denture adhesives and cleaners, dental floss and toothbrushes.

Food trucks were everywhere, along with booths and tents dispensing souvenirs. A tent selling liver and onions was doing a booming business, as were those offering free shots of heartburn relief and frozen prune juice sticks. If you weren't offering a Happy Hour, senior discounts, early bird specials and coupons, you weren't doing much business.

Hecklers were few, especially after two arrogant college students waded through the crowd carrying signs reading "Geezers Go Home" and "You Are Yesterday" and "OK Boomers." Nearby elderly marchers began to shout "OK Zoomers!" and "OK Millennials!" in retaliation, and others took up the retort.

Before the situation could get out of hand, several burly ex-Marines took care of the protesters. They issued no Trigger Warning, and when the two students emerged, sputtering and dripping from their Unsafe Space, the Reflecting Pool, the Marines turned them over on laps of willing bystanders, who administered some brisk blows to their backsides before turning them loose.

"That's called a spanking," a bearded veteran in a Harley shirt shouted after them as they slinked away. "You've probably never had one."

"Well, they had courage to come in here with those signs," said Mabel from Murfreesboro.

"That's not courage," said the Harley shirt. "That's foolhardiness."

But on the whole, even the Ninnies had enough innate politeness and respect left for their elders to refrain from their usual displays of invective, obscenities and violence. Besides, they were vastly outnumbered.

"See? Maybe there's hope here after all," said Warren from Walla Walla. "Even Ninnies might see the light some day."

§§§

"Whenever the people are well informed, they can be trusted with their own government."

–Thomas Jefferson

TWENTY-NINE
The Speech

At the podium, Emma hesitated, overwhelmed by what she had wrought, by the mass of humanity spread out before her.

"What am I doing here?" she wondered in alarm while Crash Cooley sang the National Anthem. "I am on sacred ground, dedicated to our greatest president, on the very spot where Martin Luther King spoke, where Marian Anderson sang in a landmark civil rights concert."

But she had come this far, and had to press on. She had spent hours on her speech, practicing and rehearsing, and the time was now.

"Greetings, my fellow rebels," she said in a thin, timid voice that fortunately was amplified and boomed out over the crowd.

A million people who were getting their first glimpse of Emma O'Doud, who had adopted her as the voice of their frustration, their dissatisfaction, their rebellion and revolution, and now their aspirations, roared back their approval.

Encouraged, she ramped up her voice:

"I'm Emma, and we are here to take back our country!"

The thunderous roar that exploded down the Mall set windows rattling in the Smithsonian's Natural History Museum a mile and a half distant, and at Ford's Theater, even farther, and as far away as the Capitol building and House and Senate office buildings, where nervous congressmen cautiously pulled window curtains aside, straining to see and hear what was happening.

Even the president came to a White House balcony to look, but was quickly ushered back inside by Secret Service agents, conditioned to suspect dangerous militants might be lurking anywhere, even among this geriatric crowd.

A chant began, and swelled into a cacophony of deafening voices.

"EM-MA! EM-MA! EM-MA!"

Emma had to raise her arms to quell the din.

"We are able to be here today because the First Amendment of our favorite document says the government shall make no law abridging freedom of speech, or religion, or the press, or the right of the people peaceably to assemble and petition the government for a redress of grievances.

"It's the First Amendment for a good reason. So it's the first one the Ninnies want to get rid of!"

This time the roar rolled across the Potomac to the national cemetery and Arlington House, where an anxious caretaker glanced at his watch, wondering why distant cannons were going off at this hour. Despite the dead air, the little flags at thousands of tombstones suddenly fluttered.

"EM-MA! EM-MA! EM-MA!"

"Listen to us, Congress and America," Emma continued when the chant died down. "We are here peaceably assembled, emphasis on *peaceably*, to air our grievances.

"We are the voices of a glorious yesterday. We are the real Americans, the shopkeepers, the housewives, the farmers, the tradesmen, the veterans, the professionals, from big cities and small towns all across this glorious land. We are old-fashioned, to be sure, but we are as certain as the sunrise that all that is new is not necessarily good.

"Yes, we fear that our values are slowly perishing. We come from a generation of morals and ethics and religion, of hard work and patriotism. We are here to send up a last cry, a last warning, from a fading, vanishing generation

"EM-MA! EM-MA! EM-MA!"

"We believe in God, in hard work, private initiative, liberty, free enterprise, civil discourse, aspirations to a better life and country, in being responsible for yourself. We value life, the individual, economic freedom, a country where people are encouraged to reach their full potential, to dream as big as they dare, regardless of race, creed or color.

"Our generation can remember a time of apocalyptic war and economic devastation, and also a time of prosperity, plenty, security and bright promise. We have lived through both. For some of us, our earliest memories are of the hardships of a terrible Great Depression, and then of a long, costly war that touched and tore at our families and friends, a time when America stepped in and literally saved the world from tyrants, savage cruelty and eternal darkness."

A new chant began. "USA! USA! USA!"

"We grew up at the best possible time, a time when the world was getting better; not worse. The Russians were obnoxious, yes, as usual, but we were confident we could take care of that bunch of amoral socialist thugs, or to use their old favorite word, hooligans. And we did. But beware, the evil of their socialism, their ambition, is not dead. Just look around you, listen to what is being said by a growing class of idiots. Yesterday the threat was Russia. Today it is China. Or both of them, plus terrorist goons.

"We are a generation that loved our country, raised our children to be honest and civil; we studied and innovated and led our nation into a technological age. We endured tough conditions like outhouses, party lines and cloth diapers. We had cave-man devices like typewriters and telephone booths, and way back, we needed a crank to start our cars, and I don't mean crazy Aunt Tillie in the back seat."

Emma paused briefly to let the laughter die down.

"At the time, we didn't know they were tough conditions. It was just the way it was; we didn't know we were deprived. Today, we would be "economically disadvantaged" and "victims of capitalistic oppression" and "casualties of our culture," and the relentless do-gooders would be at the door trying to move all of us into foster homes."

"EM-MA! EM-MA! EM-MA!"

"We know the words to the *Pledge of Allegiance* and the *Star-Spangled Banner* and *America the Beautiful.* We wore the uniform of our country proudly. We might even shed a tear when we sing our anthems and see our flag stretching in the breeze. We have fought for them, many of our brethren died for them, and we will lay down our lives again to keep treasonous socialist/leftist/progressives from trampling our heritage and pushing us into another Depression, or worse.

"We will not stand by anymore and watch the degradation of our nation, the decline in civilized language, the rising entitlement mentality of those who expect something for nothing, a political system paralyzed by a new climate of hate, by revisionists who would rewrite history to their own ends.

"We curse those who disrespect our nation, its ideals and its emblems, we condemn the dolts who buy into this rising tide of socialism and communism. The very Earth trembles in revulsion at the thought of a socialist America!

"We will not stand here and watch while subversives, even in high places, smear, slime, tear down and disrespect every ideal we were taught as kids."

"EM-MA! EM-MA! EM-MA!"

A small group of young protesters tried to muster a counterargument.

"Geezers go home!" began a thin chant again on the edge of the crowd. "What do we want? Socialism! When do we want it? Now!"

Emma heard, and pointed at them.

"Grow up, you ignorant twits!" she shouted back. "Wake up! Shut up!"

She looked out over her crowd and raised her arms in supplication, like a preacher imploring divine assistance. They responded as one, with their own taunting chant.

"WAKE UP! GROW UP! SHUT UP!"

The din and commotion set off ripples in the Reflecting Pool; marchers cooling their aching feet there had to get out or get soaked.

The twits never had a chance. Vastly outnumbered, the counterprotesters shrank away in retreat, some of them trying to hide among the impressive statues at the nearby Korean War Memorial, but they were hauled out by security people and charged with trespassing at a national monument.

Emma watched them go and continued:

"To younger generations we say: We have lived what you have read in history books, so listen to us. We have something to say, the wisdom that comes with years, with experience. We have been young, like you; you have not been old, like us, so listen. We are tough. We lived for years without cell phones or the internet; we found our way without a GPS; we stayed in touch with family and friends without social media."

Emma grinned as another titter swept through the crowd.

"We are the Golden Generation, and it is time to take our stand. This is a battle for minds, for survival, against a mob of miseducated, misled, misguided misfits who would surrender our culture, our traditions and our heritage, who envision a utopia that on close inspection is made of smoke and mirrors and unicorn farts, except farts are now illegal."

Emma paused briefly again for laughter, and then continued with her solemn message, aimed as much at a bitterly divided Congress as at her followers..

"We will not let a bunch of bubble-headed, ignorant, treasonous twerps destroy our country. No more! It is time to fight back. Our side has been too reserved, too polite, too mannered, too Old School, for way too long. Why? No more! We are fighting a force that has no morals, no ethics, no principles, and one goal – to gain power and never let it go. They want to shut down all opposition, create their own dictatorship."

A new chant began on the fringes of the crowd and soon swept through it. Now there were competing chants:

"NO MORE! NO MORE! NO MORE!"

"EM-MA! EM-MA!"

After a moment Emma raised her arms again to quiet the crowd.

"This is not about me," she scolded gently. "This is about Us! Capital U, Capital S! And a capital A, too!"

Another chant returned:

"USA! USA! USA!"

"There are a lot more like us who could not come here today," Emma continued. "But we bring their voices, too. They get it, they understand, like us, what many do not. There are people out there, AINOs, Americans In Name Only, and others, who are out to destroy this country from within and replace it with some misguided socialist vision of paradise. Socialism is not a dream; it is a nightmare, weighing down both the individual and society in a quicksand of blandness and mediocrity.

"Some day is this generation going to look around in alarm and terror and say, 'My God! What happened?' Will they be in the streets, demonstrating for their lost liberty? 'What happened?' they will ask. 'Where did it all go?' And the reply will be, well, you stood by, you *let* it happen! You made this bed. How do you like sleeping in it?

"A pox on your socialism! AINO Gonna' Happen!"

Another roar had been building as she spoke, and erupted as she raised her fist. Another chant began.

"AINO Gonna' Happen! AINO Gonna' Happen!"

"We can play the game the Ninnies play. We have come to occupy, just like *they* like to occupy. We want to occupy not only this space for a little while, but to occupy the minds of Congress and all Americans with our concerns for the preservation of our beloved country and its values.

We demand total rejection of this un-American so-called omnibus bill they are considering. It is a bill worthy of the Politburo, or the Chinese Party Congress.

"We are a generation that helped build this nation into a colossus, and we will not stand by while Ninnies and socialists and communists try to tear it down! We have been pushed around and ignored long enough. The socialist bill they are considering is a stain on the American soul.

"It is time to take our stand! Listen to us. We are crying, Enough! Enough!"

"ENOUGH! ENOUGH! ENOUGH!

Emma looked out over the throng again, took a sip of water, and then got to the meat of her message.

"So hear us, political parties and Congress and especially the Ninnies.

"We are here to take our country back. We reject treasonous socialist concepts. Here is our answer.

"We call it a Gray New Frontier. Ignore us at your peril!"

She had to wait for a minute before continuing, while the familiar "Em-ma! Em-ma! Em-ma!" chant gradually dissolved into a new one:

"GRAY NEW FRONTIER! GRAY NEW FRONTIER! GRAY NEW FRONTIER!"

Emma looked out over a colorful scene. There was not much gray about it. American flags waved everywhere. The throng was one massive blend of red, white and blue. Here and there a grandchild waved a miniature flag. A toy poodle whose fur was dyed in alternating stripes of the national colors struggled in a grandmother's arms.

"These are our demands," Emma shouted above the din. The crowd fell silent.

"First and foremost in our Gray New Frontier: Cease your constant bickering and infighting and do what we have sent you here for – to improve and protect our nation. Cooperate! Compromise! Do the business of the nation! Think of your country instead of your party. Do your damn job!

The throng roared again.

"We want an uncontaminated government, free of politicization by the party in power. Keep your meddling hands off of the FBI, the CIA, the IRS. Restore the public's faith in them. If you can't trust them, who *can* you trust? Corruption and dishonesty are the biggest enemies of democracy: When you destroy trust in critical agencies, you destroy trust in America itself.

"And while we're at it, we want fraud and corruption and waste eliminated in all those government programs. Imagine the savings! Does anyone police the money they spend? Who's watching the public store, anyway?"

Emma's appeals were hitting a nerve. The crowd's collective voice was growing in volume.

"GRAY NEW FRONTIER! GRAY NEW FRONTIER! GRAY NEW FRONTIER!"

"We want national security, which means a strong military and a sensible, practical police presence. Do not ignore the crouching wolves who are just outside our door, encouraging dissension and division, waiting for signs of weakness in our resolve and in our defenses. Security includes protecting our internet from hackers and computer fraud and identity theft, from enemies intent on stealing our national and corporate secrets or disabling our infrastructure.

"It is long past time to return to our ideal of promoting the 'common good,' and bury forever those who strive to divide us by emphasizing our differences.

"We want compulsory national service after high school, whether military or civilian work. A year or two in the service of your country won't kill you. What better way to instill patriotism and appreciation for the many blessings that have been bestowed on us, on this favored land? This is not a free ride. You owe your country. Pay it forward, pay it back!"

Emma's appeal resonated loudly with this crowd, many of whom had served in the military. Another mighty roar went up.

"PAY IT FORWARD! PAY IT BACK!"

"We want a new respect for law enforcement, for the police. Try living in a society without any, except those you are likely to hear pounding on your door in the middle of the night. Do you want to call a grief counselor or therapist when your car is stolen, or a Fascist mob is screaming on your lawn, or your crucial pharmacy has been burned down by rioters, or your child is taunted and mugged while walking home from school?

"We are going to take back our culture, which we have abdicated to public schools and communist university professors, to a partisan press, to a dissolute Hollywood, to sinister social media snoops constantly intruding on and trying to influence our lives and decisions. We have abdicated control to agencies devoted to turning out a steady stream of new little loyal socialists."

"ENOUGH! ENOUGH!"

"We want to reinvent a public school system that is turning out too many ignorant and uninformed citizens, unaware and even deceived about the honorable history and underpinnings of this country, oblivious to its basic civic functions. We want an end to authoritarian colleges that impede the free flow of ideas, squelch discussion, preach and permit hate for America, who are so preoccupied with its perceived faults that they have lost sight of the basic goodness and idealism of the great American Idea. They are trying to turn a generation of students into flag-burning traitors to their families, their country and their ancestors. What kind of college abdicates to anarchists?"

"EM-MA! EM-MA! EM-MA!"

"NO MORE! NO MORE! NO MORE!"

"We want an end to a press that has become a stranger to truth, objectivity and impartiality. We want a return to an objective Fourth Estate, a watchdog over government abuse, one that presents all sides of a story, one that gives us the evidence to make up our own minds. We are not so stupid as to need their biased, partisan reporting to make intelligent decisions.

"We want closed borders and our immigration rules enforced. We are not against immigration, but we *are* against illegal aliens flooding and overwhelming our social service agencies and receiving from their Ninnie patrons the right to vote and other benefits that some of our own citizens do not enjoy. Create a fair system where people get in line and wait for their opportunity. What kind of country flings open its borders to trouble and chaos? And while you're at it, English is our language. Press two for a tutor or a language course to help you learn it."

"GET IN LINE! GET IN LINE! GET IN LINE!"

"We want you to separate the truly needy from the shiftless, lazy and listless, from the welfare cheats and druggies and manipulators. We respect the truly needy and indigent and handicapped. But we no longer want to pay for the growing culture of Free Stuff. Can't find work? Report to a government job, or join the military. Why is it demeaning and damaging to your self-esteem to insist that you be responsible for yourself, to take a job? Isn't it demeaning to take money from others for doing nothing?

"We want a crackdown on the professional loafing class. There are millions on unwarranted food stamps, phony unemployment and disability benefits, or who pay no taxes and game the system for benefits they are not entitled to. If you want steak and $20 burgers, get a job. Let's have mandatory drug testing before and during welfare."

The crowd roared.

"GET A JOB! GET A JOB! GET A JOB!"

Emma paused and stepped back from the microphone when it began to shriek from feedback, and while a technician adjusted the sound. Then she picked up where she left off.

"We demand respect and adherence to our Constitution and the Bill of Rights. No better system has ever been created. Put God back in America, where the founders put Him, but believe whatever you want. Religion and its ancient laws teach compassion, and provide a brake on lawlessness and immorality. We want a return to an atmosphere of civility, where other opinions are heard and respected.

"We want a new emphasis on promoting and preserving the concept of families. Stable families are the bedrock of a successful society. But our kinds of families do not include Big Brother. Break up Barney, the Big Snooper! It is an un-American monopoly with insidious power!

"EMMA! EMMA! EMMA!"

Emma was getting hoarse, but pressed on:

"We are told we are intolerant. Yes, we are intolerant, intolerant to an extreme, of cultures, peoples, views, religions that would destroy us and our way of life. We have plumb run out of tolerance for enemies we are not supposed to name, for fear of offending someone. Well, we are not afraid of offending terrorists, parasites, traitors, racists, communists, scoundrels and assassins.

"Our precious gift of liberty is not self-sustaining; we must regularly feed it, breathe new life into it, be forever vigilant. Do those apathetic, indifferent citizens among us really think they will not be affected if our enemies succeed in obliterating America? Wake up!"

"WAKE UP! WAKE UP! WAKE UP!"

By now the crowd also was getting hoarse.

Emma rolled on, building toward her climax.

When it came, the response was thunderous.

"In our Gray New Frontier, we want term limits for you yokels in Congress," Emma said, pointing down the Mall toward the Capitol. "No more lifetime careers at the public trough. Six terms for the House, two terms for the Senate, then go back to making an honest living."

Emma began to talk faster, fearing that the rest of her message might be drowned out by the rumble that she could hear building at the edge of the crowd.

"And while we're at it, we will require that you have the same retirement and health care and pension plans that the rest of us must buy," she shouted. "No more voting raises for yourselves, cutting deals with your lobbyist buddies. You will obey all of the same laws you impose on the rest of us!"

The rustle of shouts had gradually become a thunderous roar, the biggest so far. Emma had her finger firmly on the public pulse.

"NO MORE! NO MORE! NO MORE!"

"ENOUGH! ENOUGH! ENOUGH!"

Children covered their ears. Startled flocks of birds abandoned their perches in the trees and blackened the sky. Across the river, at the Tomb of the Unknown Soldier, tourists looked skyward at the sudden rumbling. The two solemn soldiers passing each other in the Changing of the Guard ceremony never blinked.

"And while we're at it," Emma continued above the roar, "we want limits to these endless presidential campaigns, which seem to start the day after the last one is over. And here's a thought: Let's restrict all of the candidates to the same amount of campaign money."

Sebastian, watching with his father from behind Emma's podium, marveled at the reaction his grandmother was provoking from this enormous throng. Glancing back over his shoulder, he wondered idly if maybe Lincoln himself wasn't stifling an urge to get up from that chair and applaud.

A woman in front picked up Emma's cue and yelled the ultimate threat, "Go green! Recycle Congress!" and the crowd took up the chant. Far down the mall, at the House and Senate office buildings, nervous congressmen watching on TV shuddered, locked their doors and then piled heavy office furniture in front of them.

Emma took another sip of water and cleared her throat for the finish.

"In our Gray New Frontier, we want to put the past behind us. Let us look forward, to America's full potential, to a glorious future, to a New Beginning. We want to start again with a new Revolution, just like the first one, opposed to tyranny and oppression of any sort, a revolution that will fight to preserve the best of our past, the elements that made us a great nation, while welcoming and adapting the new realities of a different age.

"Call us naive, call us unrealistic, but we want a return to tolerance, to decency, to manners. We cherish this country made up of diverse people who have come here from all over the world seeking a better life and who now have so much in common, especially a shared love of freedom and liberty. Let us live in harmony and peace in the Promised Land."

Emma looked up, pointed again at the Washington Monument and the Capitol Building in the distance.

"You do not want to mess with us or ignore us," she warned. "We, your elders, your seniors, your matriarchs and patriarchs, have had enough. You will satisfy our demands, or maybe we will have to do something drastic, like stop paying our taxes."

A collective gasp ran through the crowd. She must be kidding.

"What do we have to lose?" Emma said, laughing. "As they say, life in prison is hardly a deterrent to us anymore. Besides, according to the Ninnies, the world will be coming to an end in a few years anyway…"

"EM-MA! EM-MA! EM-MA!" ENOUGH! ENOUGH! ENOUGH!

Those closest to the Washington Monument felt it shudder slightly when the immense sound wave of applause, cheers and stamping feet swept down the mall and washed over it. Alarmed tourists at the Air and Space Museum headed for the exits when Charles Lindbergh's *Spirit of St. Louis*, suspended by cables from the ceiling, began to sway.

The mighty roar shook windows again in the halls of Congress and the warren of bureaucracies spread across the capital. Congressmen and bureaucrats trembled at the heretical thought of an income tax strike.

Spontaneous dancing broke out everywhere along the mall. Cyril and Samantha from Syracuse did a schottische around the new statue of Ninnie hero Peregrine Shufflebottom, newly celebrated as the first leftist in America at Jamestown, which had displaced a likeness of the despicable "Indian fighter" Daniel Boone. Then the nearby crowd, led by Cyril and Samantha, pulled Shufflebottom down, and splashed red, white and blue paint on it.

It was the only incident of vandalism during the entire Ramble.

"USA! USA! USA!"

Emma quieted the crowd one last time and added a sober warning to her message.

"To this generation we say, 'You have been entrusted with a precious gift, the gift of democracy, liberty, freedom. The fate of America is in the balance. Do not squander it, do not let this light go out, or you and your descendants will answer to history! You are the heirs of the Greatest Generation. Do you want to be known to posterity as the Foolhardy Generation?"

And to Congress, she issued the ultimate threat:

"Make no mistake. There is a lot of life in us yet. If you ignore us, if you dismiss us as irrelevant, we will be back, we will run against you! We certainly are experienced! And our children and grandchildren are ready behind us!"

"WE'LL BE BACK! WE'LL BE BACK! WE'LL BE BACK!"

In a congressional office building, where a birthday party was underway for a senator now in his 70th year in Congress, the attendees huddled around a TV set, watching this grandmother who had brought a rebellious mob to their doorstep. When Emma issued her threat, the combined intake of breath from the congressmen, all gasping in shock at the same time, snuffed out all 95 candles on the cake. The senator, mouth agape, staring vacantly into space, mumbling to himself, spittle dripping from his chin, never noticed.

Emma herself, in a clear, striking voice almost as good as Kate Smith's, led the crowd in the closing anthem, *God Bless America*.

Then, pointing toward the Capitol building, she shouted, "Now, let's make sure they hear us! Let's go!"

§§§

"A patriot must always be ready to defend his country against his government."

–Edward Abbey

THIRTY
The Showdown

Swarms of patriots, seniors and juniors alike – Emma's Army, Emma's Freedomfolks – rambled down Constitution Avenue toward the Capitol Building, arms linked, singing patriotic songs.

Veteran Capitol watchers said it was the biggest march ever, bigger even than the civil rights march of 1963. It also was the most orderly.

"Oh dear. I hope I'm not being irreverent," said Sister Mary Margaret from Marquette, looking back over her shoulder while she marched, "but I don't think the pope gets this many people to St. Peter's Square on Easter Sunday."

Hundreds of thousands lined the avenue to watch this grand spectacle as it wound its way toward the Capitol. Parents brought their children to see a phenomenon that might never be repeated.

Vendors roamed in and out of the crowd, selling American flags, T-shirts, snacks and patriotic novelties. One enterprising young woman was doing a brisk business in tattoo stickers and bumper stickers reading "Go, Granny, Go!" and "Geezer Power" and "I Rambled to the Rumble!"

Another hawker's stock of "Oldie but Goodie" hats sold out in minutes. Many children wore "My Grammy Is Fire!" T-shirts.

The tension had built slowly throughout the morning as people jockeyed for position along the curbs for the best view. Many set up lawn and camp chairs and made new friends of their neighbors while they waited. It could have been a small-town Fourth of July parade, but for the size of the crowd and the majestic dome of the Capitol looming in the background.

Finally came the shout from down the street that everyone was waiting for.

"Here they come!"

'Don't Get Me Started'

The throng pushed forward toward the curb, craning their necks, straining to be the first to see the police car lights signaling the arrival of this gaggle of geezers, as the *Courier-Transcript* snidely put it. And then they began to pick up the first strains of a familiar march melody, *Stars and Stripes Forever*.

Coming into view, out in front of the grand spectacle, was an energetic 75-year-old drum majorette, Dolores from Davenport, leading the Golden Notes Senior Citizen Band, a marching unit cobbled together on the spot from former band teachers and other retired musicians, picking up where they had left off not that long ago.

Dolores had not lost much since her days fronting the band back at Davenport High School in the '60s. She wowed the crowd with her moves, strutting and preening in her plumed hat and tassels, from one side of the street to the other, twirling her baton tantalizingly in the faces of little children, and then throwing it high in the air, catching it effortlessly on the way down as they ducked for cover. It was her high school homecoming parade all over again.

Percy from Peoria and Herman from Hackensack had brought their instruments to the Ramble, thinking they might be useful somewhere along the way.

Percy, hesitantly fingering the valves on his cornet, had lamented, "I haven't touched this thing in 30 years." Herman nodded. "Last time I played the trombone was in my hometown little theater production of *The Music Man* in 1968."

The Golden Notes director had taken note, and persuaded the two that they might be more useful carrying the big Golden Notes banner instead.

Behind the band were three classic convertibles from the 1950s.

Grand Marshal Mordecai Bumbleton, Supreme Court justice, beamed at the crowd from his perch on the back seat of a 1959 Cadillac Eldorado.

"I haven't had this much fun since that roller coaster at the 1938 Iowa State Fair," he said.

Next came Emma herself, in a robin's-egg-blue 1959 Ford Sunliner.

"That was the first new car we ever owned," she had told someone, and overnight, Floyd from Flint, an auto dealer, produced one for the parade.

Country music star Crash Cooley waved to fans from his 1952 Cadillac while his new hit, *Rambling to the Rumble*, which was sweeping the nation, blared from a speaker in the grill.

"I think Hank would be proud." he said.

Then came retired Marine Corps Col. George Patton Collins, out in front of a huge contingent of veterans, each massed behind their flag-bearers – Army, Navy, Air Force, Marines, Coast Guard. Collins himself carried Old Glory, rippling in a fresh breeze that had sprung up off the Potomac.

Collins was ramrod straight as usual, eyes forward, struggling to conceal his slight limp. The only blemish to his perfect military posture was a huge smile.

The veterans marched proudly, most in uniforms that didn't quite fit anymore, singing along to their service anthems when strains of the marching band's *Marines Hymn* and *Anchors Aweigh* and the others reached their ears.

News and police helicopters hovered overhead. Small planes pulled banners with inevitable messages such as "Fairfax Mall Open 'Til 8" and "Bargain Days at Ben's Toyota." Another trumpeted, "Go Geezers!"

Then came the mass of humanity that had turned out for Emma's Ramble on Washington, 30 or so abreast again, arms linked, pushing on toward the Capitol, a crowd as diverse as America but united behind one common cause – to take back their country.

Masons walked arm in arm with Knights of Columbus. Baptists walked with Catholics. Blacks walked with whites, Latinos with Asians, auto mechanics with nuclear physicists.

Medical researchers linked arms with plumbers, professional athletes with high school sophomores, doctors with debutantes, soldiers with pacifists, shopkeepers with housewives, Green Bay Packers fans with Chicago Bears fans. There was an attempt to bring Red Sox fanatics together with Yankee supporters, but both sides protested that they could not go quite that far.

A group of students from Hillsdale College in Michigan befriended and marched with a lonely pre-med student from a notoriously liberal California school. He claimed he was the only known conservative on the campus, perhaps in the entire state system.

There even were a lot of old-time Democrats, the kind before the party lurched left, walking arm-in-arm with Republicans and Libertarians.

"I think Hubert Humphrey would have been here," said Delbert from Duluth.

Some of the seniors wore sweaters and scarves, to ward off the 'chill' of a 78-degree fall day.

Here and there among the marchers was a parade float, adding humor, whimsy and music to the holiday atmosphere and the colorful spectacle.

Emma was amazed and impressed at the ingenuity of some of her followers.

"Look at these things!" she said excitedly to Sebastian. "How did they manage all this at such short notice?"

Some of the marchers had brought parade material with them; others made it up on the spot out of paper mache, chicken wire, bedsheets and anything else they could scrounge.

A group from Kansas rode a farm wagon float pulled by a tractor and featuring Betsy Ross. Betsy was not sewing the first American flag, but pleating a red, white and blue gallows noose to hang a Karl Marx likeness kneeling beside her.

Another float was a Boston Tea Party tableau, with patriots throwing Ninnie manikins overboard instead of tea.

"Are those real Ninnies or dummies?" shouted a straight man in the crowd.

"Same difference," came the answer.

A third was a home-made but decent replica of the Mayflower, under a sign reading "Plymouth Rocks!" Aboard was a Massachusetts rock band of lively octogenarians and septuagenarians calling themselves The Pension People, who performed their own lively version of "Y-M-C-A," but reworked as "V-I-A-G-R-A." The Pension People were fronted by an energetic 85-year-old from a popular '50s group, who pounded out *Johnny B Goode*, among other classics, on an upright piano.

Emma did not want to know how they procured a piano.

Some marchers strutted in distinctive apparel or performed along the way.

The Codgers, a delegation of seniors decked out in vintage baseball uniforms, their name spelled out in a familiar blue script across the front of their jerseys, passed baseballs back and forth in a comic unison drill. Now and then a ball got away and was claimed by a child in the crowd. A small group from California marched under the banner "Golden Old

Goats from the Golden State." A contingent from North Dakota, billed as "Forty Fabulous Fogeys From Fargo," performed precision, unison drills with their walkers, wheelchairs and canes.

From the back of a pickup truck, a barbershop quartet from Utah calling themselves "Four Coots in Suits" belted out old chestnuts like *The Sweetheart of Sigma Chi* and *Let the Rest of the World Go By.* And from Embarrass, Wisconsin, performing on the back of a flatbed truck, came a folk music tavern trio billed as "Caesar's Wheezers and Geezers," reworking the old favorite *Walk Right In* into a lively *Ramble Right In.*

Decorated golf carts, some occupied by circus clowns, weaved in and out among the marchers and passed out treats to children. And that group from Wisconsin that had traveled to the march on riding lawnmowers paused every now and then to perform intricate figure-eight maneuvers and wheelies. A few were talented enough with their machines to get them vertical briefly, in what they said was a double-axle, and one even rolled her machine onto two outer wheels in a tricky move she called the Quadruple Klutz.

"I must say," said an impressed onlooker tourist from New Zealand, "you Yanks certainly have a strange but delightful sense of humor."

Following behind the marchers, in a lineup of buses three abreast, were Emma patriots not nimble enough anymore to manage the trek to the Capitol. The decorated lead bus had been turned into a float by a group from Georgia, and featured a Rosa Parks lookalike at the wheel, driving a gang of white Ninnies restricted to the back seats.

§§§

At the Capitol, in a scene that had been preapproved and prearranged with security officials, contingents of quite orderly seniors roamed the building or fanned out to nearby streets and the congressional office buildings, seeking out the offices of their representatives.

Not all of them were to be found. Many suddenly had been called away to committee meetings. Others needed to make a quick trip back to their home districts. One claimed he was needed urgently at home because his arachnophobic wife was trapped in the bathroom by a spider she had just spotted outside the door.

'Don't Get Me Started'

The cowering congressmen, senators and bureaucrats who remained were reluctant to emerge from their dens and burrows. But some of the elders found their prey anyway.

"I know your mother, and she would be ashamed of what you are doing," yelled Noreen from New York, shaking a finger at her trembling congressman. But then she realized what she was saying.

"But the problem is, you are not *DOING* anything!"

A suspicious Marine Corps veteran glanced twice at a furtive figure slinking down a corridor. When he plucked a wig, false nose and glasses from the man's head, he found Pemberson Prittchard, congressional leader of the Ninnies, underneath.

"I'm... I'm... I'm on my way to the annual Ninnie Masquerade Ball," he stammered by way of embarrassed, feeble explanation.

"Well, that would actually make some sense," said the ex-Marine. "A whole room full of phonies and disguised frauds."

Emma herself cornered her own congressman, a former student of hers, hiding behind a potted plant, and dragged him out by his ear into the light of day. The mortified official looked like a frat boy partier who had just been caught up in a tree, peering into sorority house bedrooms.

"Did you learn nothing in my history and civics classes?" Emma thundered at him. "You spend more time conniving to get re-elected than you do in legitimate actual government activities."

Emma recalled that this congressman was the same student who once thought civics was just an automobile, who couldn't write a literate sentence, and could not find his own state on a map.

"Might still be true," she mused, and found herself wishing that they had never done away with dunce caps and dunce stools.

Constituents found some of their congressmen in unlikely places. Senator Snodbruster from South Carolina had to be dragged out from his hiding place, crouched behind the statute of Sacagawea in Statuary Hall.

"I lost my glasses back here," he stammered, offering no elaboration as to what there was to read on Sacagawea's buttocks.

Rep. Brashbottom of Rhode Island was posing as a waitress in the House Members Dining Room, and proved immediately that she was a natural. She interrupted Rep. Philibuster's hilarious story by asking for his order just as he got to the punchline, and then came back to inquire if everything was all right precisely when everybody in his party had their mouths full.

Senator Flibberty from Washington was confronted outside, waiting for the taxi that would take her to the airport for a critical ten-day, tax-payer-financed junket to The Netherlands, where her party would study whether wooden shoes from sustainable forests were superior to environmentally harmful models made from platypus hides and synthetic materials, all this to be sandwiched between crucial visits to art museums, canal boat tours and gourmet dining in opulent tulip gardens.

Up and down the corridors of the office buildings, the seniors pursued their quarry. Some of them had to be flushed out of restroom stalls, others from hastily-convened committee hearings, still others from back-room huddles with aides and lobbyists.

Outside, on the sidewalks and in the streets, angry seniors paraded, bearing signs saying, "We Are Coming for You," and "Reduce, Replace, Recycle our Reps." Many chanted new slogans they had picked up from Emma's speech – "Enough!" and "Gray Lives Matter!" and "No More!" and "Wake Up!" Most chilling of all to the politicians was the repeated cry, "We'll be back!"

It was dawning on the congressmen that they were up against a very formidable force, a movement that might upset their status quo forever. Each was seriously reassessing their re-election chances and strategy in the face of a fierce but orderly mob and powerful voting bloc that was threatening to run against them.

"Whoever heard of such a ridiculous thing?" lamented Sen. Klingerton of California. "Next thing you know they'll want honest elections, one-man-one-vote, tamper-proof ballots, a ban on lobbyists, an impartial IRS, that kind of pathetic nonsense."

§§§

A feeble countermarch to the Ramble on Washington was set up at the last minute by a small group of motivationally deficient, delusional young people with degrees in Interpretive Dance, Intercultural Studies, Male Toxicity, and Cultural Diversity, who crept out of their parents' basements, anxious and excited about what they hoped would be a chance at some free food, free drugs and maybe free sex.

230

But only six people showed up, hardly enough to advertise as a very convincing counterblow. Many potential counter-marchers had evaporated, shrinking in alarm before this sudden, threatening display of elderly outrage. Those who didn't stay in their basements fled toward Canada, where several prominent legislators proposed building a wall of ice to keep them out.

"Next thing you know they'll be sneaking in and seeking asylum," one of them said. "And you know what happens next. Pretty soon they'll be overloading our social support system, demanding free food, free education, driver's licenses, the right to vote, the whole shebang.

"Crimes will soar and we'll have to set up sanctuary cities where our own citizens can be safe from them. No thank you.

"And besides, we don't have enough basements to handle all of them."

The counter-protesters never had a chance against this army of wily, wise, finger-wagging seniors.

One young laggard Ninnie cynic, cowering behind a mailbox at the corner of Constitution and Pennsylvania while the marchers went by, told another, "Listen, all we have to do is wait them out. It won't be long before they're all gone, one way or another."

Mildred from Moline, a marching librarian, overheard them.

"Oh, wake up!" she shouted, waving her little American flag in their faces. "Your indifference and ignorance are dangerous. Do you even appreciate what you have here? We need you to pick up the torch, to light the way to the future. It's all up to you now."

The young Ninnie shrugged. "Not my problem," he said, in the usual bored tone of the indifferent, irresponsible and disinterested. "I have other priorities. I need to tend to my cannabis garden, cultivate my beard."

"Yes, it is your problem, our problem," said his more sensible companion. "If we don't do it, who will?"

Mildred the librarian nodded. Indeed. Who?

But the march had caught the attention and admiration of many of the nation's other young people, who marveled at the determination and strength of their parents' and grandparents' convictions, their willingness to go to such lengths and extremes to preserve the foundations of the country they loved.

Emma had met many of them on the Ramble. She was not as pessimistic as some others. She knew there was a solid core out there of young patriots. As for the others, she believed that eventually they would do as other generations had done, that they would recognize the realities of the world and embrace better solutions to its problems, that eventually they would just Grow Up.

"Let them have their adolescent crush on socialism," she told Sebastian on their way back to their bus. "They will find out soon enough what it's like to be jilted, ditched, betrayed, double-crossed, by someone or something you believed in and trusted."

God forbid they might ever actually have to live under socialism, she mused, even though it would be a sure cure for their misplaced idealism. A fatal cure.

§§§

Emma had one last stop to make before she could head for home. She had to settle up with the law.

The elderly judge who had allowed her to post bail of $1 for that scuffle at the Jefferson Memorial now winked and smiled as he dismissed all of the charges against her.

"You stay out of trouble now, you hear? You don't want to build up a long rap sheet that will come back to haunt you some day, hurt your chances for a great career, for promotions."

He grinned and added, "It's about time somebody did what you did." Then he asked for her autograph.

The clueless, taunting kid that Emma had pushed into the Tidal Basin was fined $495 by the judge for despoiling a national landmark, and faced jail time for nonpayment until Emma persuaded the judge to let him off. Then she gave him money for his bus fare back home.

"You remind me of my grandmother," he said, shaking her hand. "I think she was somewhere out there in your crowd."

The flag-burning professor she scuffled with was fined $876.89 on two charges of polluting the environment and setting a fire in a public place without a permit, plus 30 days to be spent scrubbing anti-conservative graffiti off of walls in public places. Then he was docked a month's pay by his college when he showed up 30 days late for classes.

She made another brief stop to revisit her jailers, who were ready with prune juice toasts and a huge cake decorated with 86 candles and the American flag.

"That was daring," Emma told Sgt. O'Rourke. "Lucky they didn't set off the fire sprinklers."

"We wanted to get some of those naked male dancers in here for you, too," said O'Rourke, "but we weren't sure your heart could take it."

Emma signed her release papers in a bold, cursive hand. The senior partner of the prestigious Washington law firm, specialists in elder law, which had offered its *pro bono* services to "extract her from her circumstances," as they put it, was on hand to say goodbye.

"You have been an inspiration to all of us," said the graying, distinguished emissary, kissing her hand in a grand continental gesture. "By the way, do you have any plans for dinner?"

Emma blushed, and politely declined.

"Wait'll I tell Sebastian about this. I haven't been hit on in 60 years."

§§§

Emma looked around in wonder as she boarded the coach that would return her to her old life.

The grand adventure had finally ebbed late in the day, as the gray senior tide of ramblers gradually began to make their way back to the buses that would take them home, to Omaha and Odessa, Texarkana and Toledo, Pawtucket and Peoria, and everywhere between.

She left D.C. knowing she had given voice to millions of patriots who joined her in speaking up and standing up for the America they loved.

A last straggler, Phyllis from Phoenix, spotted Emma.

"We're all so happy we did this," she said. "We want to thank you for inspiring us, for giving us a voice, for putting this all together, for everything you did. My grandkids now think their marching grammy is the coolest person they know. They think I'm 'fire'. And 'lit.' I slay!"

She shook Emma's hand, then instinctively knew that was not enough, and embraced her instead in a tight hug.

"I think we did this just in time," Phyllis said, grinning. "The problem with being over the hill is that now we start to pick up speed."

Emma's last view of the National Mall was of a bored city sanitation worker, aimlessly pushing a broom over the empty protest and rally grounds. There was nothing to sweep.

The seniors had picked up after themselves, just as they had always told their children and grandchildren to do. The mall was cleaner than when they arrived.

§§§

"I love my country. It's the government I'm afraid of."

—Anonymous

THIRTY-ONE

The Aftermath
December 15, in a year not too far away

After her horde of followers dissipated, Emma returned to a new life. She did not go back to Arthritis Acres, but took up residence in a new, comfortable condo in a community of conservative seniors.

She was a celebrity now, with a book contract and her own TV show and product endorsements. In Philadelphia, there was a new bronze statue of her in front of Independence Hall, shaking her finger at a cowering congressman.

A hamburger chain introduced a new menu item, the Emmaburger. There was a song, "Emma Rocks the Capitol" and even a dance, the "Emma Ramble."

For several years hence, "Emma" would be the most common name given to girls. She was a regular guest on TV talk shows, and even showed off her singing voice on a TV talent show called "Seniors Got Talent." She finished second, was offered a recording contract, but declined.

"I would have a very short career," she said.

In the face of growing hostility inspired by the marchers, Congress withdrew the Ninnie omnibus bill from consideration, and in the next election their majority evaporated. Many of the marchers had indeed been elected to Congress, as well as some of their children and grandchildren. A new coalition, the Common Sense Party, infused with a dose of new and old blood, took control in a landslide

Things were very different.

Many of the Gray New Frontier demands had become bedrock platform planks of the new party and enacted into law. "Gray" had become the perfect compromise word, the perfect solution, the perfect position, in many disputes and disagreements – "part white and part black!" Emma observed.

A new sense of peace and harmony descended on a country that had had enough of constant political bickering, infighting, racial confrontations and protests, and just wanted to get back to being a model for the rest of the world, a place where ambitious people could stretch their minds and talents and find a piece of the American Dream.

Democrats and Republicans became civil to each other. Conservative leader Throckmorton Silverton, a Presbyterian minister, replaced Pemberson Prittchard of the Ninnies as Speaker of the House and subsequently was delighted to accept an invitation to officiate at the wedding of Prittchard's daughter, Persimmon, to a conservative talk-show host.

Police and criminals reached an uneasy truce and kept a wary eye on each other. Sgt. O'Rourke in D.C. helped a reformed but talented financial swindler, Pangborn "Ponziboy" Plumgully, get a legitimate job on Wall Street after his release from the penitentiary. An astute and straightened-out Plumgully soon ascended to the top ranks of the corporate hierarchy.

In the Twin Cities, Maxie from Minneapolis, a toxic male policeman, successfully courted and wed Sarah from St Paul, a toxic feminist protester, and they lived happily, if toxically, ever after. They had met during a street riot organized by fanatical "inclusionary" zealots protesting the lack of electricians in the plumbers' union, and during which the plumbers' union hall had been burned to the ground.

Overnight now, "ethically disoriented" people were again called just plain dishonest crooks; the "economically inactive" were now jobless or unemployed; global warming and climate change events became cyclical weather and natural disasters again; the "motivationally deficient" returned to being just plain lazy, and the "alternative facts" of the Ninnies were given back their old name of simple old-fashioned lies.

People no longer screamed "racism" and "white privilege" at every perceived affront. "Racism" was gradually losing its pejorative meaning, and for most people the word "race" now only brought to mind thoughts of the Kentucky Derby, the Preakness, the Indianapolis 500 and the mad dash to the restroom to avoid picking up the restaurant check. "White Privilege" had given way to "American Privilege."

The most popular colors in the new spring fashion lines were interchangeable combinations of white, black, yellow red and brown.

But the hottest new fashion colors by far were various shades of gray. Stealing a page from paint companies, designers came up with imaginative popular hues called Overcast, Misty Coast, Ocean Swell, November Sky and Prison Cell.

A popular new commercial showed three eggs – a white one, a tan, and a dark. When they were cracked open – all the same.

Immigrants now stood patiently in long lines at border stations, filling out papers to enter the country legally. Schools and colleges began teaching good manners and patriotism and respect for the opinions of others. Two conservative speakers who dared breach the wall of hostility at a liberal California university actually received some polite questions and applause and were hosted at a reception later.

You no longer needed 14 passwords to access your websites; tech wizards had adapted alcohol breathalyzers into an infallible means of identifying you by your breath.

This had a beneficial secondary effect. If you drank too much or used illegal drugs, the equipment would not recognize you until you were sober and clean. In extreme cases, it would not allow you access until you used some mouthwash.

Welfare and food stamp rolls plummeted. Everybody who needed a job had one. Congressmen who found it hard to get by on their newly reduced pay and benefits and limited corruption prospects took second jobs as janitors and high-rise window washers. When they had to pay the same as everybody else for their health care, they turned out a very efficient, inexpensive national health care plan in a day and a half.

The Big Brother behemoth called Barney was broken up into little pieces. You now were free to choose your own political candidates, and a healthy exchange of ideas resumed. You could now go to the bathroom without fear that Barney would be in the stall, too, and tell you that your stool looked suspicious and "click here for a lab analysis."

Isolated pockets of Ninnies remained, but they had largely retreated to culverts under railroad tracks and other places where most decent, sensible people did not go anymore, such as red-light districts, nuclear waste landfills, Florida sinkholes and red tide beaches.

One of the first bills to be taken up by the new Congress was the Common Sense Reparations Act, which aimed to provide compensation to all those who had been inconvenienced, damaged or offended by the policies of the Ninnies while they were in power. But it was tabled when the Government Accounting Office determined that the reparations could run into the quadrillions.

"And besides," said one Common Sense Party leader, "wouldn't a push for revenge make us no better than them?"

As it turned out, the country did indeed soon tire of the socialism fad, just as it had discarded over the years other worn out and exhausted concepts like zoot suits, mood rings, ant farms, telephone-booth-stuffing, conical bras, flagpole sitting, goldfish swallowing, Pong, and overexposed, washed-up celebrities.

"Now it's up to your generation to make sure we don't make another terrible mistake," Emma told Sebastian. "You must preserve a way of life that is the envy of the world, a way of life that ignorant, dunderheaded twits might again try to replace with a never-neverland utopia."

Sebastian now was a high school freshman preoccupied with girls, bathroom humor and food, in that order, and was running for president of his class.

"I am proposing a Free New Frontier for my school," he informed his grandmother with a straight face. "Free food, free backpacks, free books, freedom from homework and grades, plus a new name, Mediocrity High. Just like my socialist idols."

Emma looked at him suspiciously.

"You're not too old yet, you know. You keep that up and I will give you a free spanking and disown you at no charge."

Christopher had done extremely well in his business, so much so that the chain of computer repair stores that he created had been bought out for millions by a high-tech conglomerate. He had been offered the position of CEO, but declined.

"Actually, I'm thinking of retiring myself," he told his mother. "I can afford to do what I want now for the rest of my life."

"Why, that's wonderful," Emma said with a twinkle. "By all means, let me pick out a nice comfy retirement home for you."

'Don't Get Me Started'

George Patton Collins came out of retirement to become president of a military school, where recovering helicopter parents now sent their snowflake, buttercup children to learn something about the realities of life. The matriculation rate at his school was 100%.

Deuteronomy Diaz set out to find his own American Dream, just like his parents had, and succeeded. He founded a successful building services company, which he called The Wizard of Diaz.

New conservative convert Simper Squance turned his transformation into a crusade to bring other wayward, listless basement dwellers back to the truth. He cruised former Ninnie neighborhoods in a speaker truck, imploring these lost souls to "Come out, Come out! It's safe now!"

§§§

Arthritis Acres itself was no more, having disintegrated, as socialist efforts always do, into confusion, arguments, resentments, finger-pointing, lethargy and malaise.

It now was a rehabilitation/detoxification center for recovering Ninnies.

Comrade Stallingski led a few remaining diehards to California, the last Ninnie refuge in the country.

He picked out a lovely freeway underpass in San Francisco as their last socialist paradise and survival shelter.

Each diehard adapted well to the new environment.

Professional politician Park Barile declared himself mayor and set about establishing agencies governing water supplies, health and safety, and freeway underpass behavior. He also divided the one-quarter acre plot into five legislative districts.

Lazuli Leech immediately applied for welfare benefits in all five districts.

Sunflower Squance, happy to be back in San Francisco, sought unemployment benefits on grounds that there were no jobs to be had in any of the districts.

Prof. Budleigh Salters protested that the site was too close to Columbus Avenue for his taste, and mounted a campaign to move elsewhere.

Horace Aappel set about establishing a secret wi-fi network and immediately began snooping on everybody else.

And Slant Greeley misreported everything that was happening in the new Ninnie enclave in his new newspaper, the Underpass *Undertaker*. In an attempt to attract new residents, a front-page photo in his first issue tried to pass off the Japanese Tea Garden in Golden Gate Park as a typical view in the new underpass site.

Rocky Tosterone and wife Nurottica moved to a better location, a scenic wastewater reclamation plant with a view of Alcatraz, and it was a year before the rest knew they were gone.

California, now officially called Mexifornia, had seceded and become a sanctuary state run by socialists and illegal immigrants.

Its Third-World economy soon collapsed from mismanagement.

Once-enchanting San Francisco degenerated even further into a trashed and trampled encampment of homeless druggies, welfare cheats, gangs, criminals and illegals.

Yosemite National Park became a lone refuge for remaining sane and sensible Californians, who established their own militia to protect the natural wonder from homeless, marauding Ninnies looking for a new place to over-regulate, trash and despoil.

The U.S erected a wall from Mexico to the Canadian border to keep the remaining Ninnies quarantined.

California and its allies, Oregon and Washington, eventually sued for peace, and the military soon restored them to normalcy.

The three renegade states sought foreign aid from the US, which demanded assurances first that they would not revert to their old profligate ways.

New rumblings along the San Andreas Fault were panicking California residents, many of whom tried to climb the wall, but other states insisted that they be sprayed first to prevent the Ninnie infection from ever spreading again. Even so, they were not allowed to gather in groups larger than four, had to quarantine for a year, and wear masks.

They also had to sign waivers forever forsaking their bizarre views and beliefs.

§§§

Emma often wondered if all of her efforts, the blog, the Ramble, the confrontations, had been worth it, if she had done the right thing.

"How do I know if this new atmosphere of hope and optimism is going to last, if the socialists and Progressives have finally been exterminated for good?"

It occurred to her that she knew somebody who might have an answer, somebody who was close to some influential people. Perhaps she could prevail on their long friendship…

"Harry," she mused one day not long after returning from the Ramble, "tell the folks up there to send a sign that we got through, that we're doing some good, that our America, the land they have always blessed, is going to survive…"

That evening, setting out with Christopher and Sebastian to watch the sunset, she stopped suddenly and gasped as they came to the end of the path.

Emma began to laugh. Then the laughter became sobs. She fell to her knees and had to cling to Christopher's legs to steady herself. Christopher and Sebastian turned to look....

Emma slowly got to her feet, wiped the tears from her cheeks, and grinned.

"Close enough," she said.

EPILOG

in a year not too far away...

Harry had stopped his regular visits to the station, down there just behind the gates, after someone pointed out that he shouldn't really be checking the arrivals every day. It didn't look good. Why did he want to rush things? Maybe she was enjoying the time she had left. So now he wandered by only occasionally.

And then one day there she was, looking around, bewildered, carrying a scrapbook, a little American flag pin in her lapel...

THE END

ALSO BY DAN CHABOT:

Godspeed: A Love Story

The Last Homecoming

Available at Amazon